# Innocent Hostage

## by

## Vonnie Hughes

This is a work of fiction. Names, characters, places, and incidents are either the product of the author's imagination or are used fictitiously, and any resemblance to actual persons living or dead, business establishments, events, or locales, is entirely coincidental.

**Innocent Hostage**



Cover Art by *Kim Mendoza*

The Wild Rose Press, Inc.
PO Box 708
Adams Basin, NY 14410-0708
Visit us at www.thewildrosepress.com

Publishing History
First Crimson Rose Edition, 2014
Print ISBN 978-1-62830-629-3
Digital ISBN 978-1-62830-630-9

Published in the United States of America

**Toeing the inside of each stair tread** he climbed the stairs that led to the bedrooms. As he got near the top, he hesitated. More perfume, different from the smell of soap powder hung in the air. Tania's perfume, strong and poignant. It was called Chloe. He ought to know. He'd bought enough of the stuff.

He stopped. Was she here? Had she been here? That stuff lingered for a long time. Their apartment had stunk of it for weeks after she'd left.

"Tania?" he whispered.

A disturbance in the air was his only warning. He ducked as something whizzed over the top of his head. Then he was shoved aside as a dark figure pushed past him. Breck clutched at the banisters, his feet shooting out from under him on the slippery carpet. Shit! Scrambling to his feet, he bounced down the last couple of stairs and chased the stocky figure careening down the hallway.

His quarry wrenched open the front door. Dusk had settled and it was almost dark outside. He managed to grab his attacker's coat and began reeling in the interloper like a fish. But the man wriggled out of his plastic raincoat and fled towards a blue pick-up truck waiting at the curb. His balding head gleamed under the streetlights. Someone inside the vehicle leaned over and flung open the passenger door, revving the engine just as Breck aimed a solid punch at the back of the attacker's neck. Reeling against the car door, the man half-collapsed on to the front seat of the truck, his legs hanging out the door. The driver floored the accelerator and the blue truck jerked out from the curb as if the driver was unfamiliar with the gears.

# Praise for Vonnie Hughes

"Terrific, Vonnie. *LETHAL REFUGE* is a MUST read."
*~Sloane Taylor, Author*

~*~

"Read the excerpt and just had to have it, Vonnie."
*~Rita Monet, Author*

~*~

"A witness struggling to cope, a man who needs to stay away and can't seem to keep his personal feelings separated…welcome to *LETHAL REFUGE*. This is an emotional and thrilling romantic suspense novel…A heated romance, staying ahead of danger, and these elements make for a nail biting thrill ride. Ms. Hughes delivers a tale that captures readers' hearts. If you're a fan of romantic suspense, keep this story in mind."
*~Siren Book Reviews*

~*~

"I don't want to talk too much about how the story is developed, for fear of spoilers, but I will say that I was genuinely scared in places and I suspected some characters, then acquitted them, then suspected them again, more than once. In short, I was impressed. The title and cover didn't let me down! If you like your romance spiced up with life-threatening danger, or you like your crime spiked with love-under-fire and hot sex, I'd say, give Vonnie Hughes a go."
*~Imelda Evans, Wine, Women and Wordplay*

Chapter One

Breck Marchant's cell phone and pager buzzed simultaneously.

Game on.

As he dragged his canvas bag out of the closet, he tucked the cell phone under his chin. "Uh, huh?"

"Report to intersection of Verbena and Eskdale," a voice barked. The caller clicked off.

"Eskdale. Not far from where Kit lives," Breck muttered to himself. "Hope the boy is safe at preschool." Then common sense asserted itself. Why wouldn't his son be fine?

He grabbed his car keys off the table and slammed the apartment door behind him. As he charged down the stairs, he tugged on his Armed Offenders' Squad jacket. He'd collect his weapons and the rest of his gear at base.

Clamping the blue beacon on the roof of his SUV, he revved her up and nudged into the traffic flow, then muscled his way into the outside passing lane. As he crashed an orange light, his cell phone rang again and he frowned. No further contact until they were on scene was the golden rule. Had the situation already been defused and the call-out canceled? Taking his foot off the accelerator he leaned towards the mike, expecting to be recalled. "Marchant."

"Baz here," said a voice he knew well. Baz Asquith was his supervisor, a senior sergeant whose ambitions were taking him out of the Armed Offenders Squad and into the CIB.

*This could be the call he'd been waiting for.* Breck badly wanted Baz's job. Like Baz, he wanted to climb out of the herd. If he headed up an AOS squad, he had a good chance of being selected for Special Tactics, the crème de la crème of law enforcement. Lord, what wouldn't he give to get into ST.

"Marchant, report to me before you fit out." Baz's voice had lost its usual drawl. "How far away are you?"

"One minute."

"Right." The phone went dead.

Breck frowned again. Something wasn't right.

As he approached the intersection, he saw Baz standing apart from the vans and tents being erected on suburban lawns by members of his team.

Leaving his vehicle in the shade of a sycamore tree, Breck grabbed his bag and loped over to join Baz.

"Marchant," Baz greeted him. "You're not needed on this one. But you might like to observe."

Breck took a step back. Whatever this was about, it sure as hell wasn't promotion.

"I'd prefer you not to be here at all, mate," his boss continued, "but I think you'll insist on staying."

Breck looked at Baz's tanned, worried face and his stomach clenched. "What's this about?"

"Hostage situation," Baz answered after a slight hesitation. "Breck—it's your son. Kit is the hostage."

## Chapter Two

Breck tasted the tinny flavor of fear on his tongue. His hands clenched around the handle of his canvas carry-all. He needed to hold on to something, and the bag was the only thing available. "How the hell…?" he croaked.

"His stepfather has him," Baz explained grimly.

"But what the fuck is Marty holding him hostage for? It doesn't make sense." Breck struggled to find a kernel of logic among the questions jangling in his brain. "Kit's not worth anything to anyone except—"

"Except you," Baz said. "Marty's after you, I reckon. We haven't heard a word from Tania. Don't know if she's inside the house or not."

Breck wondered fleetingly if this was one of his ex-wife's little games, then discounted the notion as absurd. No. Tania liked to play around with the emotions of the men in her life, and she had a nasty streak a mile wide and some suspect friends, but she was a good mom. She wouldn't endanger her children.

He glanced down the road. All he could see of Marty and Tania's house from here was a strip of front lawn. But on the roof of the house across the road, a sniper settled himself and his gear behind the chimney.

"What happened? I mean," he licked his dry lips, "who gave the alarm?"

"The next door neighbor heard a lot of banging and shouting and then she heard a kid crying, so she phoned us. By the time the blues got here, Marty was standing on the front steps with one arm wrapped around Kit and a .308 in his other hand."

Breck sucked in his breath as a pearl of sweat trickled down his face. Marty had never been renowned for his calmness and the idea of an angry, armed Marty was terrifying.

"I have to be here, Baz," he heard himself saying, but his voice was muted as if he was hearing sounds under water.

"Sit down, Breck. Now," Baz ordered.

Breck sat. The chilly, damp earth soaked through his coveralls.

"We'll get Kit safely out of there," Baz assured him. "You know we will. We've done it again and again. Just because it's Kit this time won't make any difference to us. But it *will* make a difference to you and that's why you can't work the scene."

"I understand," Breck mumbled. His senses were dulled, as if he'd been slugged by a heavyweight with a vicious right hook.

All he could think of was Kit, his son, the boy Tania used as a bargaining tool for leeching money out of him. Kit—the boy Tania said was difficult, just like his father.

He'd let Tania have custody of Kit because she knew what she was doing when it came to raising kids and he, Breck, didn't have a clue. Kit was much better off with Tania, even though some of her behavior was questionable.

The guilt of three years swamped Breck. Since

Tania had married Marty, Breck had been worried about Kit. But had he done anything? No.

By God, he'd like to take that half-witted Marty Kerr and sling him against a brick wall till his—where the hell was Tania? He struggled to his feet, using the sycamore trunk as a prop. "I understand your orders, Baz. But I need to be involved in some way."

"No."

He grabbed Baz's arm. "Baz, I'm begging you. This matters more than you know. I've let that kid down…"

"Baloney. Let's not go there. You'll have to stand by in case Marty wants to bargain with you. But you're *not* part of the operation. Here are the others," Baz said, looking over his shoulder.

Breck released his grip and stepped back, clenching his hands into fists so hard his knuckles cracked. If he went against orders now, not only would the whole operation be compromised, but his job with the AOS would be over. He had two reasons for living and they were both at stake at this very moment.

Baz waved to the other operatives to kit up inside the tent set up on a civilian's front lawn. Abel, Breck's best friend, gave him the thumbs-up as he disappeared through the tent flap.

"I have to go, Marchant. Stay here. I promise I'll get word to you every step of the way. We've got the best negotiator in the business arriving shortly. Now remember—you need to be here for Kit when it's over, so hold it together."

Yes. That's what he had to do. Be here for Kit. So long as Tania didn't try to keep him out of it. He grabbed hold of Baz's sleeve again. "What about

Tania?"

"She might be involved, for all we know."

Breck reeled back. No. Tania was a terrific mom. She used to laugh at Breck's inept attempts to change a diaper, and refused to let him read stories to the little fella because she said his gravelly voice would frighten the dead. She'd been a bitch to live with, but she wouldn't endanger a child.

Breck snapped out of it to realize he was on his own. Baz raced across the road to the HQ tent to talk to a police sergeant. Breck hunkered back down beneath the sycamore tree and put his head on his knees. The earth smelled of spring and life. How could it smell so fresh on such a terrible day? No grass grew beneath the spreading branches, so perhaps the smell of new growth was deceptive. Like a lot of things in life.

What had set Marty off this time? Marty had never done anything like this before but the guy sure had a short fuse. Even Tania, who adored him, acknowledged it took very little to upset Marty's world. How could Breck ever have thought Kit was safer in their household than with him?

Because Tania had told him numerous times that Breck's background had not prepared him for fatherhood, that's why. His demanding, high-achieving parents had left him doubtful of his abilities in that field. And ordinary police hours were bad enough, but coupled with his being on-call for the AOS, Tania had decided that Kit was better off with her.

*And you agreed. It was easier for you that way Marchant, wasn't it?* his conscience taunted. He rubbed his forehead, trying to rub away the worry. They sure as hell couldn't have remained married after what he'd discovered about her. He was a cop, for God's sake.

"Breck Marchant?" inquired a pleasant female voice. It was redolent of crisp apples and green meadows.

"Yes?" He glanced up just in time to receive a stinging slap across the face.

"How *could* you?" the voice on the end of the hand exclaimed. "How could you let it get to this?"

"What the—?" Breck began. He peered at her through watery eyes. For a small woman she packed a heavy wallop. He rubbed his jaw. "Who the hell are you?" He scrambled to his feet.

"Ingrid Rowland. And before you deny all knowledge of me, think again."

He thought. He thought that his day, which had started out so promisingly when he'd done his workout at the gym, had turned to custard. Now he had a madwoman slapping him and he didn't even know who—yes, he did. Shit! She was Kit's preschool teacher. He remembered that mane of astounding silver-blonde hair that she kept tightly under control. He remembered thinking that she looked as though she kept a lot of herself under control.

"Of course I remember you," he said grimly. "What are you talking about?"

"As if you don't know! At first I thought it was a case of neglect caused by overwork. Cops! They're all the same—lousy parents. But you just don't care, do you? You dumped Kit on your ex-wife and that abusive sonofabitch, and stood back and let it get to this. Poor little Kit."

Christ, his conscience and Ms. Rowland were hand-in-hand.

To Breck's horror, the woman's hazel eyes filled with tears that she blinked away, scowling. She didn't like showing weakness. Okay, he understood that. It didn't make him feel any better.

He opened his mouth, and then shut it again. Finally he managed, "If you were a man, I'd thrash you for that."

"No doubt," she rasped. "That's all cops understand. Violence."

"Don't come at that crap, lady. I was way past those accusations years ago. Tania used to lay it on thick—"

"Tania!" Ingrid Rowland spat the name as if it were a curse.

Breck stared at her. What *was* the woman trying to say? On their two prior meetings she had at least seemed reasonable. He'd made sure he registered Kit himself and paid over a semester's tuition in advance in order to bypass the Tania money pit.

At first glance he'd thought her very pleasant and charming. An understatement. If he'd had the time and the wherewithal to pursue a relationship, Ingrid Rowlandson would be his pick. But she was no doubt already in a relationship. She had a sort of fragile shine to her that made him want to bask in her approval. She looked as if she belonged in a fairytale, not a preschool. It made a man want to shield her from the world. Huh. Looks could be deceiving.

The second time he'd seen Ms. Rowland he'd been too rushed to do more than wave a thank-you as he hustled Kit out the door. It hadn't been his regular custody day—those were few and far between—but it had been one of those rare days when Tania had phoned him out of the blue and told him, "We don't have time today to run around after your son. You'll have to collect him from preschool at four o'clock."

Breck had been on his way to a debriefing and had no recourse but to take Kit with him. The poor kid had cooled his heels for two hours in the watch-house. That incident had underscored how ill equipped Breck was to look after his son. Tania was quite right.

He stared at Ingrid Rowland now, puzzled. "I don't understand. What have you got against Tania?"

****

Ingrid Rowland looked into the clear grey eyes and wondered how this guy got by in the world. He was a dream to look at, and from what little she'd managed to glean, he was excellent at his job. But as a father and husband he was an unmitigated disaster. Or so Tania Kerr said. Ingrid had not encouraged Tania to enlarge on that. Gossiping with adversarial parents was not professional behavior and could only lead to disaster. Also, she knew Tania of old. 'Untrustworthy' was Tania's middle name.

But Ingrid wanted to help Kit, one of the loneliest, nicest little boys she had ever met. She was determined to fight on his behalf, even if Breck Marchant took a chunk out of her.

"Tania is probably a good mother to Pixie and Bobby, Mr. Marchant. But haven't you read *any* of the notes I sent you about Kit? I was just about to deliver another one this morning when—" She shrugged, indicating the police presence.

"Notes?"

Ingrid glowered. Was the man as obtuse as he sounded? Then she told herself to cut him some slack.

Only a hundred yards away his son's volatile stepfather was holding the little boy captive. Marchant was probably finding it hard to concentrate. She reached out a hand and touched his arm, then snatched it back. The man's forearm was hard as a rock, but she'd felt the telltale tremors in his muscles. And he wouldn't want her to know about that.

She looked at his face, creased with lines of despair and her heart softened. "You don't know anything about the notes, do you? I *did* wonder. That's why I waited till Kit said your next custody visitation was due. I was going to telephone you this weekend."

Brechon Marchant snorted derisively and glared at her.

*Now* what had she said that was so wrong?

"Next custody visitation," he mimicked in a sing song voice. "Did Kit tell you just how many 'custody visitations' I've had this year, Ms. Rowland? Did he?" he snarled. "Two. That's all I've been allowed."

She gasped. "Oh, dear. You see, Kit told me all about those visits. He told me what you do and where you go. Last month, he told me about going dolphin watching and to the Easter Show and…" She trailed off, looking at Breck Marchant's face. "It's all make believe, isn't it?" she finished weakly. "Kit lied to me."

The anguish on Breck Marchant's face was almost unbearable.

"We talked about doing those things," he whispered, "but Tania and Marty had other plans for him. I didn't dare rock the boat—"

"Breck?"

Damn the interruption. Exasperated, Ingrid turned away. She wanted to hear his story. There was a lot more here than met the eye. She'd been sure he was yet another cop who was so busy looking after business, he neglected his own. Like her father. But now she wasn't so sure.

****

Breck turned quickly to meet Baz. "Here." Baz was holding out a ballistics vest. Breck shrugged out of his jacket and tugged the vest on over his shirt. He closed his mind to his conversation with Ingrid Rowland. The important thing right now was to do whatever it took to get his son out of this situation. "Has Kit asked for me?" he asked Baz.

Baz shook his head. "No. Kerr wants to speak to you."

"Oh, hell." Breck's heart plummeted. Even though Kit must be frightened and desperate, he still hadn't wanted his father. Or perhaps Kerr wouldn't let him talk to anyone.

"Follow me. The PNT want to speak to you." Baz meant the Police Negotiation Team attached to the squad. "You're not talking to that bastard until we've figured out a way to get Kit away from him. Kerr asked if you were on the call-out team and I told him you were sent home because of your personal involvement. The principal negotiator told him he'd have you brought back to the scene."

Breck followed Baz into the mobile HQ van, a huge bus furnished with enough electronic equipment to back up the national grid.

"Marchant, sit beside me and tell me everything you know about Kerr." The principal negotiator was all dark edges and angles. He signaled to Breck to take a seat in front of the screens curving across the front of the interior of the bus. Breck could see several close-ups of Marty Kerr sitting on his front lawn cradling a .308 across his knees. Kit was nowhere to be seen.

"Where's Kit?" Breck jumped back up again. "What's going on?"

"Sit down!" the PN barked like a drill sergeant.

Breck sat. He knew he'd better shut up or they'd work out a way to cut him out of the picture. That didn't mean he had to like it.

"Your boy is inside," the negotiator said in a quieter tone. "I'm Jack Tanner, by the way." He stretched his arm out in the cramped quarters and shook Breck's hand, then returned his attention to the screens. "Kerr sent the boy inside to fetch him a beer. I guess it's hot sitting out there in the full sun."

"But Kit's only four! He won't know what to do."

"Oh, yes he does. He's done it before, I'd say." Jack Tanner nodded towards the far screen.

And there came Breck's little Kit trotting out of the front door of the house, carefully carrying a can of Steinlager for his stepfather. The operator zoomed in for a closer look and everyone could see the pinched, closed look on Kit's face.

"Poor little devil." The dog handler who'd come in behind them stared at the screen.

"Oh, Christ," Breck whispered, unable to take his eyes off the screen. "What is going on in that household?" He hated what he was seeing, but he couldn't look away.

Jack Tanner shuffled his chair back to beside Breck's and began questioning him. There was a team of five inside the bus including the camera operator, Baz, Jack and the dog handler whose dog was chained to a bar across the doorway. But Breck heard nobody except Tanner. The man was relentless in digging out every last detail Breck could recall about the Kerrs. He finished by asking, "Why does Kerr want you out there, facing him? What have you done to him?"

"Nothing yet," Breck growled.

"Look, Marchant, you've pissed this guy off somehow. There must be *something* in your history together to set this off."

"You don't understand, Tanner." Breck realized a second too late he should have called him 'sir.' "Kerr doesn't need anything to set him off. He has a hair trigger."

"I don't suppose he has a firearms license for that weapon."

Breck allowed himself a small, bitter smile. "I doubt it."

"Someone check the arms register," Tanner ordered. Then he added, "So you don't know what you've done to annoy him, and you don't know why he's using your son as a shield. What a crock, Marchant."

Breck kept his eyes down as Tanner hammered away at him. He knew the way the game was played, but Tanner had it all wrong.

"There has to be something," Tanner persisted, "because from what I can see, he's set this whole thing up to get at you. And where the hell is Tania Kerr?"

Breck raised his head and watched Marty on the screen as the man screwed around, looking back over his shoulder to check on Kit.

"I have no idea, sir. I haven't seen any of them for three weeks," Breck explained. "Last weekend I was supposed to collect Kit and take him to the zoo, but Tania phoned the day before and said Kit was feeling off-color." He shrugged. "I don't know whether it was true or not. I advised them to take him to the doctor, and I drove past and dropped a check off in their letterbox that evening. Just in case he had to go to a specialist."

"When you were there, did you see anything unusual?"

Breck shook his head. "It didn't look as though anyone was home. I'd been on afternoon shift and it was full dark by the time I got there. There were no lights on in the house. I phoned next morning to check on Kit, but nobody answered. That doesn't mean much though. They've got caller ID so they may have decided not to answer. So you see, if there's anyone with a grievance here, it's me."

"Do that a lot, do they?" Jack inquired. "Brush you off, I mean."

"Sometimes." Breck had no intention of telling the negotiator how bloody frustrating it was to phone up day after day asking to speak to his son and end up talking to an answer phone. At other times Tania would stonewall him. She'd say that Kit wasn't available— that he was playing in the park with his stepsister or had gone to the shops with Marty.

And he had done nothing to upset the equilibrium because he knew he wasn't worthy of being a father. Tania was a far better parent, much better for Kit than he'd ever be. Instead of insisting on his parental rights, he'd usually gone and worked out at the gym or joined the others at the Flagpole for a few beers. Over the years he'd got quite good at shoving down hard at the despair eating away inside him.

Tanner looked at him for a moment, chewing over what Breck had said. "Okay," he said at last. "Here's what we're gonna do."

One by one Tanner outlined all the likely scenarios, and then together they planned responses for each possibility.

The meticulous way the man worked eased the vise around Breck's heart. They were by no means out of the woods, but with Tanner around, Kit stood a better chance of getting away from Marty. *But would he escape unharmed?* Yes, of course he would. He would be okay. Breck refused to contemplate the alternative.

Various members of No. 4 Unit crossed back and forth in front of the cameras and every single one of them gave Breck the thumbs-up. The tightness around his chest eased. They were all behind him. Nobody in the unit had ever been in a situation like this before. Breck sat back in his chair. He could help best now by shutting up and letting Tanner do his job. A hushed quiet settled in the van, interrupted only by soft electronic beeps as Tanner input data into a laptop.

Breck kept his eyes glued to the screen and saw Kit sit down obediently beside Kerr again. The kid tried to lift the tab on the can, but Kerr laid his rifle down and impatiently ripped the top off while at the same time aiming a slap in Kit's general direction. As if it were an ingrained habit, Kit dodged the blow and sat a short distance away from Kerr, his face impassive. Marty's arm snaked out and yanked him closer. Kit's shoulders huddled and his head bowed.

Breck ground his teeth.

Tanner looked up. "The most important thing,

Marchant," he said, "is to let Kerr think *he* is calling the shots. We respond to him, and we only initiate communication if it looks as though Kit is in—well, if he's in real trouble."

"He's in real trouble right now." Tight-lipped, Breck glared at Tanner.

"Actually, mate, I think it's *you* who's in real trouble. Kerr is using young Kit as a means to an end."

"He's already done so to the tune of about $30,000 over the past couple of years," Breck muttered. "I knew I was a cash cow for them, but I did it for Kit. It looks as though the only money that was used for Kit was the preschool fee. Probably to get him out of the house. Preschool!" Breck said suddenly, standing up. "Where's that preschool teacher?"

Jack Tanner stared at him. "Huh?"

"Here," said a voice from the doorway.

Everyone turned.

"What the hell are you doing here?" Tanner demanded. "Get rid of her," he snapped at a cop talking to the dog handler.

"She's got clearance," the cop said. He nodded towards Baz who was hunkered down a few yards away, talking to some of the members of Unit Four.

"This lady knows Kit well," Breck explained.

"She's in the way," Tanner objected. "You know your kid better than anyone else, Breck. He—"

"No I don't," Breck ground out. "Miss Rowland sees him nearly every day."

A beat of silence, then Jack Tanner recovered. "Gotcha. This changes things. If we can divert Kerr, will Kit run to you or Ms. uh…Rowland?"

"I don't know." Breck looked down at his feet.

To his surprise, Ingrid Rowland approached him and patted his arm as if she were petting a piranha. "He talks about you all the time, Mr. Marchant. He'll head straight for you."

Breck raised his head and stared at her. He felt like a condemned man who'd been given a reprieve. "He talks about me?"

She nodded, the long silver-blonde hair swaying around. "Like I said before, he talks about the places he goes with you…uh…"

"You mean he talks about the places we plan on going till Tania puts a stop to it," Breck said bitterly.

The officer manning the phones interrupted them. "Kerr's just phoned Central and they've patched him through."

Tanner shot over to the camera. "Damn. He's still holding the rifle in the crook of his arm. Okay, time to parlay." He sat down with the phone, eyes narrowed, staring at the screen. Breck presumed he was trying to evaluate Marty Kerr's mood.

"That you, Marty? I'm Jack Tanner and you'll be talking to me today. So here's my number. Any time you—"

He was interrupted by some angry quacking on the other end of the phone. Breck distinctly heard the words "bloody Marchant" and "fucking kid" before he mentally closed it out. He had to keep calm and not worry about Kerr's outbursts if he was to help Kit. Heaven knows, he'd heard them often enough. Cursing was Marty's preferred method of communication. He glanced at Ingrid and she gave him an encouraging nod.

"Sorry, Marty. No can do." Somehow Tanner managed to sound disinterested, brisk and cooperative all at once. "He'll be back here soon and he may talk to you then. But if he doesn't want to, I can't force him to. He'd probably talk to Kit. We'll just have to wait and see."

To Breck's amazement, Tanner clicked off the phone. On the operations Breck had been involved with, he'd never heard a negotiator behave like this.

Ms. Rowland voiced Breck's fears. "B-but what if he gets really angry now and hurts Kit and—"

Tanner shook his head. "He's after Marchant. The boy is the means to an end."

Breck prayed Tanner was right.

He was. Ten minutes later Marty rang back asking for Breck. This time Tanner gestured Breck over to the speaker-phone. The conversation was relayed throughout the caravan, through the speakers on the AOS team's helmets, and at Central. Breck cringed inwardly. The idea of the whole world knowing about his problems was embarrassing. But he had to swallow the embarrassment and save Kit.

"Kerr?" Breck inquired.

He received back a string of invective. Following Jack Tanner's instructions, Breck asked, "What can I do for you, Marty?"

"Send Tania back, you sonofabitch. I know she's with you. Tell here to get back here now or I'll—"

"Gotcha," Breck jumped in before Kit got to hear what was going to happen to him. His heart ached for the blameless little boy he'd thought was living a normal life with reasonable parents. If he and Kit survived today he'd take the boy home, and no matter how bad a parent he was, he and Kit would muddle through. To hell with the Family Court and to hell with

Tania. What a bloody fool he was. He should have known better than to trust Tania in the first place. *Concentrate, Marchant, concentrate on the job in hand,* he told himself. *There'll be no future for you and Kit if you don't get this right.* "I'll try to—" he began to say, but Tanner leaned over and cut the phone off.

"Don't promise him what we can't give him, Marchant. Why does he think Tania's with you?"

Breck shrugged. "I've no idea."

Baz's voice boomed through the speakers. "At least that answers one question. Tania's not there so that's one less person to worry about on site."

Breck didn't give a damn about Tania. Tania had always been able to take care of herself. And he was beginning to wonder if she hadn't set this scene up.

"What about the other two children?" Ingrid Rowland asked.

Breck jolted. He'd forgotten Pixie and Bob, the other two kids in the Kerr family. Pixie was Marty's daughter from a previous relationship, and Tania and Marty's son Bob was barely eighteen months old. Breck knew very little about them, only what Kit had told him.

"If Tania left, wouldn't she take the kids with her?" Jack Tanner asked.

"I'm not sure," Breck said.

"Oh, she'd take Pixie and Bob all right," Ingrid Rowland said grimly. A trickle of sweat dribbled down the side of her face to disappear inside her collar.

Breck sympathized. The back of his shirt was saturated with nervous sweat even though the aircon kept an even temperature inside the trailer van.

"Marchant. He's back again." Tanner was

gesticulating over Ingrid Rowland's head.

Breck spun around in his chair. On the screen he saw Marty with his cell phone to his ear. His voice rang through the speakers. "Put Marchant on. Must be frantic by now about his poofy little boy."

"He's here," Tanner replied. "Just a moment." He flicked the hold button and handed the phone to Breck. "Find out what he really wants. Maybe it's not about Tania at all. Maybe it's something else. Usually I'd say we spin it out, but this has gone on too long."

Everyone inside the van looked at Kit, sitting beside Kerr. His head drooped in the spring sunlight, and the grimy hand plucking at grass-blades trembled.

Breck flicked the switch. "I'm here, Kerr. What can I do for you?"

"Get Tania on the phone."

"She's not here. She's never been here. If she's disappeared, then it's nothing to do with me."

"She's with you all right. She said that even if you were a nosy, sanctimonious ponce, at least you earned good money. The bitch. Just because I lost my job. I know she ran to you."

"No, she didn't because she knows damn well I'd never have her back at any price. Use your brains, Kerr," Breck replied, deviating from Tanner's set piece. "Since our divorce, the woman has played me for money to keep you lot in luxuries. There's no way she'd get past my front door."

It was quiet while Kerr regrouped, then "Get me another beer," they heard him say in an aside to Kit.

"How many does that make?" Tanner asked the video technician.

"Five. Starting to get to him."

"Yeah," Tanner agreed.

On the screen they watched Kit trot in through the open front door, heading for the kitchen at the back of the house.

Baz's disembodied voice spoke one word. *"Now."*

Breck leapt to his feet. Inside the trailer, all eyes were glued on the screen. Everyone watched as three members of Unit Four fanned out and approached the house from the rear. Behind them, the remaining members crouched at the ready. Then in a rush, Baz raced forwards and pulled Kit to safety. The Unit melted away into the trees at the rear of the property. Marty Kerr neither saw nor heard any of it as he chugged down the last swallows of his beer.

"Oh, God." Breck thunked down on to a seat and closed his eyes. Relief thundered through his head. From a distance he heard Baz calling, "You there, Breck? Kit's asking for you. Get over here."

Breck peered out the door of the trailer and saw Baz with Kit perched on his shoulders, standing beneath the spreading branches of the sycamore tree. As he stumbled outside, he could hear Jack Tanner talking to Marty Kerr. "Marty? We spoke before. This is Tanner here. We've got Kit so—"

Breck didn't hear the rest. He raced across a couple of lawns and hurtled over someone's garden to get to Kit.

Chapter Three

As Breck clutched his son to his chest, he wondered how things had come to this. Although Kit had his head buried in Breck's shoulder, he was amazingly composed for a little boy who'd just been held hostage by his stepfather. No tears. Breck wasn't sure if the boy realized how precarious his situation had been until he whispered, "Daddy, was Marty going to kill me?"

Breck gulped and fumbled for a reply.

"Of course not, Kit," Ms. Rowland's composed voice responded from beside them. "He's angry at everyone because he lost his job, so he's trying to get back at the world."

Breck gazed at her with gratitude. He doubted Kit understood her explanation, but her calmness was what the boy needed. She was one hell of a woman. "Thank you," he mouthed over Kit's head.

She nodded in acknowledgment.

"Can I go home with you now, Daddy?" Kit asked.

Breck hated the way his son's voice quavered over such an ordinary question. Between them, he and Tania had made Kit hesitant and fragile. And Breck knew that of the two of them, he was more to blame. If anyone should understand the value of a secure childhood, it was he. To think he had once vowed to himself that no child of his would endure what he had lived through.

Now he must make it up to Kit. He'd take his son home and love him, even if he wasn't an adequate parent, and even if his cramped apartment didn't have a front lawn. Somehow he'd dig deep and give Kit the secure, loving childhood he'd never had.

He coughed to clear his throat. "Yes, of course. We'll be together from now on."

Kit's solemn grey eyes surveyed him, and then a tiny smile flickered at the corners of his mouth. He quenched it quickly and dipped his head.

Breck looked at Ingrid Rowland, wondering if she'd seen that ghost of a smile.

She had. She smiled back at him, and he felt as if he'd accomplished some great feat of courage. Lord, the way a smile could light up that woman's face. For a moment he savored the warmth, then he bent down and lifted Kit up to perch on his shoulders, the same way Baz had done. Kit had seemed to like that. He turned to thank Ms. Rowland and she was right at his elbow.

"Kit, honey—I probably won't see you at preschool tomorrow because you and your dad will have to talk to the police and make plans about what you're going to do. But I'll see you there Monday, okay?" She was telling Breck she expected to see Kit on Monday come hell or high water. And she was giving Kit the security of knowing that he'd get past today. She patted Kit's leg. Breck marveled at how she seemed to understand instinctively what to say. Some people were made to have kids, and some weren't.

As Breck turned away, he thought of something. He went to dig in his pocket and realized he was still wearing his bullet-proof jacket. "Ms. Rowland?"

Again the hundred watt smile. "Ingrid," she said.

"Ingrid. Here's my card. My private number is at the bottom. If you want to call us…I mean—"

"Thank you," she murmured, when he ran out of steam. "And in return—" She fished around in a handbag the size of a small continent. Muttering under her breath she pulled out a couple of books, a box of crayons and a stuffed tuatara lizard. He smothered a grin. The necessary adjuncts of a preschool teacher, no doubt.

"Aha!" She pulled out her wallet and handed him a card.

He memorized the private phone number before putting the card in his pocket. He'd always been good with numbers and knew he wouldn't really need the card. But it comforted him to know he wasn't alone in caring for Kit. Holding on to Ingrid Rowland's card was like holding on to a talisman.

****

Two hours later he'd bought a bunk bed and arranged to have it delivered. A quick dash into a couple of department stores netted some clothes for Kit along with a few toys and puzzles. Kit trotted at Breck's side, holding on to his hand, saying nothing. Breck knew that Baz or possibly Harley Max, the overall AOS manager, would be trying to contact him. But he'd left his cell phone turned off. Of course that was a no-no, but they'd have to understand that right now Kit came first.

Kit stared through the shop window of a bookshop. Remembering Ms. Rowland's bagful of books, Breck detoured to the children's section. "You choose," he told Kit, watching to see what sort of books appealed to his son. Precious minutes ticked by as Kit hovered over the huge selection. He finally cut his selection down to two books titled 'When I'm Feeling Happy' and 'When I'm Feeling Sad.'

Breck swallowed hard and said matter-of-factly, "We'll take them both." He knew Kit couldn't yet read the words, but the sentiments inherent in the bright pictures obviously appealed to the boy. "I couldn't have chosen better myself," Breck said. An inner voice cautioned, "And how would you know what books a child wants to read, Marchant? You were the despair of your parents. Hell, you couldn't even read till you were eight." All too vividly he remembered the endless hours of squirming in front of his parents as they held up flash cards, trying to get him to read simple words like 'tree' and 'dog.' He was a fine one to take his kid into a bookstore.

"Thank you," Kit whispered in a wispy little voice when Breck handed him the plastic bag of books to carry. Breck looked down at his son. He couldn't put off the real world much longer. Soon he would have to attend a debriefing and contact his solicitor, but these two hours with his son had given him a glimpse of what he'd been missing. Tania and the Family Court could get stuffed. He'd fight them both tooth and nail before he let Kit out of his protection ever again. If he had to, this time he'd reveal his suspicions about Tania's tawdry little occupation.

As he bundled Kit into the SUV, the boy asked, "Are we going to eat today, Daddy?"

Breck cursed his own stupidity. Here he was pontificating to himself about how well he'd look after Kit, and he hadn't even *fed* the child. "Sorry, tiger," he said, trying for a casual grin. "Subway, here we come. Uh…I guess your Mom gave you breakfast this morning?" He wasn't sure how to ask exactly when Tania had disappeared.

Kit shook his head. "When I woke up, Mom, Pixie, and Bob were gone," he said matter-of-factly. "Same as last month."

"Last month?" Breck pricked up his ears. "Mom went away last month too?"

"Uh, huh." Kit gazed out the window as they exited the ramp out of the parking building. "She said it was his last chance. If he didn't…didn't…something to do with ships, then she'd do it again."

Breck scoured his mind, wondering what a ship had to do with Tania and Marty. They had left Subway well behind before he clicked. "Did Mom say something like 'shape up or ship out'?" he asked. Kit had a mouthful of prosciutto and lettuce on Italian bread, so he just nodded.

Breck thought it sounded familiar. Tania had said the same thing to him about his working hours. But he could swear she adored Marty. She'd always been happy to tell the world she'd found her soul mate. She sure as hell had never made any comments like that when she was married to *him*. He tried to suppress a smug smile. The very reason she'd cited for the breakdown of their marriage—that his work hours didn't jive with being a husband and father—had now reared up to bite her on the bum. Seems it wasn't so crash hot when your partner didn't have a job at all.

Breck finished his sub and stuffed the paper bag into the trash receptacle. Then he switched his cell phone back on. He'd been off air now for almost three hours and he'd never been that unprofessional before. If he wasn't careful, he'd be without a job too.

Sure enough, there were messages backed up the wazoo. He'd check them out at home. Normally, he'd flick over to loud speaker, but with Kit in the car, well…the boy had had enough trauma for one day. He didn't need to hear how the authorities were dealing with his stepfather.

When Breck elbowed open the apartment door with his arms full of shopping, he got the shock of his life.

"Where the hell have you been?" Baz stood with arms akimbo in the hallway. Breck's tiny living room was full of cops.

"How did you get in?" Breck asked inanely.

Baz looked at him and cast his eyes up.

"Stupid question," Breck muttered to himself. Walking through to the bedroom, he dumped his shopping on the bed. Kit hung back, holding tight to his books and his bottle of OJ. He stared at all the people and blinked.

Breck realized that Abel's wife was here too. "Sorry, Jace. Didn't see you amongst all the navy blue. What are you doing here?"

"Finding a temporary solution to your problem, I hope," she said, smiling.

"Okay!" Baz shouted. "Now he's here, we'll start the debriefing." The buzz of cross-conversations toned down.

Breck's eyes went to the whiteboard set up in the corner of his living room next to a laptop that was flicking through a video of this morning's operation. Shit, Kit shouldn't be watching this. "Uh, Kit, how about a nap? Or you could read those books we bought.

Bunk down on my bed until yours is delivered." Did four-year-olds take naps? He expected mutiny from the boy but his son obediently turned away and headed for the bedroom. Breck guessed Kit was no keener on rehashing this morning's events than he was.

"I'll look after him," Jace offered.

"Thanks, Jace. You're a real trouper," Breck said gratefully. As he shut the bedroom door behind her he heard her say, "Cool books, Kit. Let's read about how everyone gets sad sometimes. Even mommies and daddies. And children. Especially children."

****

Two hours later, the debriefing finished. It was the most efficient debriefing Unit Four had ever held.

"Brilliant!" Baz exclaimed. "Forget Central. In future we'll meet here and do without all the paraphernalia."

Breck hoped not. It had just dawned on him that his apartment was full of hungry, thirsty people and he didn't have a scrap of food in the kitchen. His shopping expedition with Kit had been for clothes and toys to make his son feel comfortable. He'd have to race out and buy some food. Kit would probably wake up from his nap ravenous. This fatherhood thing was damned hard.

"Munchies!" caroled Jace, and in she strode with a tray of savory bites. They were gone before she set the tray down. She laughed and sent Breck to fetch more from the kitchen. He stood there, open-mouthed, at the sight of wall-to-wall food and drink in his kitchen. Jace and Abe, he thought. What fantastic friends they were. And the rest of Unit Four weren't far behind, even if they *were* treading crumbs into his carpet and yelling out for more beer.

"Here's to good results!" Baz shouted. "And here's to Breck Marchant, the new leader of Unit Four!"

Breck damn near dropped the tray he was carrying. He set it down carefully. "You know something I don't?" he asked Baz.

"Maybe," Baz grinned, his round, good-humored face creased into wrinkles of amusement. "I'm off, boyo, and as of next week, you're the man."

He'd got it! He'd got the promotion to team leader! A tentative grin began slowly, and then spread across his face from ear to ear. He punched the air. "Yes!!"

The whole Unit cheered. "Go, Marchant!"

Someone touched his hand and he looked down. "Daddy?"

Oh, God. His heart plummeted. For a few seconds he'd forgotten all about Kit. He could feel his grin cracking into a thousand pieces. "Hi, son. Come and eat something." Breck stretched out a hand to his son.

He would never take over as leader of Unit Four. Today he'd become a solo parent and Kit was his main responsibility. Being leader meant even longer hours. On top of normal police duties, the leaders of the AOS units were responsible for operational policy, planning, debriefing and reporting. Harley Max, the District Commander, would never look at a solo parent as a unit leader. And he'd be right.

How could Breck cope with all that and one small boy too? Oh shit, oh shit. He felt his smile waver as his stomach turned over. In his mind's eye he could see a roaring bonfire, and in the flames, all his plans for the future were burning brightly.

He let the party racket on around him and

concentrated on Kit, making sure his son was not awed by the roomful of cops. Breck noticed that Jace seemed to take it all in her stride. She said to him quietly, "Don't look so worried. I've got a temporary solution for you."

Breck turned to her and thought once again how damned lucky Abe was. Well, almost lucky. Abe had told him they weren't able to have kids, but that didn't stop them from volunteering their time to a couple of kid's charities, and last year they'd applied overseas to adopt. They'd be great parents, not like him.

Jace reminded him of Ingrid Rowland. She was pretty too, and she had the same calm, capable mien around kids that Ingrid had. He preferred Ingrid's softer style though. With Jace, what you saw was what you got. But he had the feeling that Ingrid Rowland had hidden depths. He liked that in a woman.

Jace leaned over and snaffled a piece of sausage off Kit's plate. Kit grinned up at her. "Breck, until we're given the go-ahead for the adoption, I can look after Kit outside of his normal preschool hours." She dipped the sausage in the puddle of ketchup on Kit's plate. "How's that for a bargain? I get a kid to play with and you get peace of mind."

Breck stared at her, his heart full. "I couldn't let you—"

"Of course you could. Who fielded all our calls from Russia last year when we were going through the initial adoption visit? Who did extra duties when Abe had flu last year? Huh?"

Breck smiled. "Abe would do the same for me."

"Yep. So that's the plan. I'm sorry I can't promise you anything permanent because we may have to drop everything suddenly to fly to Russia. And Breck," she laid a hand on his arm, "I'm really sorry about the promotion thing. Something will come up."

Breck shook his head and tried to grin. His throat was so tight he had to swallow so he could speak. "Thanks, Jace. But I don't understand. You work part-time. How can you—?"

"Not any more. Since we applied to adopt, I've become a full-time housewife. And very boring it is too."

Yes. Breck could imagine quick-silver Jace whizzing through the housework by nine a.m. and getting antsy for the rest of the day. Her home gym was probably taking a pounding.

"Well...I—"

"Done," she said, getting up. She waggled her fingers at him and strolled across to where Abe was watching them. He gave Breck the thumbs-up and put his arm around Jace.

Breck blinked hard. He'd been alone for so long he'd forgotten he had good friends-—really good friends—in the unit. When his marriage disintegrated, he'd gone within himself. The other members of the unit had partners and wives and he'd been a fifth wheel. Anyway, he hadn't wanted to socialize. Socializing had always been painful for him, but while Tania was there she'd made things easier.

Yeah, for a short time he'd had it all, and then it had been taken away. Okay. He probably didn't deserve it anyway. That's what his parents would say. They'd made him work for every little privilege, and if he didn't get the privileges, well then...he hadn't deserved them. And if that hadn't worked, they used the cupboard. His stomach squeezed just thinking about that damned cupboard.

He didn't intend to bring Kit up the same way. He respected his parents but he didn't like them and he sure as hell didn't love them. He would never use the twin weapons of guilt and shame that they'd used so effectively on him. No, he loved Kit and he hoped that over time, Kit would come to love him.

Having to forego promotion was devastating, but as he'd learned before, time healed most things. And at least he still had a job, which was more than Marty Kerr had.

He shoved a smile on his face and looked down at his son. "Think you'll enjoy spending time with Jace?"

Kit nodded, his mouth full of sausage. "Cool."

Cool? Kit was recovering rapidly.

Breck grinned. A genuine grin this time. He was in for a hell of a ride, but it would be worth it to know that Kit was safe and happy. When Kit was in bed he'd contact Harley Max to thank him for the opportunity he'd been offered. He ran his side of the conversation through his mind. He always found that planning conversations helped. He would explain why he had to refuse it, but not go into detail. He doubted Harley Max cared a fig about a lowly senior constable's domestic problems. Perhaps if Breck hinted that his decision had been forced upon him, Max might give him another chance sometime in the future. Perhaps. And perhaps pigs flew.

His cell phone vibrated in his shirt pocket and he tugged it out. There was so much noise he couldn't hear the ring tone and he strode into the kitchen to answer it.

"It's Ingrid Rowland here. I was just checking up

on Kit. How are things?"

The fairytale lady. She'd been on his mind all day. Just sitting there quietly. She was that sort of woman, not intrusive, just…there. Thrilled that she'd phoned, he felt an uplift in his spirits. "Kit's doing really well, Ingrid. We've been keeping busy."

"So I hear," she said, her tone as dry as aloes. "I didn't realize I was interrupting a party."

Oh, hell! All the noise the unit was making probably sounded like a rip-roaring party from her perspective.

"No. That's just the guys from—"

"Tell Kit I phoned. Bye." She clicked off.

Damn it! He needed this woman's cooperation and she'd just bounced him. The lady was a little too quick off the mark. "Jeez, talk about jumping to conclusions," he muttered to himself. Her disapproval stung.

"Who are you talking to, Daddy?" Kit was standing at his elbow. The kid crept around like fairy-dust. Must have caught a sprinkle from Ingrid Rowland.

"Ah, that was Ms. Rowland. She wanted to know if you were okay."

Kit waited.

Breck surrendered. "Okay, she wanted to know how you were, but she also got mad at me. She thinks we're having a party and she considers it's inappropriate after what you've been through today. At least, I suppose that's what she's so angry about."

Kit shrugged. "Mommy and Marty have lots of parties. Sometimes Mommy says 'thank you, Breck' and she sort of lifts her glass up—you know."

"Oh, does she?" *And this was the environment I left Kit in.* He'd forked out more and more money hoping

Kit would be the beneficiary, but he'd never asked for a reckoning. It served him right. "Well, never mind," he said. "Let's go and have some more sausage."

Since he was on day shift, he'd work all that sausage off in the gym early Monday morning.

## Chapter Four

Ingrid Rowland jabbed the phone back on to its recharger on the kitchen counter. Just as she'd first thought. She shouldn't have been swayed by his concern for Kit at the hostage situation today. *Any* man, no matter how bad a father he was, would be concerned in such circumstances.

"That's what comes from admiring a nice set of pecs," she admonished herself. "Great body, handsome lived-in face and no sense of responsibility." Well, he must have *some* sense of responsibility, otherwise he wouldn't be a cop. But like many cops, his responsibility was toward the public, not his own family.

Like her father. He'd been a cop too, wedded to the job, so her mother always said. Marla ("call me Marla, darling. 'Mom' and 'Mother' sound so *old*") had asked him to leave when Ingrid was four. Not that Ingrid could remember it. The man was so seldom around that no particular day stood out as different. All she could remember was a tall guy who laughed often. But that might be wishful thinking because her stepfather took life seriously and didn't laugh a lot.

Ingrid hissed in a breath and pulled a face as she sat down at her desk in the corner. She had no right to be critical of Tom Rowland. Everything she had, she owed to him. Tom had been crushingly generous since the day her mother had married him. She'd had the best that Tom's money could buy, right down to a private school education. Then he'd wanted to pay for her university fees, but she'd baulked. Her parents' unrealistic suggestions for her future had spun around esoteric careers such as being an antiques valuer or an events planner. But Ingrid knew her limitations, and anyway, she didn't *want* to do those things.

Although she liked Tom, she couldn't connect with him. She was sick to death of hearing from Marla "how much we owe Tom." Ingrid thought that if he loved them as he professed to do, there should be no "owing."

Preschool teaching suited her just fine. Even so, her parents had made sure that when her training was completed, they'd purchased an elite private preschool for her. In her more uncharitable moments, she wondered if they'd done that so her job did not reflect badly on them. "Our daughter teaches at a preschool" didn't have quite the same ring as "our daughter owns an élite private preschool."

"You are an ungrateful, spoilt brat, Ingrid." She snatched up the attendance register and flipped the pages so fast the paper was in danger of tearing. She marked Kit Marchant absent and typed up a note describing today's events for future reference. She sighed. She'd put off doing the dreaded monthly accounts as long as she could, but now came the reckoning. Which bills could she manage to pay this month? She might have no mortgage or leasing costs, but the ongoing expenses of running a preschool were horrendous. Taxes and local government fees ate up a chunk of the budget. Keeping up with trends was the killer, but to compete with the opposition she had to have the latest equipment so as to be on top of everything.

Sometimes she wished she'd defied her parents and gone to work for one of the big public centers as an ordinary teacher. It would be glorious to flop down on the sofa after work, slam the door on her responsibilities for a few hours, and curl up with a good book. Or join her buddies for a drink at one of their favorite watering holes. Better yet, have time to spare for a casual date now and again. Someone like Breck Marchant with his damn-you eyes. She didn't approve of his parenting skills, but he was easy on the eye. Just made for a casual fling.

Yeah? Who was she kidding? She didn't do casual.

And then there was the black dog hanging over her that would jump up to bite her if anyone inquired into her background.

Glaring at the stack of invoices on her desk, she stuck out her tongue at them.

****

Two days later, Breck took Kit back to preschool. He'd managed to wangle day duty for the next six weeks, which made life easier.

Once Marty had been taken away, the blues had checked through the Kerr home searching for other firearms and clues as to Tania's whereabouts. They'd dropped off a carton of Kit's belongings at Breck's place. "At least we've got some of your stuff," Breck had said to Kit. "We'll get the rest later when we're allowed in."

Kit peered into the box. "It's all here," he said, scratching around inside the carton.

Breck opened his mouth, and then shut it again. What the hell had Tania done with all that money?

Screwed up in the bottom of the carton, Breck discovered some preschool notices explaining the school's policies on clothing and healthy lunches. He checked through his son's meager possessions to ensure he had the right clothing for the coming week, and then set to work to make a ton of food according to Ms. Rowland's edicts. He didn't have a damn clue what 'cheesy-mites' and 'orange pick-ups' were, so he skipped those.

On Monday morning at 7:25, he and Kit arrived at the Rowland Private Preschool squeaky clean and shining bright. Kit wore his little grey shorts and Rowland brand T-shirt, and in his backpack he carried his Rowland-approved morning snack, lunch and afternoon apple pieces. Breck was pretty sure he had everything licked, but he'd learned before that being too cocky could lead to a gigantic stuff-up, so he approached Ingrid Rowland warily.

"Good morning," she greeted Kit sunnily, but she turned to Breck with a glare that could have burnt dry grass at the tag end of summer. Oh, brother.

"You go on in and put your lunch in the fridge, honey," she said to Kit. "I need to speak to your Dad."

Kit looked anxiously at Breck. "Is that okay, Dad?"

Inwardly Breck sighed. He couldn't rid Kit of his anxiety to please. Every time the kid wanted to do something, he checked with Breck first. "Sure. That's what you're here for, son," Breck said, then grinned. "Have a good day, Kit. Jace will pick you up at 4:30 and I'll collect you from her place at 5:30. Okay?" He poked Kit in the chest and Kit grinned back. "Okay!"

he yelled and surprised everyone, especially himself judging by the shocked look on his face. Breck laughed and Kit ran inside.

Breck jumped into speech before Dragonlady Rowland got stuck into him about Thursday night's 'party.' "Here is an authorization letter from me, together with a photo of the lady who will occasionally drop off and collect Kit," he said crisply. He didn't tell her it was only a temporary measure. What she didn't know wouldn't hurt her. "I'll deliver him to preschool and collect him most days, but it depends on my shifts," he explained to the fairytale princess with dragon eyes. If looks could kill…

She relaxed a little. "Good. I'm pleased you've got someone responsible lined up."

His blood boiled. What was she insinuating? That he was irresponsible? That she was surprised he knew a responsible person like Jace?

"Look, Ms. Rowland." He purposely hissed out the 's.' He was *not* going to call her Ingrid. "I don't know why you think I'm incapable of caring for my own son, but get this." For emphasis he prodded a finger against her chest. Oops. He felt his face redden. He'd barely missed a very lush and inviting part of her anatomy. "Sorry. But just because Tania spoon-fed you crap about me, doesn't give you the right to judge me. Okay, I agree I'm not the world's best father, but I'm doing the best I can. Now that Tania has disappeared, I'm all Kit's got. And Jace is the best possible person to take care of him when I can't be there. Kit likes her. I like her. Hell, *everyone* likes her."

He threw up his hands in frustration and glared at Ingrid, daring her to disagree. To think he'd thought she looked like a delicate fairy princess. Well, she did actually, but she had the disposition of a Rottweiler. "And I've got a question," he added.

"What's that, *Mr*. Marchant?" She hissed out the sibilants much better than he had.

"Who are the Wiggles and what the hell is granola?" he growled.

Chapter Five

Breck was beginning to get the hang of this father thing. It wasn't as difficult as Tania had made it out to be. Kit was still way too anxious to please, rather like a Labrador puppy, but he was getting better. Their household was not what you'd call 'typical' but they managed. Fortunately, neither of them was fussy about fancy food or dust bunnies. Just as well. Breck didn't have time in his schedule to worry about cordon bleu cookery and clean windows. Sometimes he wondered what Natasha, his parents' old housekeeper, would think about his efforts. She'd probably just laugh.

Gradually Kit began to mention little things about his life with the Kerrs. The Kerrs hadn't had a 'typical' household either. Kit had commented on the arguments between Marty and Tania in a matter-of-fact voice. It sounded as though the making-up sessions after the arguments were as explosive as the arguments. Breck's face burned when Kit asked him one day, "What did Mommy mean when she said 'suck me'?"

He shrugged. "Not sure, son. So tell me, what did you do at preschool today?"

But Breck wondered about those arguments. It sounded as though Tania and Marty had not been getting along so well for quite a while. If Tania really had left Marty, why had she taken Marty's daughter with her? She had no claim whatsoever to Pixie. Ingratiating, precocious Pixie was Marty's daughter from his first relationship. Breck had only met her a couple of times, but he thought it was a good thing Pixie had taken after her mother in the looks department. Pixie's mom had just up and disappeared one day, leaving a cryptic message. Left with a two year old, Marty had quit his job to live on a single parent's benefit and had no doubt been very comfortable until Tania came along and shoved him into taking a job. Not that that was the way Tania had described it. She had warbled on about finally meeting her 'soul-mate.'

But now Marty had lost that job and Tania had left him, taking his kids with her. Did Tania intend to come back? Perhaps she was teaching Marty a lesson in her own inimitable style. Or was her absence more sinister than that? Had something happened to her and the kids? God, he hoped not. Tania was…Tania, but those kids were so little.

"Where did Marty work?" Breck asked Kit.

But Kit just shrugged and looked away. He was four years old and his life with the Kerrs had consisted of staying out of their way and keeping his eyes and ears closed. Breck gave up trying to get more information out of him. Anyway, it might be better for the boy if he put that time of his life aside and concentrated on his future.

The following day they were sitting at the breakfast table when there was a loud knock on the door.

Kit jumped and stared at the door. "Do you think that's Marty, Daddy?"

"No. Marty's in prison, Kit. You know that."

"What if he got out?"

"Open up!" a voice yelled.

Breck crouched down next to Kit and whispered, "I don't know who this is. Why don't you grab your breakfast and take it to the bedroom? Keep the door closed."

His face twisted in fear, Kit scuttled away.

Breck cursed under his breath. The boy was just coming out of his shell and this had to happen.

"Who is it?" he asked, his face pressed against the door.

Someone shoved an ID up against the fish-eye lens. Detective someone. He opened the door and was pushed aside as two detectives strolled in, followed by a uniformed cop. Without another word they set about searching his apartment. The lead detective's arrogance had Breck grinding his teeth. The guy indicated the first room to be searched with a careless flick of his wrist.

"Show me that ID again," Breck said to him. "When I lay a complaint, I want to know who I'm talking about."

The guy's eyes narrowed and he tugged the ID out of his top pocket. He was shorter than Breck and Breck purposely looked down his nose at him. "Detective Sergeant Alan Moffat," he read aloud. "Thank you." He leaned forward and jammed the card back in Moffat's pocket. Startled, Moffat jumped back out of reach.

Breck turned his back on Moffat and went to sit beside Kit who was huddled on his bed, his eyes big with fear.

Was this search anything to do with work? Not likely. That would be handled by Harley Max. So it must be to do with the Kerrs. He kept quiet to see how the scene would play out, forcing himself to keep cool and holding tight to Kit who was tensed as taut as a bowstring.

Twenty minutes later, they still hadn't found whatever it was they were looking for.

"I'm gonna be late," Kit wept.

"Miss Rowland will understand, Kit. Don't worry."

Kit being late for preschool was the least of their worries. What the hell was this about? If Kit hadn't been here, he'd have had that rat Moffat in a headlock. Cops had rights just the same as ordinary citizens and this guy had no search warrant and no manners. He needed to be taught a lesson. His 2IC and the uniformed cop kept casting anxious glances over their shoulders as they searched. They were uncomfortable with the proceedings.

"Okay. You'll have to come with us," Moffat said.

"What? What about my son?" Panicked, Breck glared at the detective.

Moffat shrugged. "Surely you've got someone who can look after him."

The detective constable looked a little more sympathetic. Breck figured he had kids of his own. "Is there someone you can call to come get him?" he asked.

Jace. Had to phone Jace. With Kit watching anxiously, he dialed Jace and Abe's number. No answer. Oh, shit.

Kit tugged at his sleeve. "Miss Rowland. Phone Miss Rowland. She could collect me. She won't mind."

Breck chewed his lip. "She has to teach, son. She can't just up and leave school at the drop of a hat."

"Yes she can. There's Mrs. Lennox and Miss Martin there too."

Oh. He hadn't given any thought to the fact that the princess had assistants. Of course she did. Would she help him out? Probably not. But she'd help Kit out. He dialed.

"Be there in ten minutes," she said crisply after he'd explained the situation. And she was as good as her word. "What's all this about?" she demanded of Moffat, the second she put her foot in the door. "What do you think you're doing, terrorizing Kit? This boy has been through a traumatic experience recently. *What* did you say your name was?"

Breck stood back. The fairy princess had spine to spare. Good on her. He had to be careful what he said at this stage, not knowing what was going on. But as a disinterested member of the public, Ingrid could say what she liked. She looked at the bedroom closet where the cops had tossed clothes aside and pulled out every drawer in the big chest of drawers. "I take it your housework isn't usually this slack?" she said, raising her eyebrows at Breck.

"You take it right," he answered.

"What the hell are you looking for?" she snapped at Moffat.

Moffat opened his mouth and closed it again like a goldfish. Before he could say a word, she was off again. "Must be mighty small if you expect to find it in Breck Marchant's drawers." Then she realized what she'd said and blushed an unbecoming scarlet.

Moffat didn't even get it because he was so startled at her outburst. But the uniformed cop smirked and looked down at his boots.

"I'll take Kit to school with me now," she promised Breck. "Do you want legal representation or is that something you cops sort out among yourselves?" The way she said 'you cops' reminded Breck of the day she'd bailed him up while Kit was a hostage. She sure hated cops. But he was grateful she'd come to his aid.

"Oh, I don't think it will come to that," Moffat rushed to tell her. "We just want to ask him some questions about…about Tania Kerr."

"Can I help? I've known her for some years."

Everyone stared at her.

"You have?" Breck asked.

"Mmm. We did our graduate diploma of preschool teaching together."

And that had been one of the reasons Breck had thought it prudent to leave the parenting up to Tania. Not only was she a natural, she was qualified.

"But Tania never qualified." Ingrid added.

Breck raised his eyebrows. "What? I didn't know that."

"I think you'll find there's a lot you don't know about Tania."

The men raised their eyebrows. Ouch. The fairy princess didn't like Tania one little bit. Breck wondered what had happened between them.

"So," Moffat frowned. "Would you have any idea where Tania might be?"

Ingrid looked down at Kit who was holding tight to her hand. "Sweetie, clean your teeth and wash your hands. Don't forget to check that your backpack is ready."

As soon as he was out of hearing, Ingrid looked Moffat in the eye. "Talking about his mother in front of him is about the most callous thing I've ever heard. I've no idea at all where she is. But hasn't it struck you that

Tania has managed to get two men into trouble? Marty got so hyped up he did a stupid thing, and now you're taking Breck in for questioning over her disappearance. Two birds, one stone. Clever."

*And so are you*, Breck thought. *You know Tania very well.*

"I see," Moffat said, obviously not seeing anything at all.

Miss Rowland took Kit's hand. "Come on, Captain Kit. You and I have work to do, my man." And delicate, sweet little Miss Rowland stomped out the door.

****

Breck discovered that Moffat's animosity had its roots in Harley Max's admonitions to tread carefully with one of "his men."

"We got an anonymous tip-off," Moffat's 2IC, Detective Peters, explained to Breck when Moffat left the room to collect a video of the interior of Kerr's house. They'd taken Breck to headquarters to question him. Moffat could just as easily have questioned him at home without all the drama, but Harley Max had ruffled Moffat's feathers when he'd told him that the tip-off was a crock. Moffat's own boss, Detective Inspector O'Halloran, had stirred the pot when he'd agreed. So now, not only was Moffat pissed off at his superiors, everyone was pissed off with Moffat.

Detective Peters grinned. "You could steal the Holy Grail now and everyone would turn a blind eye. He'll have to watch his back in future." Peters settled in for a gossip, leaning back against Moffat's desk. "He tried to join the AOS, you know, a couple of years ago. Didn't get to first base. Couldn't get the requisite three recommendations."

Breck snorted. "No surprises there. His temperament wouldn't be a good fit."

Peters sighed. "It's not a good fit around here either. He's applied for a transfer, which is fantastic."

Breck grinned.

Moffat came back and Peters subsided.

"We got a call from a disposable cell phone," he explained to Breck. "The caller said that if we wanted to find Tania Kerr, go and look at your place."

"I'd already figured that out," Breck said drily. "And the only one who persists with that idea is Marty Kerr. Better check on his phone privileges."

"We did. He doesn't have phone privileges. He made his initial call to a lawyer, and he hasn't communicated with anyone since then. He's had one visitor—his brother. But the guy only visited once, on the day Kerr was arrested."

"How did the brother know he'd been arrested?" Breck asked.

"Christ, it was all over the TV. Big news."

"I guess." Breck didn't know anything about Marty's brother but he decided right then and there to do some checking of his own.

"So…" Moffat was determined to shake something out of this debacle, "when did you see Tania last?"

Breck shrugged. "Not sure. About three or four weeks ago, I saw her through the window when I dropped a check into their letterbox."

"What was she doing?"

"Kissing Marty," Breck said equably. "The lights were on. It was early evening." He thought for a moment. "I spoke to her on the phone a couple of days before she disappeared."

Moffat perked up. "Did you ring her or did she ring you?"

"She rang me with the same old."

"Huh?"

"Same old 'no visitation for Kit this month because he's going with Marty to the zoo.' She used every excuse under the sun to keep me from having Kit for a weekend. There wasn't much I could do about it." He struggled to subdue the familiar anger.

"Why couldn't you? Your lawyer should have sorted that out."

Moffat spoke with the carelessness of the misinformed. He'd obviously never suffered the trauma of struggling to deal with child access issues. Breck had no intention of airing his dirty linen for Moffat to pick over. He didn't want anyone to know how scared he'd been to stir the pot, and most of all he didn't want people to know how ill equipped he was to be a parent. He mumbled that Tania was a great mom apart from her habit of stiffing him.

"Didn't you want the kid?" Moffat needled him.

Breck breathed in through his nose. "Yeah. I wanted him. What's this got to do with Tania's disappearance?"

"Just wondering if she pissed you off one time too many and you decided to take care of her once and for all." Moffat took a careful step backwards.

Peters rolled his eyes.

Breck squeezed down on his hubris and forced himself not to rise to the bait. God, *how* he longed to leap up and deck Moffat. "Look, Moffat, there's a couple of things you should know. Tania is given to disappearing. During our marriage she twice disappeared for a few days. The first time she took Kit with her. The second time she left him at home with me. Each time she came back behaving as if nothing had happened. She was a secretive woman but she was a good mom, so I let her call the shots. It seems she did the same thing to Marty. My son mentioned that a week before Marty had his little brainstorm, she left early in the morning, taking the other two kids with her. She came back the next day and even though Marty raved, she refused to say where she'd been. From what Kit told me, it generated a volcanic argument. Those two thrived on arguments." Breck had no intention of explaining to Moffat about Tania's little sideline, which was probably what had got her into trouble this time.

Moffat thought for a moment, which made a nice change. He should have thought before thumping on Breck's door and instituting a search. And he should have thought before dragging Breck down to HQ.

"What exactly were you looking for at my apartment?" Breck asked. Would Moffat tell him?

"Signs to see if Tania had been there or was staying with you, that sort of thing," Moffat answered, as if that should have been obvious.

Yeah. That sort of thing. Bloodstains. Signs of a struggle.

At least Moffat had one saving grace. He hadn't tried to interrogate Kit at preschool without an adult in attendance. He'd seen Moffat eyeing Kit as if he was trying to work out how much Kit knew about his mother's disappearance. Maybe Peters had restrained him. Breck grinned to himself. Anyway, the dragon fairy lady wouldn't have let Moffat get within an inch of any of her children. Lord, that woman was amazing. She sure fired up when she was in a snit. Which reminded him. "It sounds as though Miss Rowland might know quite a lot about Tania. You could question her again," he suggested evilly.

Moffat stiffened. "Not if I want to keep my balls," he muttered.

Breck grinned again. He must buy Ms. Rowland a present.

## Chapter Six

A week later, Kit and Breck had their timetable down to a fine art. But a teenage boy threw a spanner in the works. He got hold of his father's new .223 and took it to show some of his mates how well he could shoot. When he realized the cops were on his tail, he holed up in bush land at the back of the local public school. A really dangerous situation.

Unit Four hadn't yet had a new team leader appointed, so Breck was in command for the time being. He phoned Jace as he sped to the scene. She assured him that picking up Kit was no problem. That was one thing off his mind.

As soon as he arrived on the scene, he set up the points for his team. "The rifle's got a Pecar varipower scope. Hardly a challenge at that range," he muttered to Abe.

Abe grinned. "Be fair. When you were fourteen, you'd have thought you were the cat's pajamas if you could get your hands on one of those."

Breck snorted. When he was fourteen his father had spent hours inculcating the old 'peace not war' mantra into his son. So much so that Breck was unable to defend himself until he became a cop. He often wondered what his father would have done if someone had attacked his mother. Probably stand there and lecture the assailant till the guy was so bored he'd run away. Breck also believed in peace not war, but he'd seen the other side of the coin too often to know it didn't always work.

Unit Four took it upon themselves to give the fourteen-year old some advice. He was too frightened to do more than bluster when Abe, Breck and Turkey had quietly come up behind him and relieved him of his weapon. By that stage he knew he'd bitten off more than he could chew and had been almost pleased to see them. As Abe said, "Not all the boy's fault. His father has had a gun license for years. He should have spent some time telling the kid the gun license was a privilege, not a right."

Jace reported to Breck that evening while Breck packed a sleepy Kit into the back seat of the SUV. "Ms. Rowland gave me a superior look that said, 'The parenting didn't last long, did it?' So, I got stuck into her. I said you were carrying a heavy load, and doing it well. I told her not to judge people she knew nothing about."

Breck cringed. He hadn't told Jace about Ingrid's helpfulness on the day Moffat had questioned him, and he wasn't sure Jace was in the mood to listen anyway. He smiled and thanked her. What else could he do?

But his heart was heavy when he delivered Kit to preschool the following day. If Ingrid told him to take Kit elsewhere, he didn't know what he'd do. Kit loved Ms. Rowland. It was "Ms. Rowland says" and "Ms. Rowland likes us to…" until Breck was absurdly jealous of her influence over his son. Anyway, *he* liked Ingrid. She was a rare woman who'd come to his aid even though she didn't like him and thought he was a hopeless father. And she was a heck of a good teacher. She was nothing at all like his parents. Somehow he knew that if her kid couldn't read until he was eight years old, she'd just encourage him and cuddle him and pretend she didn't care. And once or twice Breck had been late collecting Kit at the end of the day and she'd never said a word.

He approached the gate of the preschool warily.

But Ingrid Rowland came out to greet them, taking Kit by the hand and smiling nervously at Breck. She licked her lips, and then jumped straight to the heart of the matter. "Mr. Marchant, please—"

"Breck," he said.

"Breck," she said, the same way she'd said it on the day of Kit's escape from Marty.

Breck's toes curled and he damned near forgot to breathe. He found himself grinning like a loon. *You don't spend enough time around women, Marchant, if this up-tight little munchkin can tie you up in knots. Concentrate.*

Meanwhile, Ingrid was warbling on. "Please apologize to Mrs. Carter for me. She caught me at a bad moment yesterday."

She peered at him from under her lashes. Was she checking to see if he was suitably mollified?

"My stepfather was here looking over his investment." Her dry tone reminded Breck of autumn leaves crushed underfoot. "He is insisting I raise my fees. We were in the middle of a battle royal when Mrs. Carter arrived to collect Kit. It wasn't because she was late or because you didn't come or anything like that." She smiled down at Kit. "Say goodbye to Daddy and put all your gear away now, Kit," and off skipped Kit, happy as a cricket with his new Spiderman backpack.

Ingrid Rowland turned back to Breck. "He's a new person," she said. "Living with you has worked wonders."

"D'you think so?" Was she buttering him up? He'd thought recently that Kit seemed more settled and less inclined to be watchful. But he didn't know enough about the parenting thing to be sure.

Ingrid nodded, strands of hair escaping the business-like scarf tying back her silver-blonde mane. "Very much so."

"So…" Breck inquired, for some reason wanting to keep her talking, "*Are* you going to raise your fees?"

She shook her head. "Tom doesn't understand the first thing about preschools. He sees them as a business, which of course they are," she amended, "but government subsidies apply and he never takes those into consideration. Being a self-made man, he has a certain contempt for reliance on subsidies." She sighed. "All very well if you're a millionaire."

From which Breck deduced that her stepfather was one wealthy hombre. Lucky sod. Was Ms. Rowland just dabbling in preschool work, waiting for Mr. Rich and Right to come along? He didn't think so. She seemed sincere about 'her' children. Sometimes Breck stood and watched her when he dropped Kit off in the mornings, just for the pleasure of watching the sun glint on her blonde hair as she bent down to listen to a whispered confidence from a lisping four year old. Her tone of exasperation when she'd referred to her stepfather had not been lost on Breck. All was not well in the Rowland dovecote.

"Well, I'm very glad the fees are staying the

same—"

"For the time being," she interrupted quickly. "I can't promise they won't rise in the foreseeable future."

Unease stirred inside him. "Can you define 'foreseeable'?"

She eyed him, and he had the uncomfortable feeling she knew how much he earned, right down to the last cent. He rushed into speech. "I've been thinking about a new place to live. Bigger. With a lawn, maybe. And a dog for Kit." Christ, he couldn't stop babbling. Well, he *had* been daydreaming about those things, but Ingrid Rowland didn't need to know that.

Her eyes lit up, little chips of green shining through the hazel. "Oh, yes! I know what you mean. I'd *love* to have a place of my own." Then the light went out of her eyes. "But it will be years before I can afford it."

"Wouldn't your father buy you a place?" Breck asked, and then wished he'd kept his mouth shut. Her life was no business of his.

She stiffened. "My stepfather, you mean," she snapped. "In a heartbeat, he would. But I want to be free of any more ties. I'm sick of being obligated." She looked as though she'd sucked on a lemon.

Good for her. Independence was a precious thing, he could attest to that. He'd checked himself out of school before his parents found out and taken a part-time job at the wool stores beside the Auckland wharves in order to shake himself free.

"So menial," his father had said with disgust.

But he'd figured "menial" was what he needed. He hadn't been so big in those days and he'd intended to succeed at Police College so he'd needed the hard physical work to build him up some.

As soon as he neared the acceptance age he'd applied. With his heart in his mouth, he'd slaved over the paperwork at the Central Library. And that was where he'd met Abe. Abe had coached him and he'd coached Abe and together they got through training.

Breck's parents had washed their hands of him. After all their hard work he wanted to be a *cop*?

"I understand," he said to the fairy princess.

Her eyes searched his face. She nodded.

Something inside him unfurled. This woman and he were on the same wavelength. What if…? No, don't go there, Marchant. She deserves better than a struggling single parent cop from a dysfunctional family.

****

That night, still thinking about Ingrid Rowland, he drove into his allotted parking space beneath the apartment building. Kit was sprawled out asleep in the back seat, his safety restraint cutting into his stomach. Outside, only a sprinkle of stars dotted the sky and clouds obscured the moon. The basement parking area was as black as pitch. The super had neglected to fix the two fluorescent tubes that had been flickering on and off for a couple of weeks now.

Wondering what he could fling together for dinner, Breck jumped down from the 4WD straight into a punch that sent sky-rockets exploding in his brain. In the distance he could hear Kit struggling out of his seatbelt yelling, "Dadd-ee!! Dadd-ee!!" but fog clouded Breck's brain and swirled in front of his eyes. He couldn't seem to move. His eyes wouldn't focus but his hearing went on full alert to compensate. A slight hitch in breathing and the scrape of a sneaker on asphalt had him ducking down.

"Dadd-ee!" Kit yelled again and Breck heard a click as Kit escaped from his safety belt.

Terror gripped him by the throat. Nobody was going to take Kit away from him. "No!" he managed to croak, and then Kit cannoned into him. In one movement Breck curled himself over his son and dropped to the ground. He squinted up at the dark figure looming over them and punched upwards, the full force of his anger behind the punch. His fist connected and the figure staggered back. Still too stunned to move, he stayed where he was, a sitting duck. His eyes swiveled, trying to gauge where the next attack would come from. Then an almighty wallop slammed him between the shoulder blades. The breath whooshed out of his lungs. Choking and gasping for air, he prayed the assailant wasn't carrying a knife.

Nearby a car door slammed and an engine revved. The warmth of car exhaust brushed his skin and he raised his head in time to see a battered pick-up truck fishtail its way out of the car lot. Without giving way, it roared into the traffic flow to the accompaniment of blasting horns. As it turned, Breck caught a flash of color under the streetlights. Blue.

"Daddy?"

Hell. He was crushing Kit into the asphalt. "Sorry, Kit." He dragged himself to his feet, groggy and disoriented, using the SUV as a prop. That had been some punch. It had been years since he'd been sucker-punched. He touched his chin gingerly. Warm blood coursed down his chin and neck and dribbled over his fingers. So, not just a fist. A knuckle duster.

He staggered into the apartment with Kit trailing

behind, towing his backpack and Breck's satchel.

Breck locked the door and turned on the lights. Then he crouched down unsteadily to examine Kit. "Sure you're okay, son?"

Kit stared at him, his eyes round with wonder. "You saved me, Daddy," he said solemnly. "Just like…like—" He gave up trying to find an analogy and buried his face in his father's shoulder. Then he started and pulled back. "Ugh! There's blood all over you!"

There sure was. Breck's tee shirt was soaked. It stuck to his skin. He tried to stand but the effort was too much for him. He settled for crawling on his hands and knees and collapsed on to the sofa just as his cell phone rang. "Shit," he muttered, struggling to sit up.

"I'll get it, Daddy." Kit dived into Breck's satchel. He fished out the phone and to Breck's shock, gabbled away like a pro. "Hi, Ms. Rowland," he chirped.

Breck groaned. The woman would think he stumbled from disaster to disaster.

"Ms. Rowland, can you come over? Daddy's sick. A bad man tried to hurt us."

"Hell! No, son. Don't tell her that!" Breck tried to grab the phone.

Too late. Kit had already shut the phone down and set about emptying his backpack and Breck's satchel. "Lie down, Daddy."

Breck lay back, wondering where his submissive, quiet little boy had gone. This kid was taking over. He almost grinned in spite of his spinning head. It was great that Kit had become confident enough to take over.

The next thing he knew, gentle hands were turning his head this way and that. "Puncture wounds," a soft voice said. "How on earth did he get those, Kit?"

Breck struggled to sit up.

"No, no. Lie down, Mr. Marchant—er, Breck."

It was the fairy lady. His stomach tightened.

"Let me see…"

He stayed still.

There was a short silence while her fingers brailed his face. His heart beat in an uneven tattoo.

"I think you should go to the emergency department," she said after a few minutes. "Two of these wounds are very deep. I think they'll need stitches. Here." She pressed a soft, damp cloth against his chin. "Are you hurt anywhere else?"

He was damned if he was going to admit that his head was spinning and his back felt as if someone had driven a tank over it. "There's a doctor I can call," he mumbled.

"Will he make house calls?" Ingrid Rowland bit her lip.

"Yes," Breck said, and lay back again. Out of the corner of his eye, he saw Kit, round-eyed, watching.

"Kit? Sure you're okay?"

"Yes, Daddy. Ms. Rowland checked me over."

"Thanks," Breck murmured.

Somehow he lost another half-hour and woke to find Doc Hargreaves bending over him, tying off a stitch.

"Hi, Marchant. We meet again," Hargreaves said. He shone a light into Breck's eyes. "No concussion."

"No. I didn't bang my head. Why am I so dizzy?"

"Blood loss. I think you ran into a knuckle-duster with sharp spikes. Stuffed up your stubborn chin but was high enough to miss your windpipe."

Breck hadn't thought about his trachea. Lucky he hadn't drowned in his own blood.

"Seen a couple of similar injuries recently," Hargreaves said. "Martial arts technique. Got any ideas who would do such a thing?"

Breck tried to shake his head but his head swam and he subsided.

"Uncle Billy does martial arts, Daddy." Kit's voice startled them. He was standing beside them, watching his father anxiously.

"Who's Uncle Billy, son?" Breck tried to sound casual, but it came out as a croak.

"Marty knows him. He's mean, Marty says."

Hargreaves raised his eyebrows. "I have to report this at HQ, Marchant."

"Mmmph." Breck wasn't going to try to nod. "I understand."

"Leave it up to Max to sort out." Hargreaves peered into Breck's face. "Hmm. See how you feel tomorrow. You're healthy enough not to need a transfusion. Plenty of fluids will do the trick."

In the distance Ingrid Rowland clattered pots in the kitchen. The doctor inclined his head, "Friend of yours?"

"Not really," Breck answered. "A friend of my son's."

Ingrid came into the room, wiping her hands on a cloth. She must have heard what he said because her lips trembled. Looking uncertain, she began to back out of the room.

Feeling like a complete bastard, Breck lay back and looked at the ceiling.

Hargreaves looked from Breck to Ingrid. "Well, if

you're staying, Ms. Rowland, could you see that Breck gets plenty of fluids to drink?"

Ingrid nodded and hurried off to the kitchen, Kit pattering behind her.

As Hargreaves packed up his gear he whispered to Breck, "Not bad; not bad at all."

Breck flushed. Hargreaves was a notorious gossip. He hoped while he'd been out cold the doc hadn't said anything that would be better left unsaid. Then again, he had just managed to both upset and insult Ingrid, so anything Hargreaves came up with couldn't possibly be worse.

"Don't want to hear from you until you come in for your next physical." Hargreaves winked, and was gone.

Breck fingered his chin. As Ingrid had surmised, the doctor had stitched two of the gashes beneath his chin. Breck hadn't felt a thing so Hargreaves must have sprayed his skin with anesthetic. The skin still felt numb.

Ingrid and Kit rattled into the room carrying trays of food and Breck struggled to sit up.

"Here, let me help you," Ingrid said, dumping her tray. She came around the back of the sofa and put her arms around him as if she were going to hug him. She smelled of lemon peel and vanilla. Startled, he froze, but she had already hoisted him up against the back of the sofa.

He tried to assemble his wits. "Where did you…uh, learn that?" he asked.

She grinned. "Night shift at a retirement village while I was at university. There were supposed to be two of us on duty at all times but it just never happened, so we learned to manage."

Lord, the little princess was strong. He would never have believed she could lift more than a cucumber sandwich.

"Kit was hungry so we dug around in the cupboards. Hope you don't mind."

She looked anxious, and he cursed inwardly that she'd overheard his comment to Hargreaves. How ungrateful could he be? "Thank you, Ingrid. I'm not very hungry at the moment, but it looks good." Must be. Kit was tucking into his food as if he hadn't eaten for a week. Breck knew his cooking left much to be desired, but hell, it wasn't *that* bad. "He *did* get breakfast and lunch, you know," Breck muttered.

Ingrid smiled. She dug her fork into her food. "It's good. Try some."

He frowned. She was talking to him as if he were one of her four-year olds.

Then she saw the expression on his face and clapped a hand over her mouth. "Sorry. Force of habit." She removed the plate from his lap and plunked it down on the table next to him.

Perversely, he now wanted to sample the casserole. Damn it. The woman must have done a course in psychology. Child psychology.

He shuffled along the sofa and retrieved the plate, his head swimming with the effort. As soon as he swallowed the first mouthful, he realized she was right. It *was* good. It wasn't like any canned casserole he'd ever had before. "What did you add to it to make it taste like this?" he asked.

"Just a bit of this and that. You know, the usual stuff."

Well, that cleared things up. What the hell was she

talking about?

"She put in some spices and stuff, Dad," Kit explained. His plate was clean. Breck suspected that if Ingrid wasn't there, Kit would have licked the plate. As a matter of fact, if Ingrid wasn't there, *he* would lick the plate. "I didn't know I had any of those things in the cupboard," he said, feeling like an idiot.

She eyed him, delicately forking up small mouthfuls. "So who stocked your cupboards?"

The penny dropped. "That must have been Jace on the day the Unit came here. The day you—" He stopped. He'd been going to say, "The day Kit was kidnapped and you got snotty about our having a party." Since Kit was listening and since she was doing him a favor, he shut up.

"Oh. That day," she said. "It must be great to have friends like Jace. I could do with some."

"You don't have friends—"

"None who I'd let near my kitchen." She finished the sentence quickly, with a snap.

What was she saying? That she didn't have any trustworthy friends? She was so hard to read. Anyway, why was he wasting his time wondering? She was a kind, helpful, okay…very pretty woman who was also his son's preschool teacher. That's all. And he wasn't in the market for kind, helpful, pretty preschool teachers. He wasn't in the market for any kind of woman, period.

Chapter Seven

Ingrid collected their empty plates. Her stomach churned with embarrassment. For one God-awful moment she had nearly admitted how lonely she was. Then she'd caught a glimpse of Breck's face and seen his closed-in expression. He didn't want to listen to her any more than she wanted to confide in him. But today she'd been able to help him and she'd almost misread the situation. Hell, she'd heard what he said to the doctor about her being Kit's friend, not his. That should have told her he didn't want her lingering around, burbling on about her life. She was an idiot.

Head down, she shoved the dishes into the dishwasher, then turned around to grab her bag and escape.

And there he was. Standing right at her elbow.

She jumped back.

"Uh, sorry to startle you. I was wondering—"

"Yes?"

"Well, I was wondering if you had any ideas about where Tania might…" He stopped. He'd probably seen the pissed-off expression on her face. She'd had Tania Kerr right up to the back teeth.

"No. That's not what I meant to say." He paused and looked as if the words were being dragged out of him. "I want to apologize for…for"—he swallowed—

"the ungracious thing I said to Doc Hargreaves. You *are* my friend, just as much as you're Kit's friend. How could we not be friends? You've helped us twice now, and you're a very nice person. It's just that the police rumor mill—" Running out of steam, he forked his fingers through his hair, then staggered back a step. "Weak as a kitten," he muttered, leaning against the counter.

"You should be in bed," Ingrid said. Even as the words left her mouth she felt a slow heat burn its way over her face and down her neck. What a buck stupid thing to say! Just for a second his eyes had flashed grey fire from beneath hooded lids. She shot from majorly embarrassed to smug in five seconds. "Enjoy the ride," she told herself. "You won't get another one."

"I need to find out who attacked me and why. And somehow I have to find bloody Tania," he muttered. "Until she's found, I'm the main suspect. Well…in Detective Moffat's eyes I am."

"The man's a dork," Ingrid said. "I mean, anyone can see…" She trailed off. Let's not go there, Ingrid. Stop while you're ahead.

"If I didn't have Kit I could do some sleuthing on my own—Kit!"

They rushed into the living room.

Kit was stretched out on the sofa, fast asleep.

Ingrid closed her eyes in relief and Breck grinned at her. Lord, he was so sweet when he gave that sexy, quirky smile. Well, perhaps 'sweet' wasn't quite the right word for a toughened cop like Breck Marchant, but there was softness in his eyes when he looked at his son, and that was sweet to see.

He sat down heavily in an armchair beside the sofa.

"Does the wound throb?" she asked. Well, duh. Of course it hurt.

"Not really, but I couldn't take on a bunch of assassins at the moment." He leaned back against the chair and closed his eyes, frowning slightly. She wanted to go to him and smooth the frown away, but of course she wouldn't do any such thing. Anyway, what was this nurturing thing that had suddenly attacked her? She cleared her throat and he opened his eyes again.

"What did you mean when you said you'd do some sleuthing on your own if you had the opportunity? What sort of sleuthing?" she asked.

"I'd like to get into the Kerr house now it's no longer a crime scene. I want to know what secrets Tania is hiding that got us into this mess."

Oh, yeah. Tania had many secrets. This straightforward guy sitting here in front of Ingrid wouldn't have the hope of a snowflake in hell of figuring out what Tania was all about. Sure, he was a good cop and was supposed to know all about clues, but even though he'd been married to her for more than three years, Ingrid doubted Breck understood just how complex Tania was and what she was capable of. Ingrid did. She'd had experience of Tania's vindictive side.

With Breck Marchant, what you saw was what you got. And that was a damned good thing. Drama queens like Tania caused mayhem wherever they went. They wrecked lives and got away with it. Breck Marchant was the other side of the coin, honest and trustworthy.

But there wasn't anything Ingrid could do to help him.

She looked at Kit, murmuring in his sleep as he settled into a more comfortable position on the lumpy sofa, his hand curled beneath his chin, and then her eyes swiveled back to Breck Marchant. His head was propped against the chair back and he closed his eyes as he chewed over how to go about investigating the puzzle his life had suddenly become.

Tania had tossed these two guys aside as if they were toys she'd tired of. Tania was the stupidest woman on the planet.

Kit was a sweet kid, and how he'd survived life with Marty and Tania relatively unscathed was a miracle. It was also a testament to Breck Marchant's influence, whether he knew it or not.

Ingrid smiled. Breck was half-asleep, his head lolling to one side, his hands relaxed and loose in his lap. The wolf and his cub, asleep, Ingrid thought fancifully. And how Breck Marchant would hate her to see this side of him.

Suddenly, he jerked awake and continued their conversation. "If someone should see me at the Kerrs' place, I can use the pretext of collecting the rest of Kit's belongings," he said.

Ingrid nodded. "Do you need a look-out for this sortie?" she asked before she could stuff the words back in her mouth.

One side of his mouth quirked. "Sortie? You're very military all of a sudden, Ingrid."

"Well, what do you call it?"

"A damn stupid idea but I'm going to do it anyway."

"Okay. Can I help with this damn-stupid-idea-but-you're-going-to-do-it-anyway?"

He chuckled. "You are not at all like you look, Ms. Rowland. You're an adventurer at heart." Then he sobered. "There's no way I can let you become involved. If I'm caught I can easily talk my way out of it, but I'd hate to have to explain what you're doing there."

So what did he think she looked like? She was dying to know. She cleared her throat. "Are you telling me to butt out?" Her question lacked bite. He was probably right. "Okay. But perhaps I can give you some ideas of where to look. At college Tania had lots of little heart-to-heart chats with me. On her own terms of course. I figured she was buttering me up to help her with assignments and stuff."

Breck grinned. "No flies on you, Ms. Rowland. Did you help her out?"

"No," Ingrid said tersely. "I don't like being played. I have enough of that with my parents." Then she thought of the consequences of her refusal to oblige Tania and the resultant fallout.

"You too, huh? Parents can be the very devil. That's why I'm determined to do my best for Kit." He stood up. "And I'd better get the boy to bed. Tell you what, I'll ask Jace if she'll mind Kit for an extra hour or so tomorrow, and after work I'll call in at your place. I'd appreciate your telling me everything you know about Tania."

"Here's my address." She scribbled it on one of her cards.

After casting a quick look around the parking lot, he handed her into her car as if she were made of spun glass. But as he bent down to say goodbye he staggered and had to grasp the luggage rack on the Fiesta's roof to hold himself up.

"Go to bed," she told him, this time without

blushing furiously.
    "Yes, ma'am."
    She grinned and drove away.

Chapter Eight

Nervous excitement warred with fear in Breck's stomach as he crunched over the broken paving stones that led to Ingrid's small apartment block. He looked at the paint peeling off her front door as he pressed the doorbell.

She lived more frugally than he did. This wasn't a very salubrious neighborhood; in fact, he'd call it a damned dangerous place to live. Auckland didn't have as much crime as many large cities around the world did, but this suburb was renowned for middle-of-the-night police call-outs. He'd been here a time or three. He wondered what her parents thought about where she lived.

"It's unlocked. Come in!" she called.

Unlocked? What was she thinking?

He barged in. "Jesus, Ingrid! You shouldn't leave your door unlocked like that."

She shrugged. "I knew you were coming. You're a cop. If there was any trouble, you could sort it out. Besides, everyone around here knows me. It's safe."

He looked at her, opened his mouth and shut it again. She had changed out of her school clothes into a tight pair of jeans that hugged every curve. Small she might be, but she had curves. Oh, boy, did she have curves.

To get his eyes off the curves he glanced around her apartment. Like his, it was furnished by A-Mart and second-hand shops. But she had plants everywhere and on one wall the setting sun caught the highlights in an old oil painting of a violent storm at sea. He stepped closer to peer at it. It looked valuable, but what would he know?

"My grandfather left that to me," she said from behind him. "My father's father."

He spun around and almost plastered himself against those curves. Bad idea. Well, excellent idea, but he hadn't come here for that. Ingrid was a special lady, no doubt about that, but he had his hands full with Kit and his job and he wasn't looking for…for…temptation. Besides, he doubted she even liked him, let alone thought about him that way. She seemed to have something against cops.

"Uh, so what ideas did you have about Tania?" he asked, desperately.

Her shoulders rose and fell as if she'd sighed. "I wrote a list of things to look for. Hope it helps." She turned and bent over a low table in a corner of the room.

He didn't avert his eyes. He couldn't touch but he could look, couldn't he? His hands curled a little as if shaping themselves to cup her backside.

"Here."

He was so damned busy salivating he didn't realize she was handing him a piece of paper. Heat burned up his neck and into his face. The princess was a bit red in the face too. But she didn't stand back when he took the paper out of her fingers. In fact, he could have sworn she was issuing an invitation to look as long as he wanted.

Nah. For sure he had it all wrong. Why would a pretty, intelligent woman with her background be interested in slumming it with him? He glued his eyes to the list.

"What does this mean—look for any documentation pertaining to Bobby?" he asked, frowning. What did the kid, Bobby, have to do with Tania's disappearance?

"She once hinted to me that Bob mightn't be Marty's son."

"Holy shit! She sure likes to live dangerously. But that might just be one of her tales. He looks enough like Marty, I guess, although I've only seen the boy a couple of times."

Ingrid tilted her head, thinking. He was amused to see her twist a strand of silver-blonde hair around her finger. She looked all of ten years old. Then his eyes dropped lower. Nope. Not ten years old.

"Yes, hard to tell. Did you see what I wrote about her favorite hidey-hole?"

Breck nodded. "She used to hide things in the laundry cupboards when we were married too."

"You knew?"

"What can I say?" He spread his hands and grinned. "I'm a cop."

She didn't smile. Instead, she stared at him as if searching his face for something she did not find.

*Sorry, Ms. Rowland. Many people have found me wanting. Guess you're just another. Sure, I knew she hid papers in the laundry cupboard. And when I found out what those papers were, I discovered just how evil Tania could be. We had the most almighty row and that was the beginning of the end.*

"And?"

He shook his head. "I dealt with it." He looked at the list again. "Who is Angela?"

"I don't know her surname. Tania was friendly with her when we were training; in fact, from a distance they looked rather similar. I suspected they were cousins. But we were in different classes so Tania never introduced her to me. If you want, I'll look her up in the registered teachers' handbook. But if you haven't dug up anything on her, then I guess they didn't keep in touch."

"No class photos?"

"No. Not for preschool training. Anyway, it's worth a try to see what I can find."

"Of course it is."

"Don't patronize me! You didn't know about Bobby or Angela and you were *married* to her." Hands on her hips, she stood four square, her chin in the air.

Oh, hell. He hadn't meant to sound condescending. He'd been distracted because like a thunderbolt he'd suddenly realized he was much more interested in spending time with Ingrid Rowland than looking for Tania. This silver-hot attraction wasn't good. It could get him into all sorts of trouble. He wasn't in her league, and he was never one to play above his weight. If he didn't get out of here, she'd see his tongue slurping the floor.

Perhaps if he kissed her, he would get over this pointless yearning. She would slap his face, or their kiss would be less than world-shaking, and then they would go their separate ways. Be the same as they had before. Acquaintances.

Ah, what a pathetic excuse that was. He was lonely, that's all. Lonely for someone to share all the ups and downs with. And Ingrid rang all his bells. That sexy little backside in those tight jeans and that silver hair that hung down her back like a translucent waterfall turned him on like a halogen globe.

And he was going to leave right now before he got into trouble.

He took a step towards her. Then another.

Then somehow she was in his arms, tucked tight against his chest. She didn't resist. Not for a second. He held her warmth and savored it. "Ingrid, I-I'm not sure if we—"

She stood on tip-toe and raised her face to his.

He lost it. Completely. He covered her face with soft kisses and then jumped straight in. God, those pliant lips were heavenly. And addictive. Her arms tightened around his waist and his pulse leapt, drumming up a demand he struggled to crush. Don't startle her, Marchant; she's not the sort of woman you devour. Slow-dance into it.

But somehow he couldn't slow down. As Ingrid pressed closer and closer, crushing her breasts against his chest, he knew she must be able to feel his hard, hot erection against her stomach. And she wasn't slowing down either. Boy, could she kiss. She was exploring every inch of his lips, over and over, sensitizing his skin with her soft hesitancy. His blood boiled with anticipation and—he had to let her go. *Now*.

He pressed one last kiss to the side of her neck and eased back, holding her loosely, careful not to give the impression of rejection. God knew the last thing he wanted to do was stop.

Her head drooped on to his shoulder and he freed one hand to stroke her hair. *Say something, Marchant.*

"That was—that was uh…"

"Amazing?"

He tried to grin. "That's the word I was looking for."

She freed herself and stood back. "Thank you," she said unexpectedly.

She sounded as though he'd given her a gift. Thank you? He couldn't remember ever having been thanked for kissing a woman. When he was fourteen Marian Sinclair had kneed him in the groin because he'd kissed her ear. He'd been aiming for her lips but at fourteen his expertise hadn't had time to develop. When he'd worked in the wool stores the boss's daughter, three years older than he, had cornered him and planted a humungous wet one on him that had brought him to his knees. Then she'd flounced off, grinning over her shoulder at him.

Tania had seemed to take his kisses for granted.

One thing was for sure. He'd never before felt the zing that Ingrid's kiss had fizzled through his blood at light speed. Ingrid Rowland was one interesting woman.

"Uh, this is awkward," he blurted.

Blushing like a beacon she murmured, head down, "Enjoyed it. Much."

Breck sagged in relief then backed away before he grabbed her again and took it further. Much further. Time to go.

"Oh, yeah. Me too." He sighed. "But I think it's time I went. I'll uh…let you know what happens at the Kerrs' place."

"When do you plan on going?"

He opened his mouth to answer but his eye caught the title of a book tucked into her overflowing bookcase.

"What the hell?" He strode over and tugged the book out. Beside it were two more, written by the same authors. A & J Marchant. He dragged them all out and dumped them on the table, disappointment sitting heavy on his shoulders.

Ingrid stared at him. "What is it?"

"You using these books as manuals?"

"Well, sometimes I refer to them, but not often. Too esoteric for me. They're standard textbooks for student teachers—" She broke off as realization struck. "Marchant," she said slowly.

"Yep. My loving parents."

"I don't understand. You sound bitter. You should be proud to have such famous parents."

"Oh, when I was little I was real proud. Everywhere we went, people knew them, spoke their language. I desperately tried to live up to their standards. But I couldn't. I couldn't read until I was eight, and it wasn't my parents who taught me to read, but Natasha, our cleaning lady. I wasn't musical and I sure as hell couldn't recite, so I couldn't do party tricks for my parents' little 'evenings.' As I grew older I realized I was a sort of social experiment for them, a control platform on which to base their educational theories. And I failed them."

"What the hell are you talking about?" Ingrid's voice grew harsh. "Do you know how fortunate you were to have two parents who cared about you? Who wanted you to succeed? In their first book they mention their son and praise his achievements. They describe how they've used the same techniques they used on you for other people's children. How can you denigrate them?"

"If you only knew, Ingrid. How do you measure success? What about happiness?" His heart pounding, he knew he sounded neurotic but he couldn't stop. All those years of trying to shake free of their bloody tentacles and they were still ruining his life.

"Success and happiness are two different things, Breck."

He turned away from her. "On that we agree. Remember that when you're following their tenets. Good night."

He still had the presence of mind to snib the lock before he shut the door behind him. Before he shut out the image of Ingrid, hands on hips, staring at him. Before he shut out what might have been.

Chapter Nine

Ingrid stared at the closed door. What had just happened? One moment they were sharing a momentous kiss, the likes of which she'd never felt before. The next he was simmering with anger over—what?

Sick to her stomach, she stood in the middle of the living room feeling like a fool. All she'd done was mention how fortunate he was to have such caring parents and wham! He'd gone up in smoke. A slow anger simmered inside her. Who the hell would want to pursue a relationship with such a touchy guy? Everyone had issues, but Breck Marchant was the king of issues. Huh!

She stalked over to the table and picked up one of the textbooks. Checking inside the front cover she could see no dedications, no photos. What did A & J Marchant look like?

The foreword in the first book referred to their son in a humorous way, saying that at first he was the only child they'd had available to test out their formative ideas on so that their conclusions had been largely subjective. In the second book they acknowledged various public and private schools that had submitted selected groups of children for them to study, to help advance their theories and methods to the next stage.

Ingrid raised her eyebrows. Inadvertently they sounded as if they were studying specimens in a zoo. The conclusions at the end of that book were impartial and detached, but that might just be their writing style.

Lord, they'd taught Ingrid her craft. She believed in them. Stuff Breck Marchant. He had her doubting the people who'd been the basis of her training, the experts she referred to even now when she struck a sticky problem.

She flicked to the foreword on the third book. Here she discovered that Anna and Jeremy Marchant were conducting further control 'experiments' on larger groups of children, but by now they were fixated on the 'products' of private schooling only. Why? Had the public school children not come up to scratch? "Listen to yourself," she scolded. "He's got you imagining things that don't exist." Just because Breck seemed less than thrilled with his upbringing, didn't mean there was anything wrong with his parents or their methods of research.

So why *did* Breck react so badly to the mention of his upbringing? What had happened? She sank down on the carpet and flicked through the third book. This was the one her lecturers at university had mainly used. It was full of techno jargon that the Marchants' had devised.

She got up and sat in front of the computer to do a Google search. This time she found some photos. She leaned forward. Oh, yes. Breck Marchant was their son. He had his mother's damn-you grey eyes and his father's unruly hair. Those were the same intense grey eyes that had burned with anger such a short time ago. There the resemblance came to a screeching halt. Anna and Jeremy sat bolt upright, shoulder to shoulder, in a formal pose. Ingrid doubted that Breck had ever been formal in his life.

She clicked through their website. No mention of Breck. Just the studies they'd undertaken over the past twenty-five years interlarded with layers of techno-speak.

Maybe Breck had a point. Being brought up by these two rigid-looking academics could not have been easy. Especially when one took into account Breck's loose-limbed gait, the dark hair that flopped over his forehead no matter how hard he tried to school it, and his diffident manner.

And maybe she was way off beam. She knew she had a bad habit of second-guessing people. It had become a defense mechanism in the difficult years after her father had left home. Or more correctly, after Marla had thrown her father out of their house. Way back as far as Ingrid could remember, her mother had been depressed. To try to keep her on an even keel, Ingrid had learned to second-guess Marla's mood swings. But when Tom Rowland arrived on the scene, the depression had sloughed off Marla the way you'd peel off a wet coat. For that, Ingrid was immensely grateful. That was the main reason she'd been content to go along with whatever her stepfather suggested. Until a few years ago when she realized her parents took it for granted that she would live her life to their dictates. It had been a terrible struggle to break away from their benign dictatorship.

Had Breck Marchant suffered similar treatment from his parents? Or had there been something more sinister?

She went to bed early and lay there, wondering how she could find out more about the Marchants. She was just drifting off to sleep when she remembered his words about Tania: "I dealt with it." What had Tania done that he'd had to deal with?

****

Before commencing his reconnoiter of the Kerr's premises, Breck tried to coax some information about "Uncle Billy" out of Kit. Kit, however, was coping with his traumatic experiences with the Kerrs by blocking out all thoughts of them.

"Uncle Billy?" he asked blankly.

"Yes, you mentioned that he did martial arts, remember?"

Kit flicked his father a glance and pretended to be absorbed in pushing his dump truck around a corner of the sofa.

So far Breck had resisted attempts by the police psychologist to interview Kit. He'd wanted to give Kit breathing space, considering all that had happened recently. But perhaps he'd been wrong. Lord, this parenting thing was difficult. If only he knew why Natasha had disappeared. She would be invaluable at keeping Kit on an even keel. Dear Natasha. After all this time he still missed her.

He dropped Kit off at Jace and Abel's and arrived at the Kerr's house as the sun set. The living room was dim, the curtains pulled across the windows to keep sensation-seekers from peering in. Somewhere in the house a clock ticked loudly, its metronome-like rhythm getting on Breck's nerves.

Where should he start?

He'd never broken into anyone's house illegally

before. During his second year on the force he'd had to break down a door when they'd suspected there was a dead body inside. But he'd had a couple of other cops with him and it was done on orders from his superiors. Sure, a couple of times with the AOS he'd had to move stealthily into position as the team settled themselves for a long wait, but that was not inside people's houses. Mostly they hunkered down in garden sheds or garages; more often on high vantage points.

Leaving the back door ajar, he stood listening. If he got caught he would say he was looking for more of Kit's belongings. Even so, it was a thin line he was treading. The normal course of action would be to go to the North Shore cops to pick up a key. But he wanted to keep a step ahead of that dick-brain, Moffat. If Moffat got to hear that he'd requested a key, the idiot would presume the worst.

Tip-toeing down the hallway, he felt like an elephant trying to walk on eggshells. Only the tick-tick of the clock and the faint squeak of his rubber-soled shoes on the floor tiles broke the silence. He worked on controlling his breathing, the way they did on a mission. This was a lot more nerve-wracking than any call-out.

He paused. Some of the cartons stacked at the end of the hallway had been opened and tossed aside. He didn't think the cops would have left the place so untidy. His squad rarely left a mess when they instituted a search. The strange thing was that even though the house had been locked up for a couple of weeks, there was a pleasant perfumed smell in the air.

He pushed open the laundry door and discovered the source of the smell. Laundry powder was scattered over the floor and the hard-to-reach top cupboard doors stood open. Tania's hiding place was bare.

Breck stepped over the sprinkle of soap powder so as not to leave prints and turned in a circle, looking around the small room. The lock was still snibbed on the inside, so nobody had entered from the garden. Whoever had been here must have had a front door key.

He blew out a breath. This was getting complicated. What was going on with the Kerrs? Had Tania's past caught up with her? Or was it something more recent?

He'd follow Ingrid's advice and search for anything pertaining to little Bobby. Then he'd scarper. Something was very wrong here.

Toeing the inside of each stair tread, he climbed the stairs that led to the bedrooms. As he got near the top, he hesitated. More perfume, different from the smell of soap powder hung in the air. Tania's perfume, strong and poignant. It was called Chloe. He ought to know. He'd bought enough of the stuff.

He stopped. Was she here? Had she been here? That stuff lingered for a long time. Their apartment had stunk of it for weeks after she'd left.

"Tania?" he whispered.

A disturbance in the air was his only warning. He ducked as something whizzed over the top of his head. Then he was shoved aside as a dark figure pushed past him. Breck clutched at the banisters, his feet shooting out from under him on the slippery carpet. Shit! Scrambling to his feet, he bounced down the last couple of stairs and chased the stocky figure careening down the hallway.

His quarry wrenched open the front door. Dusk had

settled and it was almost dark outside. He managed to grab his attacker's coat and began reeling in the interloper like a fish. But the man wriggled out of his plastic raincoat and fled towards a blue pick-up truck waiting at the curb. His balding head gleamed under the streetlights. Someone inside the vehicle leaned over and flung open the passenger door, revving the engine just as Breck aimed a solid punch at the back of the attacker's neck. Reeling against the car door, the man half-collapsed on to the front seat of the truck, his legs hanging out the door. The driver floored the accelerator and the blue truck jerked out from the curb as if the driver was unfamiliar with the gears. It hiccupped along the road. Breck raced behind it, clutching the tattered plastic raincoat in one hand. The driver finally found second gear and the truck picked up speed and was swallowed in the dusk.

His chest heaving, Breck came to a halt. Two people: one man, one woman. Numberplate AC2431. The woman had hunkered low in the seat. She hadn't looked much like Tania. For starters, her hair was different. Of course, Tania often changed her hair color and style. The Tania he knew wouldn't hide from view. She liked to be seen. Except it seemed he *hadn't* known Tania at all, and a getaway driver sure would not want to be seen.

The guy was in his forties, balding and a little on the tubby side. He'd worn a grey sweater and grey trousers beneath the flasher's raincoat.

Breck snorted with amusement. Somehow he couldn't see Tania associating with an older man who wore a plastic raincoat. It reminded him of the coat that serial murderers wore to avoid splashes of blood.

He grabbed a large evidence bag out of his SUV and dropped the coat into it, then made a note of the vehicle's numberplate. The trouble was—what could he do with this information? He had no more right to be in the house than the two intruders. How could he get the information to Moffat without incriminating himself?

He went back inside the house. What had those two been up to?

After half an hour he was forced to concede defeat. Nothing whatsoever in this house could lead him to Tania and her children. All useful papers such as birth certificates and passports had been removed.

Whatever the intruders were after, they'd made a mess. Downstairs, electrical power bills were mixed up with grocery receipts. Job search downloads on computer paper rubbed noses with recipes cut from newspapers. Upstairs, baby clothes slithered off pyramids of shoes. In the main bedroom, the double wardrobe doors had been wrenched off their tracks.

And nowhere was there a single thing pertaining to Kit. It was as if Kit had never existed as far as the Kerrs were concerned.

Chapter Ten

"Good morning, Ingrid," Breck mumbled as he handed Kit his backpack. Just to torment him, today Ingrid looked as though she'd bathed in sunshine. Dressed in yellow, she was waiting for them in the carpark. At least he supposed she was waiting for them. She'd certainly homed in on them as soon as they got out of the SUV.

He swallowed. It had been three days since he'd managed to wreck their burgeoning friendship. This morning Jace and Abel were winging their way to Russia to finalize their adoption, which left him not only feeling like shit for unloading on to Ingrid the other night, it also left him in a quandary. Today he'd have to negotiate with her to see if Kit could attend preschool for longer hours. To make matters worse, Harley Max had hinted that he'd cut Breck a lot of slack recently, then he'd come right out and asked, "I need someone on standby for the graveyard shift. Can you do it?"

Breck's heart had shifted sideways. Here it was. He was staring down the barrel of a frightening decision.

"I can't leave my boy alone at night, sir," was all he'd managed to choke out.

Harley Max digested Breck's answer. "I hadn't realized you had nobody to help out," Max had said at last. "You don't have a sister or anything? Parents?"

"No-one," Breck had muttered, trying not sound like Orphan Annie.

"Well then, forget I asked," Max replied, and that was the end of the conversation.

But Breck knew it was the end of any advancement for him. He expected soon to be back in an inquiry car, cooling his heels, as his mates leapt up the career tree in front of him.

"Good morning, guys!" Ingrid sang, tickling Kit's neck.

Well, *someone* was in a good mood today. He'd better strike while the iron was hot. "Ingrid, I have a favor to ask of you."

She raised her eyebrows and waited, her head cocked to one side.

"May I extend Kit's preschool hours by one hour a day? I need to drop him off a little earlier and collect him about half an hour later each day." He was pushing the envelope. On days when Jace wasn't available he often screamed in the gate as Ingrid was packing up the last of the school equipment. Sometimes Kit was the only child still there.

Instead of answering him straight off, she leaned forward eagerly. He stepped back, smelling soap and flowers and Ingrid. Closing his eyes for a second, he inhaled.

"Oh wow, Breck! That must mean that Jace and Abe have gone to see their child? When did they leave? When are they coming back?"

She fired questions at him like pellets from a shotgun cartridge. Well, at least she was still talking to him. "Yes. This morning. In four weeks."

She grinned. "How very concise. Now, I don't know much more than I did before. Are they excited? Is it a daughter or a son?"

And in a flash he recognized something special about Ingrid that he hadn't understood before. She hadn't said "girl" or "boy" as most people did. She realized that Jace and Abe were committed to forming a family, that they wanted children of their own. Ingrid didn't make it sound as if Jace and Abe were buying a child, like some of the squad members thought. She knew what was important.

"We're going to text each other, so I'll let you know what happens."

She gave a little wriggle, reminiscent of a puppy. "I'm so excited for them, and I don't even know Abe. I bet he's a nice guy."

Breck nodded. "The best. Ingrid, about…"

"Yes, of course it's okay. I'm dying to know about the"—she lowered her voice—"housebreaking."

She certainly didn't carry grudges. She had every right to choke him off, considering how they'd parted. He was thankful that her curiosity had won the day.

He glanced around. Kit was long gone and nobody was in the immediate vicinity. He waved good morning to one of the assistant teachers, and then turned back to Ingrid. "Had a bit of a turn-up with some guy. He got away, and there was a woman driving—"

She clutched his arm, her eyes wide with shock. "Someone was there? You *fought* with him?"

"Yeah. It was the guy who whacked me with his knuckle duster. Or his twin. Same height, balding. Used the same pick-up truck. A woman was driving it."

She licked her lips. "Was it Tania?"

Breck shook his head. "Not sure. Didn't behave like her and the hair was different but with Tania, who knows?"

Her hand was still on his arm. He felt the warmth through his shirt.

"Are you all right?"

"I'm fine. Gave as good as I got. But Ingrid, there are no useful papers in the house. No birth certificates, no passports, nothing. Maybe the MPU squad took them, but I can't understand why they'd take some of the more irrelevant stuff." He wrinkled his nose. "The house reeked of Tania's perfume. Not sure if that was a red herring or not."

She smiled and took her hand off his arm. He felt the chill. "What a convoluted mind you have, Mr. Marchant."

He grinned. "I got the vehicle registration number anyway." He glanced at his watch. "Shit! Gotta go. I daren't be late. I'm in enough hot water as it is." He left her standing there and bolted for his SUV.

****

Ten hours later, Ingrid watched him as he climbed down from the SUV, the only vehicle left in the carpark besides her own. His shoulders sagged and he scuffed towards her, head down. Dog-tired. Must have been a bad one today.

"You had a call-out?" she asked.

He nodded. "Just got through the debrief. Sorry."

She wanted to help him, but she didn't know how. Hell, if her heart sank when he'd had a bad day, what did that mean? Was she seguing from Level One attraction to Level Two? She'd been on Level Two before. She knew all about Level Two. It was called unwilling attraction. He's a *friend*, Ingrid. A *friend*. She inhaled. "What happened?"

"After he'd knifed his wife and baby, he hanged himself. We—"

"Daddy!" Kit trotted towards them, dragging his backpack.

Breck straightened up. "Hi, son! Say thank-you to Ingr—Ms. Rowland."

"Why don't you guys stop at my place for dinner on your way home?" Ingrid asked. She blinked. What on earth had made her say that? It was just that he looked so weary and disillusioned. Kit would probably talk him to death and she could be a buffer between them, help to finish Breck's day on a higher note anyway. Yeah, Level Two was right. Probably already on Level Three. She was in deep trouble.

"It was going to be Macca's tonight," he admitted. "I don't have the energy to argue with tomatoes and cold chicken."

Kit giggled, swinging his father's arm. "You don't argue with chicken and tomatoes, Daddy."

Breck tried to grin. "I argue with everything in the kitchen, son."

Ingrid stuffed the next day's worksheets into her carry bag and turned to extinguish nearly all the lights, leaving only two fluorescent lights on. The bright security lights came on automatically at dusk.

"Come on, guys. You can have Macca's tomorrow. Tonight you eat healthy."

She ushered them out the door and set the alarms.

"I hear you had trouble with those at first," Breck said, nodding towards the alarm panel.

She groaned. "Don't remind me. For the first six

months after they were installed they reacted to extremes of heat and cold, neighborhood cats sauntering by, gusts of wind—you name it. Had to have them adjusted three times. The neighbors do not love me."

"You need security at your apartment."

Couldn't help being a cop, could he? Marla reckoned Ingrid's father had been like that. Always on duty, even at home. Ingrid wasn't sure if that was a bad thing or a good thing.

An hour later she decided it was a good thing. While she and Kit puttered in the kitchen, Breck phoned an acquaintance who was a wholesaler for security products. In ten minutes Breck had sketched the layout of her apartment, scanned it and forwarded it to the security expert. Within an hour they received back an assessment of his recommendations along with the cost. Okay, the cost was scary, but Breck sure got things going. As she dropped meatballs into the tomato and capers sauce, she admitted to him, "The reason I haven't done anything about security is that I'm not sure how long I'll be living here. I needed to escape from my parents and this was all I could find in my price range." *Damn it. How had that all spilled out?*

Breck looked at her for a moment then asked, "Is it okay if I put the TV on for Kit?"

"Better yet, there are kids' games on my laptop. Have a look." Anything to get him out of the kitchen. He wasn't the prying sort—not by a long shot—but she'd just opened the door to a cupboardful of secrets she'd rather have kept hidden. For some reason this man had the weirdest effect on her. She kept blurting out things that were best hidden.

He was curious about what she'd said, no doubt about it. He kept flicking sideways glances at her. But he was polite enough to respond to her attempts to steer the conversation on to innocuous topics. From time to time the serious grey eyes searched her face, but fortunately he looked too beat to worry overmuch about her comment. The man had his own problems.

"I can't continue like this," he said as they perched on kitchen stools to eat their meatballs and spaghetti. "Either I'm short-changing Kit or I'm short-changing my employers but whichever way I look at it, it's a problem that isn't going to go away. Between AOS call-outs and shift work, I just can't manage."

"What about this Natasha you told me about?"

"Nobody knows where she is. God knows I've tried to find her. One day she was working for my parents. The next day she disappeared."

"Internet search?"

"Nothing. It's as if she never existed, but she was the best thing that ever happened to me."

Kit had already finished his dinner and had rushed back to play more computer games. That was something Breck Marchant had done for his son, Ingrid mused. Kit no longer hung back and waited to see which way the wind blew before he acted.

Breck chased the last tendril of spaghetti around his plate. "It's terrifying, but I might have to rethink my career." His voice died away. It seemed he could not put into words the catastrophic problems he saw looming ahead.

"Oh, no! It can't be that bad, surely?" Ingrid laid her hand over his where he jabbed with his fork at the offending spaghetti. She looked into his face and saw raw despair. He looked like a man in shock, his skin pale and his mouth drooping at the corners. "I'm sorry. That was a stupid thing to say. It *is* as bad as that, isn't it?" She kept her hand over his. "I wish there was something I could do, but short of having Kit stay with me as much as possible, I can't see how I can help."

Breck shook his head. "He's my kid. It's my responsibility."

From his tone he may as well have said, "So butt out."

Some perverse gene in her makeup forced her to continue. "Have you considered another branch of police work?"

*Listen to yourself, Ingrid. What the hell would you know about police work?* Fleetingly she thought it was a pity she'd lost contact with her father. He might have helped. He'd definitely still be a cop, probably in the top echelon too, if her mother was to be believed. Then again, over the years Ingrid had come to realize that her mother's recollections of her first husband had gotten a little skewed. Her father might not have been as wedded to the job as Marla insisted. Perhaps he'd used work as an excuse to avoid confrontations at home. God knows, Ingrid had learned to use similar excuses. And then had to listen to: "You're just like your father."

She watched Breck as he dragged himself to his feet. She wanted to help him, dammit, even if he didn't want her help. She steeled herself for rejection. "Breck, have you thought about applying for the detective division? Sure, there'd be shift work, but there'd be a roster, wouldn't there? Or doesn't it work that way?"

"*Me? A detective?*" He snorted. "Don't wanna hurt your feelings, Ingrid, but that's the best joke I've heard all day." He gave a half-hearted laugh that turned into a sneer.

She swallowed her annoyance. "Why not? It makes sense."

"It might make sense to you, maybe, but nobody who knows me could imagine me passing exams as tough as that."

So she didn't know him well, huh? And whose fault was that? She leapt to her feet and banged the dishwasher door shut.

"I don't know what that bee in your bonnet is about, but you got into the police force and then into AOS. You must have passed a bunch of exams. What's different about applying to the detective division?"

The words seemed to be forced out of him. "I had help passing those exams. I'm no good at paperwork."

She narrowed her eyes. "How did you get to be a senior constable?" Then she realized she'd given herself away. Would he notice she'd been checking up on him?

But he was too depressed to notice her slip. "Fourteen years' experience and a superintendent's approval is all it takes."

"*Fourteen years?* And you're worried about a measly bunch of detective exams! For God's sake, Breck, surely they'd take that into account?"

"Dunno. Never thought about it. Actually, it was only eleven."

"So you got promoted on merit." Before she could control her mouth, she offered, "I'll help you with your application if you want."

He looked at her out of weary, disillusioned eyes. "Sometimes help is not enough, Ingrid. I'm very, very grateful for the offer, but it's all so…unachievable." He leaned against the kitchen counter. "It's a pipedream, Ingrid. I think I told you I couldn't read until I was eight years old. Well, you can imagine how hard study is for someone like me. But hey! I'll get by."

His arms hung loose but his fingers clenched. God, the big lunkhead was *ashamed*. Like not being able to read until he was eight actually counted in the great scheme of things.

"Good heavens, Breck! The world is full of people who have dyslexia or are barely literate or are late bloomers. It hasn't stopped them from becoming valuable citizens! Erin Brokovich, Steve Jobs, Orlando Bloom—"

He held up his hands in surrender. "Okay, sweetie. I've got the picture." Then he propped his hands on the kitchen counter behind him and looked down at his feet. He and Kit had taken their shoes off at the door as if her apartment was a luxurious penthouse. She loved them for it, but it wasn't necessary. Then her brain caught up with what he'd said, why he was looking at his feet. He'd called her 'sweetie' without thinking. A little bubble of anticipation fizzed away inside her. Breakthrough!

"If only Kit had grandparents who lived nearby," she commented.

And ruined their closeness just like that. The drawbridge came down with a wallop.

"Well, he doesn't have and he never will have. Tania's parents are dead and mine are"—he paused while he sought for a suitable word—"impossible."

She opened her mouth and shut it again. Pity she hadn't done that before.

Breck straightened up and looked through the kitchen doorway to check on Kit. "Time to go!" he called.

"Oh *gee*, Dad. I'm just—"

"Kit," Breck warned.

"I know you don't think so, but it's great that he's improved enough to argue with you," Ingrid whispered.

For the first time tonight he laughed genuinely, his head tossed back. "Ingrid! Only you could see that as positive. Pollyanna." He ruffled her hair as he walked past her to unglue Kit from the laptop.

She reached up a hand and sleeked her hair back into place, her hand lingering, unsure about that careless gesture.

And when they'd gone and the apartment was sunk in its habitual quiet, she sat down and tried to think of a way she could help Breck and Kit. There must be *something* she could do.

Chapter Eleven

Breck gazed down at his son. Kit's lashes, darker than his tawny hair, fluttered as he fought off sleep. "One more time, Daddy. Read it one more time." He yawned and rubbed his face on the pillow.

Breck grinned. He'd already read The Pirate from Mepomallawalla three times. He didn't have to *read* it. He could recite it off by heart. So could Kit. He fingered the fair hair, many shades lighter than his own. He'd seen the same colored hair in a couple of photos that Natasha had taken years ago. He, too, had had wheat-fair hair at the age of four; by the time he was six it had darkened several shades. By the time he was eight it was closer to black than brown.

Would Kit's hair be the same? He knew very little about Tania's family or his own. His father's parents had died before he was born, but his mother's parents, though very elderly, were apparently still living in a small country town some miles to the north of Auckland. When he was in his early teens, he'd raised the courage to ask Mother why he had no aunts and uncles or grandparents. To his shock she had admitted that he had grandparents who still lived in the town his mother had left at seventeen, never to look back. But when he'd asked if he could contact them, she'd thrown a hissy fit of humungous proportions. Usually it was his father who engaged in histrionics. Breck had been startled when she'd snapped, "Leave it alone, Brechon. It's none of your business."

He'd waited until they were away lecturing to search through their study and find out what his mother's maiden name had been. No luck. His parents' private papers were locked in their safe. It was as if Mother had only been born when she'd married his father.

Years later, just prior to joining the AOS, he'd searched through the National Intelligence Application as he updated his active files. He'd found nothing whatsoever on the police computer about his parents. Nothing. They'd apparently committed no crimes, instituted no court cases, and defended no court cases.

But now he had Kit to think about. Oh, Natasha. If only I knew where you were. I miss you. You were the best thing that ever happened to me. A boy needed relatives. He needed an anchor to make him feel secure. Someone like Natasha. One thing was for sure; he wouldn't approach Tania's relatives because if they were anything like Tania, Kit would be better off without them. He must protect Kit from the knowledge that his mother was a blackmailer. And a few other things. What the hell had Tania got herself into?

He leaned down and nuzzled Kit's neck. A sleepy sigh was his son's only reaction as he slid into sleep.

Breck straightened up and went over to his desk. He made notes. Marty's brother. His own grandparents. Number plate AC2431. A woman named Angela. For a moment he sat and stared into space, thinking. Then he opened up his laptop and went hunting.

****

He lost track of time and was startled when he stood up to stretch and glanced at his watch. Well after midnight. Shit. He needed to sleep. And he needed to digest what he'd learned tonight. He should have done this several days ago. Marty's brother was a very interesting character. He managed a martial arts studio near Cornwall Park. Breck found no photo of Billy Kerr on the internet, but Breck was willing to bet that Billy was balding, built like a brick shithouse and owned a blue pick-up truck.

He'd get someone in Car Registrations to look up AC2431. He wasn't able to access those records from home.

He had delved into his mother's background but could turn up nothing useful. There might possibly be something in her university records. He'd search there tomorrow.

Chapter Twelve

"I got you, Dad!" Kit popped up from behind the sofa as Breck jogged past. Their games of tag were curtailed by the smallness of their apartment, but Kit reveled in them. Breck had come to realize that like himself, Kit did not have a lot of experience playing the simple games other kids took for granted. Knowing he was unwanted by the Kerrs had forced him into the background, and at preschool he'd been too withdrawn to participate. But now he was eager to join life. Amused, Breck realized he'd graduated—or been demoted—from "Daddy" to "Dad."

As he took another turn at being the seeker, his mind churned with the details of whether he should divulge his visit to the Kerr house to the arrogant Moffat. He'd learned that AC2431 did not belong to any pickup truck. It belonged to a very old mini owned by a Miss Albertine Reynolds. Miss Reynolds had no criminal record. The only thing Breck could find on the police computer was Miss Reynolds' birth date. Miss Reynolds was closer to ninety than eighty. She sure hadn't been driving the blue pickup.

"Rrright, where is Captain Kit, I wonder?" he muttered as he poked through the kitchen cupboards. "Not here. Hmm. Perhaps in the bedroom."

A muffled squeal sounded, which meant his son

was hiding in the wardrobe.

Breck grinned. "Now let me see—" The doorbell pealed. Damn. He hoped it wasn't old Mrs. Raynor from downstairs complaining about the noise.

He flung open the door. "Sorry—"

The last two people he expected to see stood on his doorstep. His heart jolted. Clenching his hands, he stepped out and pulled the door shut behind him. No way were they coming inside.

"Mother. Father. Hullo."

"Come, come, boy. Is that all you've got to say? It's been ages since we've seen you!" boomed his father. Jeremy Marchant was, as usual, wearing a tweed suit with leather elbow inserts. Very much the university professor. He looked lean and tanned. Must have had another skiing holiday at Granada. Definitely not Whistler. "Too many damned kids there," Jeremy had once complained.

His mother had aged since he'd seen her last. The sculptured waves were no longer tinted a strawberry blonde but had been allowed to go grey. She wore another of her interminable two-piece suits with a trailing scarf but she no longer looked as vital and spry as she had a few years ago. She looked—faded. Living with his father was not easy, Breck could attest to that, but it was hard to feel sorry for her. For her the sun rose and set on Jeremy Marchant. She'd always taken his father's side in any disagreement, dismissing their son as if his opinions were worth nothing.

"We've come to check up on young Christopher. Aren't you going to invite us in?" Jeremy Marchant did not appreciate being kept standing on the doorstep.

"What d'you mean—check up?" Breck demanded.

He stood four square like the Colossus of Rhodes guarding his doorway.

"Had a phone call. Hear you're having difficulty coping with Christopher."

Hot anger boiled up so quickly he couldn't keep a lid on it. "What the hell are you talking about, Father? Have you come to stir?"

His mother looked anxiously right and left, checking to see if the neighbors were about. "Ssh, son. We're just trying to help."

"No you're not. You want to use Kit the way you used me. And I'm not going to let you. Get out of here."

"We'll be back with a court order," Jeremy Marchant said, his suave expression marred by a crease of anger between his eyes. "We have reason to believe our grandson is not being cared for properly."

The door opened behind Breck. "Daddy?"

"Go inside, son. I'll be there in a minute."

But the damage was done. Anna Marchant crouched down to Kit's level and tried to peer around Breck's legs. "Hello, darling. You won't remember me, but I'm your-your Grandma." The words seem to stick in her throat. Breck presumed her lifestyle didn't allow for ageing.

"And I'm your Grandpa," boomed Jeremey.

Kit backed away, frightened by the big voice. Breck remembered how he'd done the same thing. His father always behaved as if his life was one big act. Everything was louder and bigger and brighter for Jeremy Marchant. Breck had felt like a pale imitation of his father, even when he was grown up and taller than Jeremy. Then again, he had no desire to go through life drawing attention to himself.

His cellphone and beeper rang simultaneously. Call-out.

"We gotta go, Kit. Get your bag!"

He slammed the door in his parents' faces and rushed to the wardrobe to grab his gear. At the same time Kit grabbed his backpack and scooped up the car keys.

"Ready!" they both yelled at the same time and rushed for the door. His parents were still standing there.

"Out of the way, please!" Breck shoved past his parents and slammed the door shut. "Bye!" he yelled at them. Then he and Kit were racing towards the SUV.

Breck thumbed Ingrid's number on his cellphone as he swung out into the traffic. "You wanted to help?" he greeted her. "How about right now?"

"Okay. Where shall I meet you?"

Breck was taken aback at her matter-of-fact tone.

It was Sunday and the traffic was light. But somewhere a man had decided that Sundays weren't his favorite day if he had to spend it with family. All Breck knew was what the text on his cellphone said. "Family disturbance. Two people armed. Proceed to HQ." He chose a place close by HQ to drop Kit off. It was a long way from Ingrid's place, but he was through suiting Ms. Rowland. The bitch hadn't been able to leave well alone. She'd contacted his parents, damn her.

She arrived at the same time as he did. No doubt about it, she might be traitorous but she thought on her feet and moved fast. If she wasn't so small she'd make a great policewoman, but somehow he couldn't see her dealing with drunks outside bars and adult entertainment strips on Saturday nights.

Her betrayal bit and roiled inside him. How could she? How could she contact his parents knowing how he felt about them? He'd thought that he and she might—ah, to hell with it. He struggled to swallow his anger.

"Hop into Ingrid's car, Kit. She'll keep an eye on you until I get back," was all he said to his son. But he stalked over and leaned in her driver's window while Kit was stowing his backpack in the trunk of the little Fiesta.

"Since you are so concerned about Kit that you contacted my bloody parents, you can do me the favor of looking after him, *Ms.* Rowland," he snarled. "And if you ever try a stunt like that again, you'll wish you'd never been born."

He loped across to the SUV and revved the engine. He might hate her guts at the moment, but he trusted her with Kit. He drove away with the picture of Ingrid's dropped jaw and indignant expression in his mind's eye. She hadn't recoiled in fear, but she'd looked like a stunned mullet. Good. She wouldn't make *that* mistake again.

****

Ingrid sat there, unable, for a moment, to drive. What the heck was Breck so steamed up about? And what did his parents have to do with anything? Dismayed, she bit the inside of her mouth as she pulled out into the traffic flow. She glanced in the rear vision mirror at Kit, strapped into the back seat. She knew what she was going to do and she despised herself for it. She was going to pump Kit for information, something she always tried not to do with any of her charges. Kids were so open that often she had to stop them giving away family secrets.

Kit was a different flavor. It was like squeezing water out of chalk to get anything out of him. Nevertheless, something was very wrong here and she was going to get to the bottom of it. As she turned into the side road leading to her apartment she took a deep breath and asked, "Kit, what is your father so angry about? I don't understand."

"Grandma and someone else came. Dad wouldn't let them come in. I think they wanted to talk to me."

"But why shouldn't they talk to you? Grandparents love their grandchildren and they always want to talk to them."

"They said something about phone calls to report on Daddy. Daddy got angry." Ingrid noticed that Kit had regressed to calling his father "Daddy" again.

"I wonder what they meant about *reporting* on Daddy? That doesn't sound right." Ingrid kept fishing. Hell, if there was a piscatorial prize, today she'd win it. But she needed to know what was going on so she continued to pump Kit for information. "*Reporting* sounds serious."

"It was about me. The man said they were checking up on me." His hands clenched and unclenched on his lap.

Poor little Kit. Trouble had come to their door and he knew he was the cause of it. What a terrible situation for a child.

"I still don't understand. Did they say something else?"

"The man is getting a court nawder."

"A-a court nawder?" Ingrid was mystified. What

the hell was that? Then she slammed on the brakes and pulled into the side of the road. "Shit! *Now* I understand. Your father thinks *I* contacted your grandparents because I was concerned for your welfare. How *dare* he!" She bashed both hands on the steering wheel. "I'll have his guts for garters!" Surely Breck Marchant knew her better than that? What was wrong with the man?

Kit shrank away from her.

She struggled to rein in her temper. "Sorry, Kit. I'm really angry with your father. He thinks I told your grandparents that you two guys needed help."

"Daddy is a good Daddy!" Kit shouted suddenly.

Ingrid jumped. She had never heard Kit raise his voice before except in the playground. Then Kit kicked the back of her seat, yelling "Go away! I hate you! They are *mean* people."

Ingrid guessed the 'mean people' were Breck's parents. If they intended to get a 'court nawder' then they were mean, all right.

She put the car into gear and drove home. Kit refused to get out of the car. "I want to go home. I want Daddy." Then he began to weep with big gusting sobs that tore the heart out of her chest.

"Oh God, Kit. I'm sorry. It's all a misunderstanding." She clambered into the back seat and tried to cuddle him but he thrust her away. For the first time in her life she found herself unable to console a child. At preschool she was always able to cajole them out of a fit of the dismals or persuade them to choose another activity if they'd gotten frustrated with the one they were trying to master. But poor little Kit had had a bellyful of angst bottled up inside him for months, maybe years. No amount of cajoling was going to stem the flow of his anger and despair.

"They'll take me away from him, I know they will," he snuffled.

"Oh, no they will *not!*" she exclaimed. "Your father and I will fight tooth and nail against anyone trying to take you away from him ever again, you hear me?"

But he just looked at her with a woeful face and drenched eyes and she knew he didn't believe her. He'd been lied to before, poor little boy. She'd like to get her hands around Tania Kerr's neck and wring it until the woman's eyes popped. "Kit, I have an idea." What she was about to propose could lose her the preschool operator's license. Considering the black mark already chalked up against her, it might be the end of her career. But she would not stand by and see these two shafted by the system a second time.

"What?" Kit had grown impatient of her introspection.

"If those people—your grandparents—try to take you away, I can hide you at my place. But that's a last resort, Kit. Please don't tell anyone except your Dad, okay?"

"Okay." Kit looked out the car window. "Are we getting out?"

Ingrid sighed. He might at least have been a tiny bit grateful, considering her career was on the line. But of course he was too little to understand.

Anyway, it wouldn't come to that, she was sure of it. Breck's parents would never take away Breck's son. Their textbooks on child rearing were full of comments about how important the parent-child relationship was, how nothing could break the bond. She snorted. They hadn't met *her* father, had they?

Chapter Thirteen

Breck struggled up the path to Ingrid's apartment block, bristling with equipment he didn't dare leave in his SUV. He had checked in his weapons, but his BP jacket was slung over one arm and he hefted his tool kitbag in the other. He was spoiling for a fight. How dare that prissy bloody schoolteacher judge him? She had a bunch of kids she saw for seven hours a day so she thought she was an expert. *Try having a kid twenty-four hours a day, Ingrid. And then try to hold down a complex full-time job with everyone snapping at your heels.*

God, he felt so let down. He'd been within a hair's breadth of sinking into a relationship with her. He sure could pick 'em. He hammered on the door.

"Come in!" she called, just like before.

Still had the brains of a louse. "Kit!" he bellowed from the doorway. "Time to go. Thank you, Ms. Rowland." *For nothing,* he added beneath his breath.

Kit scuttled out, casting anxious glances over his shoulder. "Come *on,*" Breck hissed. "Let's get out of here."

The two of them raced along the path as if the hounds of hell were after them.

Breck bundled everything into the trunk and they hightailed it away from the fairy princess's castle as fast as they could.

A fraught silence hung inside the vehicle as they headed home. Breck looked at Kit. "Are you okay, son?"

"I guess."

Yeah, that was how Breck felt too. Not very good, not quite average, but okay. Breck sighed. Today's call-out hadn't been a difficult one, just time-consuming. They'd used Jack Tanner as negotiator and he'd saved them hours of difficult bargaining. The man was a genius and Breck had total confidence in him. But the whole time Breck had been lying prone on wet leaves cradling his Bushmaster, he'd had Kit at the back of his mind. And that wasn't good. He was no longer a competent operative with the AOS while his mind was wandering from the job at hand. As for his chances of joining the Special Tactics Group—well, those had been blown into oblivion.

Ingrid's offer to help him study for the detective entrance exam might have worked. If you failed, you were permitted to try again. For sure he'd fail on his first attempt. But he and Ingrid—no. All that was best forgotten. Betrayal was something you didn't get over.

He sighed. He had no way to move but down. He'd have to withdraw from the AOS and revert to ordinary police work. It would be like tearing off an arm. It took years to get into the AOS. They didn't take just anybody and the continuous pysch testing, incident evaluations and range practice caused a lot of squad members to drop out. He'd lapped it all up because he enjoyed learning on the job. He hated baseless theory, learning for the sake of learning, but if he had a physical action to relate it to, then he learned quickly.

If he went back to ordinary police work he'd take a drop in pay, but a senior sergeant's pay was not to be sneezed at. Nor would he have to worry about sudden call-outs. Shifts were rostered weeks in advance so he could make plans. But somehow he couldn't work up the energy to make plans for a future that bored him stupid.

****

Breck sloshed through the rain, holding fast to Kit's hand. "What the hell…?" A crowd of strangers milled around outside their front door, presumably waiting for them. As soon as they appeared, four pairs of eyes fastened on them.

"Who are *they*?" Kit asked, his voice wobbling.

"I'm not sure. Stand behind me, Kit."

Oh, wonderful. His mother, father and two strangers watched his approach. A short, bald guy stepped forward and held out a document. "Sir, I represent Anna and Jeremy Marchant, your parents. This is an interim order from the Family Court to surrender your son, Kit Marchant, to Child Services." Then he stepped back a pace. "I didn't realize you were a cop. Is that the AOS insignia?"

Breck nodded. He thought quickly. Which Family Court judge had been awed enough by the initials after his parents' names to issue an interim order without investigating the circumstances? One of their cronies, no doubt. The lawyer looked uncomfortable. The AOS uniform had given him pause. Breck could milk that. "Kit's been staying with his kindergarten teacher while I was on call-out. It's an arrangement we have."

The other stranger in the group peered out from behind Jeremy Marchant. "Kindergarten teacher?

Qualified?"

Breck stared hard at her. "Yes. As a matter of fact she's the manager." He was not going to mention Ingrid's name in case his parents linked it to her phone call. "Excuse me, who are you?"

"Sorry. Ann Ellis, Child Protection. Here." She thrust out a card but kept her distance. Probably because he was clanking around with a bunch of dangerous looking stuff hanging off him. Even his parents looked taken aback.

"Really? I remember contacting you people when I was concerned about Kit two months ago. Nobody got back to me. Two weeks later his stepfather held him hostage. I don't think *Child Protection* is much use to us."

"Y-you called us? About Christopher?"

"His name is Kit."

"And you're saying you have a child-minding arrangement in place?"

"Sure do. Don't we Kit?" Breck pressed Kit's shoulder in warning. "Unfortunately Kit doesn't have grandparents who live close by or I'm sure they'd care for him." He looked straight at his parents, his chin leading the way. "Except we hardly ever see them."

"Oh, come on. It's not like that." Jeremy Marchant looked like a man who saw the ground slipping away from under him. "Tania called us and—"

"*What*??"

"*Now* what's your problem? We're aware you're divorced, but Tania has always stayed in touch—"

"Don't you read the papers? What about the TV news?"

Jeremy Marchant looked contemptuously down his

nose at his son. "What on earth has all this got to do with Tania?"

But the solicitor had linked the names together. He leaned towards Jeremy Marchant. "Mr. Marchant, you never told me how you came by this information. The police are looking for Tania Kerr. She disappeared some weeks ago, isn't that right?" he appealed to Breck.

Breck nodded. He unlocked the door. "Rather than annoy the other residents, let's go inside." Already the nosy guy next door was leaning in his doorway, his nose twitching.

Everyone crowded in behind Breck and Kit. Breck felt like the Pied Piper.

"What this gentleman is trying to tell you—" Breck broke off. "Sorry, what is your name?"

"Kelly."

"What Mr. Kelly is trying to tell you, Father, is that Tania is being sought by the cops because she and the other two children in their family disappeared some weeks ago during a domestic dispute. Her husband's in gaol because he produced a firearm and held Kit hostage."

Jeremy Marchant's jaw hung open. "That can't be right. She phoned us only last week."

"Last week. You waited a week till you came to see if Kit was in good hands?" Breck struggled to keep a lid on his temper.

Anna Marchant looked anywhere but at Breck. "We were very busy, you understand," she murmured. "We were lecturing in the South Island and we couldn't get away."

"I think if you'd been that concerned about Kit you

would have arranged for Child Protection to pick him up days ago." Breck let his statement hang in the air.

Ms. Ellis patently agreed with him. She nodded and crouched down beside Kit. "Show me your bedroom, Kit."

Oh shit. Kit didn't have a separate bedroom. They were still both sleeping in the only bedroom the apartment had.

"Daddy?" Kit inquired. He had been listening, bug-eyed, to the conversation.

"Go ahead, son. Show the lady your books and stuff."

Kit took Ann Ellis's hand and trotted off.

Breck faced his parents. "You've stuffed up this time, Father. No doubt you planned to sue for custody of Kit. But in your anxiety for raw material on which to practice your educational theories, you rushed your fences."

Jeremy Marchant threw himself down on the sofa. "Mannerless as usual, I see. Sit down, Anna."

Anna Marchant looked from her son to her husband and remained standing.

"I said sit down, Anna." Jeremy Marchant's voice held an edge.

"Doesn't change, does he?" Breck said to his mother.

Anna Marchant tightened her lips. She sat down.

Mr. Kelly paced to and fro between the living room and the kitchen, his cellphone glued to his ear. "What? Say again? Oh, hell." He tucked his cellphone in his breast pocket. "Look, Marchant—"

"Yes?" Breck and his father answered together. Jeremy Marchant threw Breck a glance of dislike. A glance of dislike from this man had once reduced Breck to an insecure, trembling mess, but it no longer impressed him. Years of policing had taught him how to cut through façades and get to the people inside. "I think Mr. Kelly is talking to me. What's the problem, Kelly?"

"Unfortunately, now that the order has been issued and served, it can't be withdrawn without a further application to the court."

Breck looked out the window at the darkness outside.

"We can't do anything until tomorrow morning." Kelly said.

He looked sideways at Breck's parents, and then turned back to Breck. "I'm sorry, Marchant. Your son will have to go with Ms. Ellis tonight and we'll rescind the order as soon as possible tomorrow morning. I'll draw up an ex parte document tonight. We should be able to get it before a judge by mid-morning."

"What? No, we will *not* be withdrawing the order!" Jeremy Marchant shouted.

"We have no choice. The information given you was false and was proffered under questionable circumstances. The boy is well cared for. I am not prepared to say otherwise. I shall talk to Ms. Ellis." Kelly stalked off to find Ann Ellis.

Defeated, sick to the bone, Breck sank down on to a kitchen chair. How was he going to explain this to Kit? How could he tell Kit he'd have to go with a woman he didn't know, to a place he didn't know, where he'd be with people he didn't know? And he might see his father again tomorrow. Or he might not.

Breck choked down the lump in his throat, heaved

himself to his feet and went to talk to Ms. Ellis.

She had obviously been in circumstances like these many times. "Kit, you have to come with me. You'll see Daddy again tomorrow. Don't bother bringing anything with you. There are lots and lots of toys and books where we're going. Just get him a change of clothes," she advised Breck. "If he takes too much stuff, you may never see it again. I'm sure you understand what I mean."

Oh God. Poor little Kit. "Where are you taking him?"

"It's a foster home for short-term stayers and it's not far away. Try not to worry, Mr. Marchant."

So she wouldn't tell him where the place was.

Kit was silent. He didn't shed a single tear. Instead he clung like a limpet to Breck's legs. Ann Ellis had to unpeel his fingers one by one. Breck looked down at Kit's bowed head. There was the faintest of whispers. "Daddy?"

Breck broke. He bent down and scooped up his son. "This boy has been through a lot, Ms. Ellis. This is the last thing he needs." He was shaking. He couldn't seem to stop. Kit buried his head in his father's neck and Ms. Ellis had to do the unpeeling thing all over again.

"I'm going to go quickly now. Give me your card," she murmured.

Breck dug his card out of his jacket pocket. She grabbed it, scooped up Kit and his knapsack and rushed out of the room as if they were being chased by a pack of jackals. Breck heard Kit scream "Dadd-ee!" and the door slammed.

"Oh, God."

"Mr. Marchant."

Breck stared through swimming eyes at the lawyer. "What?"

"I suggest you get a restraining order for both yourself and Kit to keep those two"—here the lawyer jerked his head towards the living-room—"out of your hair."

"Thanks. That's good advice, even though you're acting for them," Breck murmured, trying to smile.

"Yes, well…once I've got the withdrawal of application set up, I'll call a meeting at our office and inform everyone that we no longer act for your parents. This is not the first time I've been sent on a wild goose chase by your father, but this is the most distasteful trick he's pulled." He sniffed. "I'll give you my private cell number." He scribbled on the back of his business card and handed it to Breck. "Sorry about this, Marchant. Call me anytime."

Breck nodded. There *were* some good guys around. Whoever would have thought they'd be in the legal profession? "I need to ask them about this phone call."

Kelly rolled his eyes. "How can they have missed the fact that their…what is it…ex-daughter-in-law…is missing?"

"They've always tended not to see the wood for the trees," Breck murmured.

"Must have been fun being brought up by them."

"You can say that again."

His parents were sitting just as he'd left them, bolt upright bookends on his sofa.

"We need to know everything you can remember about that phone call, Father," Breck began.

"Or what? You'll arrest me?" Jeremy Marchant's

lips tried to spread in an unused smile, but his eyes were hard.

"Hope it won't come to that," Breck said, treating it as a joke. "Anyway, I'd have to call up whoever's on duty. Can't arrest you myself. So…exactly when did Tania call you?"

"On the 27th," his mother answered. She glanced nervously at her husband. "It was last Tuesday, wasn't it, Jer?" She had an iPhone in her hand and was flicking through the apps with a long, pointed nail. "Here it is. Yes, the 27th."

"That was *six* days ago," Kelly said softly. "You waited six days before you acted?"

"We explained that." Anna Marchant looked up from her phone and frowned at the solicitor.

"You lied to me," the solicitor said softly. "You told me it was the day before yesterday, the 2nd."

"We got confused. We've been so busy…"

"Yet you were able to find the date on your iPhone easily enough just now."

"Never mind the claptrap," Breck interjected. "Tell me what she said and how she said it."

"What d'you mean—how she said it?"

Breck looked at his father the same way his father had looked at him many times. As if he was an idiot. "Was she speaking under duress? Did she hesitate? Was she parroting a message she'd memorized? Was she reading from a script? Were there background noises?"

"My son, the cop," Marchant sneered, looking at Kelly for affirmation of his opinion.

"Just as well he *is* a cop, otherwise you'd have a lot of explaining to do to some other cops who would not be so patient. Listen to your son, Marchant."

"Whose side are you on, Kelly? You're supposed to be working for us."

"That's why I'm suggesting you listen to the man. Formulate your answers carefully because you'll be asked similar questions by cops from the Missing Person's Unit soon. Isn't that right?" Kelly turned to Breck.

Breck nodded. "So, any thoughts on that phone call?"

"I took the phone call," his mother said suddenly, "and I put it on speaker phone. When she began talking about Christopher, we wondered what was going on."

About Kit. Not about Breck. Well, what had he expected?

"She said she was no longer living with Marty and that you had temporary custody but that you weren't managing well. That you farmed him out wherever you could and he looked unkempt and upset."

"And of course you believed her."

"Of course we did, boy. *We* never had any problems with Tania. We liked her. She was licking you into shape nicely when you jumped ship. Typical." His father gazed at Breck as if his son had disappointed him more than a father could bear.

Actor.

"Yes, well…I found out a few things about her that I couldn't stomach. When I confronted her, she ran off with Marty Kerr. Apparently she'd been having an affair with him for six months." Breck glanced sideways at Kelly, wondering what he thought of the Marchants' dirty linen.

"Whatever. Couldn't see a livewire like Tania lasting long with someone like you, anyway."

Breck folded his lips together tightly to prevent himself from disclosing what Tania had done. What the hell had he ever done to his father? He'd thought he was over his parents long ago, but barbs like that last one still hurt.

Kelly cleared his throat. "Back to the phone call. Any background noise?"

"Don't think so. Did you notice anything, Anna?"

"No. She sounded like her usual self. Except, of course, she was worried about Kit."

*Yeah. Sure.* "She said Kit *looked* unkempt. So she had seen him." Breck looked at Kelly. "You'd better cart them down to the North Shore Missing Persons Division to make a statement. Do you want me to come?"

"Please. And make sure you've got that card Ms. Ellis gave you in case—"

In case his parents tried to push on with their interim custody application.

****

Two hours later, exhausted and hungry, he arrived home. He opened the fridge door and peered inside. Cold pasta left over from last night. Oh happy day. He shoved it into the microwave and prepared a mugful of coffee. Sick at heart, he slithered down the wall and sat on the kitchen floor. He clasped his knees and bowed his head, wondering where Kit was, how he was faring. Was he scared? Had anyone given him something to eat?

His cell phone buzzed like a hornet. Cursing, he plunked his coffee on to the floor beside him and yanked the phone out of his pocket. "Yeah?"

"Daddy?" said a soft little voice.

Breck scrambled to his feet. "Kit! Are you okay?"

"I'm okay, Daddy. There're lots of toys here. Can I come home now?"

Another voice interrupted. "Senior Sergeant Marchant?"

So she'd looked him up. "Yes, Ms. Ellis. Is everything okay?"

"Well, there was a small incident when Kit decided to head home to you. Fortunately we have cameras everywhere so we caught up with him at the gate. I thought if he spoke to you, he'd feel better."

"Thanks, Ms. Ellis. Can I speak to him again?"

He reassured Kit as best he could. "I think you'll be able to come home tomorrow, son."

"Promise?"

"No, I can't promise because it's not up to me. But I'm fighting to get you home again, Kit. Gee, the apartment sure is quiet without you here. I can hear the clock ticking."

"I promise to be quiet as a mouse when I get home, Daddy."

Oh, God. He'd said the wrong thing. He'd made it sound as if Kit was being punished for being noisy.

"Nah, you're never noisy, Captain Kit. Except when we play tag. We're both noisy then."

Kit gave a sort of snuffling laugh. "I have to go to bed now, Daddy. Bye."

And Breck was alone with the silence.

Chapter Fourteen

Ingrid knew she was asking for trouble. Less than twenty-four hours ago the man had showed her he mistrusted her, so why was she behaving like a pyromaniac who dreads the fire but is enthralled by it? Because she was fascinated with Breck Marchant, that's why. He was a caring man who was doing his best to hold down a responsible job and bring up a kid alone. Sometimes his job must fill him with dread. He dealt with difficult, heart-rending situations every day. Some of that would surely affect him. Did he lie in bed at night going over and over what else he could have done to make things right? That was the way she read him.

He'd be awake by now. She'd call him to try and explain that it wasn't she who'd phoned his parents. He'd probably slam the phone down in her ear. The worst part was that she *had* considered it because he needed help. Then she'd asked herself the question: would you go to *your* parents for help, Ingrid? And she'd realized that she and Breck were alike.

She rubbed her gritty eyes. Not enough sleep last night. "Stop frigging around, Ingrid, and talk to the man," she admonished herself. This wasn't something she could let lie. They had to meet every day so she must try to resolve the issue. She used a pencil to tap through the contacts on her cell phone until she reached

Breck's number. She didn't know why she was using a pencil. It was as if she were trying to avoid being bitten by his anger.

"Marchant."

Ingrid took a deep breath. "Breck?"

"Ingrid? I was hoping to come and see you, but things are difficult here."

What did he mean—difficult? Before she ran out of courage altogether she gabbled, "Breck, I didn't contact your parents. Please believe me. I—"

"I know, Ingrid. And I'm truly sorry. I went crazy there for a while. It was because we'd just been speaking about my parents and…" He trailed away as if he'd run out of steam.

She breathed a little easier. She was not going to get all self-righteous with a guy who operated under the same rules as she did. "Can you find out who it was?"

"Don't have to. They said it was Tania. That set the cat among the pigeons."

"*Tania*?" God, would that woman never cease to plague them?

"Yeah. I'm leaving shortly to talk to the Missing Persons Unit again. My parents will be there too. After that I hope to get Kit back."

Her heart jumped in her chest. "Back? Someone took him? Breck, what's happening?"

"Slow down, honey. Take a deep breath."

Oh, God. Was her anxiety that obvious? So much for trying to sound like Ms. Cool & Efficient. She sounded more like a flake with a meth problem. She took that deep breath. "Sorry. Uh, what's happening?"

She couldn't believe what he told her. Kit had been taken away by Child Protection because Breck's parents had reported that he was unable to cope! And in the middle of all this Tania had reared her head. Breck's stress levels must be at an all-time high.

"Can I come with you?" she burst out. "I might be able to help."

"Well…I could use some help in regard to Child Protection, but I don't think the MPU—"

"Can you pick me up? I have to give instructions to Stella Martin about today's schedule at school, and then I'm free."

"See you in twenty minutes," he said and hung up.

She punched the air with her fist. Yes! He was letting her help him. At last he'd stopped thinking he could do everything himself. In spite of the trouble Breck and Kit were in, Ingrid felt almost euphoric. He was letting her get closer to him.

"Do you want to get closer to him, Ingrid? Do you?" she asked herself in the mirror over the washstand.

"Yes. Yes!" she answered herself. Lord, she must stop talking to herself.

She was still smiling like a Cheshire cat when his SUV drew up outside. Grabbing a wooden puzzle from the stack on her desk, she stuffed it into her bag. Kit would need something to take his mind off the last few days. It had been a wild ride for the poor kid.

"Hi," she said, bouncing on to the passenger's seat. She'd scrambled into a change of clothes and put on more makeup than usual. If she was to help Breck by facing down officials, she needed armor. Uh, huh.

Then she got a good look at him. "Did you get any sleep last night?"

He shrugged. "Some, I guess." The purple

crescents under his eyes told another story. He turned off the engine. "Ingrid, I apologize. I apologize for grabbing Kit and running, and for what I said yesterday. But Hell, we'd just been talking about my parents the day before and you'd been saying how all-fired fantastic they are. I arrived home and there they were, standing on the doorstep. I know I was way out of line, but what did you expect me to think?"

"I'd expect you to know I'd contact you first before doing such a thing. I would *never* interfere…" She trailed away. She opened and shut her mouth, feeling herself reddening. Fiddling with her handbag she admitted, "Breck, don't hate me, but I did consider it for a few seconds. Then I asked myself how I'd feel if someone phoned *my* parents and I knew I couldn't do it."

He gave her a long, considering look, those grey eyes serious and searching, then he leaned forward and turned the engine back on. "Someday you must tell me about your parents." He flicked a sideways glance at her. "I was…" he seemed to search for a word "…devastated that you'd contacted my parents. It was as if ground I'd thought was solid had slipped away under me." He cleared his throat. "I thought we—you and I—were at the beginning of a relationship that…" His voice died away.

Ingrid couldn't bear the uncertain look on his face. She stopped fiddling with her handbag and stretched out a hand to cover his where it clutched the steering wheel with a death grip. "Yes. Yes."

Looking straight ahead he said, "Yes? Yes?" with just the hint of a smile.

"You know what I mean."

"I hope so. Ingrid, later we must take some time to talk about us. Something always seems to get in the way." He sighed. "Right now I have to meet the squad leader of the Missing Persons Unit. Then I hope to be able to see Kit." He grinned suddenly. "You're my ace-in-the-hole there. I hope you brought a business card."

"I brought every damn thing I could think of to impress Child Protection. That's why my handbag is bulging."

The grin turned into a chortle. "Your handbag is always bursting with stuff, Ingrid. One of my most vivid recollections of the day Marty held Kit hostage was of you delving inside your bag trying to find something. Since then I've sort of got used to it."

She'd rather his memories of her were more personal, but what the heck. At least he paid enough attention to laugh at her handbags.

At the North Shore police station she was directed to a waiting room while Breck, his parents and their solicitor were ushered into a room filled with whiteboards and charts. The door stood open so she was able to observe Anna and Jeremy Marchant. They nodded to their son as if he was a distant acquaintance, yet their solicitor seemed to be on very friendly terms with Breck. Mr. and Mrs. Marchant hadn't noticed Ingrid, and Breck had had no time to introduce her. But that was good. She was Breck's "ace-in-the-hole," and she was happy to stay out of sight.

At first she heard only the squad leader's voice. She heard him say in an incredulous tone, "What? Nothing at all?" Then the solicitor spoke at length. Breck slouched in his chair, looking down at his shoes. Mrs. Marchant kept looking at her watch, and Ingrid was reminded of the white rabbit in Alice in Wonderland. Suddenly Jeremy Marchant stood up and waved his hands around, his plummy voice raised. The squad leader spoke sharply to him and he subsided.

Then her heart jolted as Breck turned and beckoned her into the room. Oh, no. She'd hoped to avoid this. They were both still too raw over the telephone call to his parents. She'd much prefer just to help him with Child Protection. Then she saw his anxious frown and stood. He needed her now. Raising her chin, she walked into the room.

Everyone stared. She felt like an exhibit in a glass case at the science museum.

"Sit here, Ingrid. Would you tell Sergeant Raker how you know Tania," Breck said softly.

She sat down next to him with Mrs. Marchant on her left-hand side. Anna and Jeremy Marchant peered at her surreptitiously as if trying to establish her credentials. Ingrid inhaled deeply to calm herself and was assailed with a strong perfume. Chloe. Mrs. Marchant and her ex-daughter-in-law used the same perfume. Ingrid edged a little closer to Breck. He took her hand and clasped it tightly. It felt as if he was trying to anchor her to her seat so she couldn't escape. Then he whispered, "It's okay," and her tension eased.

"How long have you known Tania Kerr, Ms. Rowland?"

And so it began. But it wasn't nearly as bad as she'd anticipated. Senior Sergeant Raker was very experienced at setting people at ease. Amused, she wanted to tell him, "You don't have to try so hard to be nice. I'll answer the questions anyway." Gradually he coaxed out of her the history of her acquaintance with

Tania. Most of it. There were a couple of things she didn't tell him.

Then he sat back in his seat. "Well, Ms. Rowland—of all the people in this room, including Breck, you've known Tania longest. My job is to establish whether Tania has disappeared of her own free will, or whether she was coerced into running away. The fact that she's taken her children with her seems to suggest her disappearance is voluntary."

"Yes, but one of the children is not hers," Ingrid muttered.

Raker stared at her blankly. "Not hers? Then whose is it? Which one are we talking about, the little girl or the little boy?"

"The little girl, Pixie. Pixie is Marty Kerr's daughter from his first marriage. I only know that because I used to teach Pixie."

"So you would have had access to the background particulars of the children. I see." Raker nodded. "Look, Ms. Rowland, I think we need to spend more time with both you and Breck." He turned to the Marchants. "Thank you for your time. I wish you'd contacted us sooner—a lot sooner."

Breck's parents bristled with annoyance. Ingrid had the impression they were used to chewing people out, but were not used to being chewed out themselves, no matter how gently.

Breck stood. He looked his father in the eye. "Have you withdrawn that order yet?"

Ingrid stood too. She intended to add her own ten cents' worth.

"It's okay. It's done," the solicitor said.

"Thank you." Breck wasn't thanking his parents;

he was thanking Mr. Kelly.

"Tell me, *Dad*. What happened to Natasha?"

Mrs. Marchant looked quickly at her husband, and then looked away again.

Jeremy Marchant stared deadpan at his son. "Natasha who?"

Ingrid felt Breck draw in is breath and for a moment she thought he might strike his father.

"Natasha Zhukov, the cleaning lady who turned out to be a teacher."

For a second, Jeremy Marchant look startled. "A *teacher*?" Then he recovered. "No idea who you're talking about." Then he snapped his fingers. "I remember. You used to sit in the kitchen with her. A witless, fat Russian woman. God knows. One day she was there, the next day she was gone. You know what cleaners are like."

Ingrid wondered. In spite of Jeremy's assumed casualness, there was a cagey wariness in his attitude. And Mrs. Marchant looked downright desperate.

Breck and Ingrid stayed where they were while his parents and the solicitor left the room. Mr. and Mrs. Marchant did not say goodbye to Breck. For a moment Ingrid saw disillusion on his face as his gaze followed them from the room. Then he seemed to clamp down on his emotions and his expression returned to its usual tight control.

"Let's get down to it," Raker said.

****

An hour later Raker had sucked them dry of every skerrick of information he could glean. At first, Ingrid was startled when Breck confessed to Raker about his illegal visit to the Kerr house, but she realized he had no choice if the investigation was to progress.

However Raker didn't turn a whisker. "Thanks. You've given me some ideas to run with. Especially that number plate. Goes without saying that if either of you hear from Tania, ask her to call me. Or find out where I can call her."

"You'll let Moffat know?" Breck asked him.

Raker grinned. "Don't worry. I'll take care of it."

On their way out of the building, Ingrid muttered, "Your ex-wife is a grade A super bitch. She contacted your parents to stir the pot. Doesn't like being off center stage." How could that damned woman play around with people's lives without a qualm?

Breck looked down at her. "It took me three years to figure that out. I've been wondering; besides trying to pick your brains, what did she do to make you so bitter?"

Ah, shit. She should have kept her mouth shut. Every time she was around Breck Marchant, she said things that were better left unsaid.

Breck's cell phone buzzed. Saved by the bell. Ingrid breathed a little easier.

"Ms. Ellis? Fantastic! We'll be there in about twenty minutes." He turned to Ingrid, grinning from ear to ear. "We can collect Kit now. It's been cleared."

Thank God. Poor little Kit. She'd almost forgotten him during the strain of the past couple of hours, but she'd bet Breck hadn't forgotten. The boy would have been on his mind every waking moment since Ms. Ellis had taken him away.

"We're meeting on neutral ground," Breck explained. Then he rolled his eyes. "Keeping it healthy. Outside the fast food court at Milford Mall."

"I'll wait in the car," Ingrid offered. "You need to see him on your own first."

"Hell, no. Ace-in-the-hole, remember?"

Oh, well. Good to know she was useful.

However when she saw Breck and Kit race towards each other like knights at a joust, she forgot about useful. Ms. Ellis, too, looked as though she was trying to swallow a greasy lump as she watched the reconciliation. Ingrid decided that useful or not, she was lucky to know the Marchant men.

Then Kit, swung up in the air by his father, spied Ingrid. His squeal echoed through the mall. "Miss Rowland! Miss Rowland!"

Breck propped his squirming son on one arm and gathered Ingrid close with the other. "There," he said as if it was the most natural thing in the world. "Now we're all together again."

Ingrid's insecurity disappeared into oblivion. Trying to swallow unshed tears, she leaned across Breck and pecked Kit's cheek. He laughed and made exaggerated smacking sounds with his lips.

"What about me?" Breck asked indignantly. His arm pressed her closer.

His tone held just a touch of anxiety, enough to give her confidence. She looked into the clear grey eyes and smiled. And kissed him on the cheek lavishly, smacking her lips for Kit's benefit.

Kit and Breck grinned twin grins and behind them Ms. Ellis cleared her throat. "Ah, I'll be on my way now."

They turned and stared at her. For a moment they had all forgotten her.

"Thank you, Ann."

When had Ms. Ellis become Ann? Ingrid watched as Breck held out his hand. "Will you be offended if I say we hope never to need your services again?"

Ann Ellis threw back her head and laughed. Then she fingered a hank of hair back behind her ear. No doubt about it, Ingrid thought. She wasn't the only one feeling the pull of the Marchant men.

As they headed back to the SUV, Kit talked and talked and talked. He must have bottled the words up and now they came rushing out, stumbling over each other. Ingrid smiled at Breck over the top of Kit's head and he gave her his slow, rare smile back. Ingrid slid painlessly into Level Four.

As they drew up outside Breck's apartment he asked, "Do you want to go straight on to the preschool?"

No. She didn't. She wanted to stay here with Breck and Kit, but especially with Breck. "I'd better go soon," she said. "It's not that the place will fall apart without me, but today is the day the new unit kicks in."

"Unit?"

"Just means topic. We work in four-week units. Today is the beginning of 'all about firemen.'"

Breck wiggled his eyebrows. "Ah, I understand your eagerness. I know how women feel about firemen."

Grinning, she said, "It's true there are some very well-built firemen at the local firehouse. They come and give talks to the children a couple of times a year. I'm always happy to welcome them."

"Uh, huh. Got one of their calendars, have you?"

She felt the heat spreading over her face and neck.

Breck laughed. "No need to answer that."

She was enjoying the banter. It had been a long time since she'd had someone to laugh with, someone who was on the same wavelength.

"Do you want to go to preschool, buddy?" Breck asked Kit.

"Yes. Got nothing to eat though, Dad."

Breck cast his eyes up. "You've got hollow legs, boy."

Ten minutes later, Ingrid strapped Kit into the car seat in the Fiesta and waved goodbye to Breck. If she were a sentimental woman, she'd say it was almost like being a family.

Chapter Fifteen

"Kit, do you know where Uncle Billy lives?"
"Uncle Billy?"
Kit was doing his usual blocking, pretending to forget everything that had transpired while he lived with the Kerrs.

Breck was curious about Marty Kerr's elusive brother. There were a zillion W. Kerrs in the phone book and on the internet. It was a time-consuming search since at some numbers he was unable to raise anyone the first time through. He made a thorough job of it and went back over those numbers. No joy. Assuming that Billy was not short for William but was simply Billy, he'd begun contacting all the B. Kerrs he could find. In the end there was only one possible lead, and it was a tenuous one. An abrupt, uninformative message was left on an answer phone at one of the numbers. "Billy's away right now. Phone back." Not exactly chummy. But the Kerrs were not a chummy bunch anyway.

He glanced at his watch. He had no more time to waste on the search right now.

He thrust his feet into his boots and grabbed his cell phone off the table.

This morning he had an appointment to talk to Harley Max about his career. Ingrid had continued to nag him about joining the detective division. Breck was still hesitant, knowing that Max would not be impressed with one of his operatives jumping ship to work for what he saw as the other side. But he had to try this option. His other options were to take demotion or quit the police altogether and end up as a security guard on half his present pay with no prospects and no job satisfaction.

He wandered over to the mirror. Looked okay. Max had a bit of a thing for spit and polish. He hoped to God Harley Max couldn't tell how shit-scared he was. His future was on the line and he didn't have anyone else to turn to for advice. Plenty of PTSD therapy, plenty of nights out with the guys. But the professional careers advisers were at Central, and he wasn't going there. Didn't know a soul over there. They'd probably have him for lunch.

Making sure Kit had his backpack, Breck checked his tie one more time.

****

"You were quick off the mark, Marchant."

Breck looked blankly at his boss. "In what way, sir?" Breck didn't think he was quick off the mark. Deliberate and plodding, yes. Quick off the mark, no.

"You haven't heard yet, have you?" Max's shrewd brown eyes examined Breck's face. "Guess your phone is turned off."

Well of course it was. He wasn't about to go into a career-making or breaking interview with a live cell phone. "About…?"

"About your old friend, Marty Kerr."

Oh, God. Don't say Marty's appeal had been successful. He waited, since Max looked as though he was dying to spread the news.

"Found knifed in his cell."

"Holy shit!"

"Pretty much what I said when the prison phoned. Kerr was such an unimportant character that it's got us all scratching our heads. Didn't get someone to off him, did you?" Max grinned.

Breck groaned. "God, I suppose I'll get another visit from Moffat."

"No, but you *will* be interviewed. You know as well as I do that we have to check every connection of Kerr's."

"Of course, but I hope nobody imagines I'd have him bumped. Why, for heaven's sake?"

"Revenge?"

"Crap. Keeping Kit on an even keel is much more important to me than revenge." Breck felt his color rise as his temper got the better of him. "God, I wish I could get the bloody Kerrs off my back permanently."

"Well, one's gone."

"No, I didn't mean—look, you don't know what's been happening." Normally Breck would not pour his heart out to a superior officer, but he'd about had enough. Enough of the Kerrs. Enough of officials who wanted to make his life a misery. Enough of teetering on a knife-edge of uncertainty about his future.

To his embarrassment, out it all spewed. He described the fall-out from Marty's short-lived siege including the attack on him and Kit. He told Max about Tania's shameful secret that had taken him so long to discover; he told Max of his suspicion that Tania was not missing at all but had chosen to disappear; and he admitted his concerns over his parents' role in the whole mess.

When he got to where he'd had to fight to get Kit out of the hands of Child Protection, Harley Max straightened in his chair. "Christ, Marchant! You should have come to see me." He shook his head.

What did that mean? That Max would have jettisoned him off the AOS straight away? Probably. Max's enigmatic stare as he sized Breck up didn't help any. Being a security guard was beginning to look like a viable alternative. With his police background he should be able to do bodyguard work or bank work or…

"Wakey wakey." Max interrupted his frantic thoughts.

"Sorry. Just wondering about security guarding."

"*Security guarding*? What the fuck…? Are you nuts?"

Breck shrugged. "That's all I'm left with. I came to talk to you about applying for the detective division, but if I'm under suspicion over Marty Kerr, I may as well bury that idea. Plus I can't be much of a cop if it took me a couple of years to realize that my wife had a nice little blackmail business going."

Max's bushy eyebrows twitched at the words 'detective division.' "You're not under suspicion. You're a good cop, one of the best we have, and we'll make damn sure you get through this with as little fuss as possible. As for your wife, you've done what you can to disassociate yourself from her activities. That's all that can be expected of any man in that position." Max examined Breck's face. "From what you said, you're finding this solo parent thing a bit rough. What are you going to do about it?"

He'd never get a better opening. Breck settled himself in his chair and launched into his reasons for requesting the interview.

"A *detective*?" Max roared. "What the hell put that maggot into your head, boy?"

"Sir, it would mean job security and it'd be interesting and…well, I mightn't pass the exams anyway."

Max snorted. "Of course you'd pass the exams. Piece of piss."

Breck shook his head. "It'd be a struggle for me. But someone has offered to help me and I can't pass up the opportunity." He shifted uncomfortably in his chair. He hadn't intended to say so much, but he'd rather talk to Harley Max than anyone else. At least Max was always fair.

The phone on Max's desk rang and he stretched out a hand and silenced it, still looking at Breck. Then he swiveled around in his chair and opened up a file on his computer.

For a second, Breck was peeved that his boss was attending to him with only half an ear, and then he realized that Max was recording Breck's words. Hell!

"You said you thought your ex-wife had been back to the house. What made you think so?"

"Her perfume. It was everywhere. This was four weeks after she disappeared. I'd have thought it would have dissipated by then." Breck wrinkled his nose. "Mind you, it's pretty powerful. Also, I saw a male and female driving away and it *might* have been Tania. But I'm not sure. The woman was hunkered down in the car seat. Anyway, the numberplate was AC2431. Raker has the details."

Max opened another window on his computer and tapped away some more. "Seems to me, the key to this thing is something between Marty and Tania Kerr. And now Kerr's dead." Max gazed at the wall for a moment, lost in thought. Then he straightened up. "What does Raker think about it?"

Breck shook his head. "Not sure. He's guarded and he's very, very astute."

Max grunted. "The way I see it, we need to look further into Kerr's life, maybe into little nooks and crannies we never peered into before. Because you're implicated, you'll have to be sidelined. I think Moffat's replacement is Detective Sergeant Tony Hull." He turned back to his desk phone and pressed a couple of numbers. Then he switched on speaker-phone so Breck could hear the conversation.

"Hull? Are you heading up to the prison shortly? I've got Breck Marchant with me and there have been a lot of unusual things happening to him lately. Possibly related to Marty Kerr. Come and talk to us before you go any further."

"Good! I was hoping to talk to him."

At least Breck thought that was what Tony Hull said. Max had the speaker-phone turned up so loud that Hull sounded like a seal coughing and exhaling. A scratching sound came from the phone then Hull continued, "Give me ten, sir. Be there soon."

"Yeah. Don't spend all day on that coffee."

Hull replied with a muffled snort and hung up.

Harley Max grinned. "You'll like him, Breck. Calm like you but with a more outgoing personality."

Talk about the Lord giveth and the Lord taketh away. First Max had called him by his first name and everyone knew he only did that to his inner circle. Then he pretty much intimated that Breck had a dull personality. Great. "Before he comes, sir—do you think I'd be any good as a detective? I mean…I'm not giving my best to the AOS at the moment and—"

A tap sounded on the door and D.S. Hull walked in. He was incredibly tall and lanky. A basketball player for sure. He lounged into the room, held out a hand to Breck and muttered, "Tony Hull," then flung himself down on the only available chair.

So much for ten minutes to discuss Breck's future. His career plans would have to wait.

Max and Breck hit the high points and Detective Sergeant Hull listened. Then he asked a couple of questions and listened some more.

Beck wondered what was going on behind those intelligent green eyes.

Hull pulled out an iPad and consulted his notes. "What was that numberplate again?" he asked, without looking up.

"AC2431." Breck rattled it off.

That had Hull looking up. "You wrote it down?"

"No. But I checked it out. It belongs to a little old lady named Albertine Reynolds. It's registered to her Mini."

"You've been busy. Certain about the number?" Hull asked.

Breck nodded.

Hull looked at him thoughtfully. "You one of those people who remembers details?"

Breck nodded again. Natasha had taught him how to compensate for his lack of reading skills. His parents had no idea that their cleaning lady had been a remedial teacher in her native Russia. To them she was just "the cleaner." Even now Breck still used some of Natasha's tricks to remember names and numbers. God, he missed her. Her jolly laugh and how she'd turned hard work into a game.

"You're a handy guy to have around," Hull commented.

Breck shrugged. "Lots of people can remember simple strands of numbers."

"Nope. Lots of people *think* they have good memories for numbers," Hull retorted.

"He wants to be a detective," Harley Max said.

Tony Hull bounced his head. "Cool. You'd be ideal. I'm here if you need help."

"Hey! Leave him alone. He's mine."

Hull raised his eyebrows at Max's outburst. He winked at Breck. "Hands off. The man wants to be a detective. Enough said."

Max looked long and hard at Breck while Hull flicked through his notes. "You're quite sure about applying to the detective division?"

Hesitating, Breck opened his mouth to reply when Max answered his own question. "I guess you are. You're one of my longest serving officers and burnout is only to be expected."

Burnout? That wasn't what Breck had been trying to say.

Or was it?

Without knowing how he got there, he found himself pacing in front of Max's desk. Burnout? Was that why juggling all the facets of his life seemed to be so damned difficult? It was a whole new world of thought. Sure, it was common enough, but because he loved what he did, he hadn't realized that burnout was a possibility.

He sat down again.

Harley Max and Hull watched him. Then Max leaned forward and handed him a sheaf of papers. "Here, Marchant. While you were pacing, I printed out the application forms for you." He grinned. "Get on to it pronto. The next intake is in four weeks and you'll be the first to be considered. In the meantime you'll be on normal duties, but call in at HR on the way out. You're due some paid leave and you need to take that before you plunge into a career change. Fill these forms out, and if you get stuck, contact Tony here. Bloody sorry to lose you from my division, but I'll be keeping an eye on you."

Breck didn't know what was more unnerving; the idea that Harley Max was 'keeping an eye' on him, or the prospect of filling out a raft of forms.

He stood, and Hull stood too. "Something I was thinking about," Breck said. "We should take a look at Marty Kerr's brother. Oh, and something else my son said made me sit up and take notice."

Hull raised an eyebrow.

"Apparently Tania had done a disappearing act only the month before Marty got himself into strife. I've told Raker about that. And I told him that she did that when we were married, too."

"Thanks. I'll liaise with Raker and we'll keep you in the loop," Hull promised. "Anything I can help you with before you fill in the application form?" He nodded at the stack of papers Breck was stuffing in his satchel.

"Not at this stage, thanks. I'm flying blind at the

moment."

Hull grinned. "You've done just fine so far. You'll be great with Max behind you. His boys do well."

"Yeah?" Breck flicked a look at his boss. "He always gave us to understand that once we left the AOS, he washed his hands of us."

Hull rolled his eyes. "Like hell. The nosy old sod has his finger in a lot of pies."

Harley Max raised his middle finger at Hull and Breck laughed. Yes, he could just imagine Max interfering if he thought he could bring some leverage to bear.

His heart not nearly as heavy as it had been when he'd arrived at Headquarters, Breck clambered into his SUV. It wasn't until he stopped at the first traffic light that he looked down at the papers spilling out of his satchel on to the seat. His stomach tightened with the old familiar fears.

Chapter Sixteen

Ingrid struggled to comprehend the latest directive from Education New Zealand. What the hell did "educative processes allied with a child's precognitive skills" mean? More red tape. The number of directives she received each month had ceased to astound her. Somewhere in a room far away, a person she would never meet spent their days constructing endless rules for preschools, especially private preschools. Oh, *how* she wished she'd not succumbed to pressure from her parents to open this school. Sure, she wanted to teach preschoolers, but that was what she wanted to do— teach. Not administrate. Not pore over pointless instructions that were better off in the trash.

The newsletter contained quotes from Breck's parents. '*A stimulating preschool environment coupled with the encouragement of an enthusiastic teacher can overcome any adverse physical or psychological influences the child may encounter outside the school.*' Yeah? She remembered reading that during training. Well, she knew better now.

What about Jimmy Holder whose mom hit the turps as soon as Jimmy left for preschool so that by the afternoon, someone else had to collect him and take him home? Jimmy was a seething cauldron of anger bubbling beneath a phlegmatic surface.

And what about poor little Eloise Driscoll whose bitter, desiccated Grandma had custody of her? Grandma hadn't wanted Eloise to mix with 'those dirty children' at a public preschool. Needless to say, Eloise didn't believe in pixies or princesses any more, yet she was barely three.

"Airy fairy shit." Ingrid snorted, chucking the newsletter aside. Then she stopped and stared at the pile of papers. If she hadn't heard Breck's side of the story and seen his parents in operation, she would still believe that crap.

"*That's* not very professional, Ms. Rowland." Stella Martin had come into the office to collect some flashcards. She stood beside the desk, grinning down at Ingrid. "Never mind. There's something outside that will make your day." She wiggled her eyebrows.

"Unless it's a check for $10,000 I'm not interested." Ingrid picked up the next letter.

"My, we *are* tetchy today. Not enough sleep last night?"

No, she hadn't. She'd laid there half the night thinking about Breck Marchant. Where was their relationship going? Was it going anywhere? *Should* it go anywhere? They were like chalk and cheese, yet somehow he got under her skin like no other man ever had. Well, there hadn't been very many other men, but there'd been enough for her to use as a yardstick. Breck Marchant went way over the top of the yardstick.

She was in great danger of plunging into a one-sided affair with a man who showed no signs of needing a woman in his life permanently. He needed a babysitter, but he didn't need a woman. And who could blame him? Tania's antics would sour the most sanguine of men. Nope. Their affair was destined to go nowhere. She sighed. "Oh, live a little, Ingrid," she muttered to herself. "Put yourself out there."

"That's what I say too," Stella said grinning. "And he's just the man to ease you gently into the dating scene."

Ingrid stared at Stella. "Who? What?" Had Stella heard her muttering about Breck? She could feel a flush beginning at her neckline and spreading up to her face.

Stella nodded towards the doorway. "Hunk. He's out there now, talking to Kit."

Ingrid leaped to her feet. "Why didn't you tell me? Do I look all right?"

Stella shook her head. "You've got it bad. Do something about it, sweetie."

Easy for Stella to say.

Ingrid squelched her fears into submission and sailed out of the office like a galleon headed for stormy seas.

****

Breck looked up from where he was showing Kit and another little boy how to hammer straight and true with rubber mallets. He inhaled. Ingrid. He'd know that subtle fragrance anywhere—sweet with a touch of bite.

"What did your boss say? Is everything okay?"

He grinned and spread his arms wide. "You are looking at a man on two weeks' leave. And no, I haven't been fired."

She grinned back. "I *told* you he wouldn't get upset if you asked him about switching to the detective whatsit."

"I think the whatsit is called a division," Breck said. He tilted his head on one side. "Nobody likes people who say 'I told you so.'"

She stuck out her tongue and Kit and his friend stopped hammering to stare at her. "*Miss Rowland*!"

Blushing, she murmured, "Sorry, boys. Mr. Marchant is being annoying."

"He's going to be even more annoying shortly. He wants you to help him to fill out a very *long* application form."

"No problem. I promised you I'd help." Then she smiled evilly. "And since you're a gentleman of leisure now, you can help me put away all the play equipment."

He shrugged. "Sure. I'd intended to help out here over the next couple of weeks anyway. May as well start now."

Ingrid beamed at him. "Not many people choose to spend their holidays at their kid's preschool," she commented.

He shrugged. "I missed out on a lot of Kit's development, and now I have an opportunity to make up for some of it." It also meant he'd get to see Ingrid every day. That was good. Very good. "But I have to fill out that blasted application form first," he added.

"It will be all right, you'll see."

She sure had a lot of confidence in him. The only other people who thought so highly of him were Kit and Natasha. Oh, and possibly Harley Max, but who knew with Max? Once Ingrid saw how he agonized over every word on the application form, she might become impatient. His parents had never lasted more than ten minutes with him, and a couple of his teachers at primary school had had even shorter leashes. Then again, they'd had a classroom full of kids vying for their attention, and a slow-witted student was probably the last straw.

"Okay. After we've shut down here, we'll go to my place and attack that application." Ingrid sounded as though she was rolling up her sleeves.

Shit. In spite of his words, he'd hoped to have a day's respite before he faced his nemesis, but Ingrid was right. It was like eating. Best to tackle the greens first before rewarding yourself with dessert.

He watched as she loped around supervising the end of day tidy-up. Kit showed Breck the list on the wall. "This week my job is to clean the whiteboards and tidy up all the marker pens. Then I have to check that the computers are switched off." He scuttled away, full of importance.

Breck glanced around, noting the amount of equipment. No wonder Ingrid seemed anxious about the running costs of the center. She was caught between a rock and a hard place, needing money from her stepfather, but reluctant to be beholden to him.

****

Two hours later, Breck was wishing he'd never listened to her. The application form wasn't just long, it was impossible.

"Why do you have to answer this stuff?" Ingrid asked as he tried to remember what date he'd left high school. "Shouldn't the HR people have all your details?"

He stared at her. He'd been so hung up on the mechanics of the thing that he'd forgotten the obvious. Of course HR had all the information they needed. He could ask for a copy of his original application and then add in his later experience. He wasn't thinking clearly.

The heat rose under his skin. "I'm a fool," he mumbled.

"Stop it! Stop it at once!"

To his shock, Ingrid stamped her foot. "Get over this 'poor little me' act. You are *not* a fool. You were given the wrong application form, that's all."

Breck stared at her in consternation.

"Your attitude pisses me off," she hissed, obviously trying not to upset Kit.

Breck didn't know what to say. Once they'd passed their initial exams for police selection, Abe had said, "Now that we've done it once, we can do it again if we have to."

At the time, Breck had thought, "Well, *you* might be able to, buddy, but I don't stand a chance." He'd been lucky with the Armed Offenders Squad. Temperament and arms knowledge was of more importance than a bunch of diplomas. Sure, he'd had to sit a rigorous entrance test and there was continuous training, but most tests were oral and physical.

Ingrid's contempt stung.

He was so damned *scared*. He only had to think about sitting a written test and he got goose bumps all over. Pathetic.

"In the morning you are going to obtain the correct application form; then tomorrow night, you and I will work on it till it's perfect."

He blinked. "You're still going to help?"

She had kicked off her shoes when they'd got home and pulled on a pair of fluffy slippers and a white sweater. Standing four square in front of him with her hands on her hips, she looked like an exasperated bunny.

"I promised you I'd help, didn't I? But *you* are

going to do most of the work, Breck. That's what it's all about."

She must be one hell of a teacher. God, that stupid saying "you're beautiful when you're angry" was more accurate than he'd thought. When Ingrid got annoyed you could almost see sparks flying through the air. He smiled.

"What? What's so funny, Breck Marchant?"

"You are. Come here."

Cautiously she came a little closer and he tugged her between his legs. "So you think I don't try hard enough, do you?" He nuzzled her neck. She didn't pull away, but she was still smoking.

"I think you hide behind your upbringing and blame it for everything that's bad in your life. But there are a lot of good things in your life too. Kit for instance. Whether you like it or not, some of what your parents inculcated must have rubbed off on you."

He shook his head. "On the whole, the best things in my life have come from doing the opposite of what they taught. The useful and good things in my life came from Natasha's lessons." He could feel the warmth of her through his jeans. He wished she hadn't used the words "rubbed off on you" as she pressed against him but he didn't think she'd yet realized what was happening. She was concentrating so hard on getting her point across that she hadn't noticed *his* point.

"Then do it for Natasha." Suddenly she stopped talking and gasped. "Oh!"

He grinned at the shocked expression on her face. What did she expect while they were standing like this?

Then her expression segued into something very different. A look of longing, of inquiry, of speculation.

His stomach muscles tightened. "Okay. I promise I will no longer use my parents as an excuse." He nudged her legs apart. "I promise"—he gave another nudge and her face reddened from pale pink to scarlet—"to ask Ms. Rowland for help only after I've explored every avenue myself. Does that please you?"

"You mean your career plan or this?" She reached down and touched him tentatively.

He sucked in his breath.

A muffled snort behind them made them spring apart as if a sword had cleaved a path between them. Then Breck stifled a laugh. Kit, snoozing on the sofa, had rolled over in his sleep.

Ingrid closed her eyes in relief. "God, I thought he was getting an eyeful. Thank goodness he's asleep."

Sexual heat shimmered through his veins. With Kit asleep, there was nothing stopping them. He reached for her.

"We need to talk."

His thoughts ground to a halt. They needed to talk like he needed to inhale sulphur dioxide. No way. When women said they needed to talk, trouble followed.

"In here." She tugged his arm and shoved him into the bedroom. Oookay. He wasn't going to object, but his little fairy princess was acting way out of character. Sure, they'd been on the boil for a couple of weeks now, but he had never in a million years imagined that Ingrid would take the initiative. He had planned a very, very slow seduction. He mightn't be good at passing exams, but he was good at planning. Now, however, it was as if the world had shifted on its axis. Confused, he tilted up her chin so he could look into her face. She still glowed redder than a traffic light. Turning her head away, she took another step, then stopped suddenly as if she'd run out of spunk.

He couldn't resist a quick glance over her shoulder. A bed took up most of the small room and surprise, surprise, there was nary a white frill or stuffed toy in sight. The bedcover was a businesslike dark green. She practically shoved him on to the bed and muttered, "Sit down."

"I've had more romantic invitations, but I guess sitting down will do for a start." Then he caught the anxious, frightened look on her face and wished he hadn't been so flippant.

"Please don't," she said. "I have to say this first."

"I'm sorry, Ingrid. What is it?"

"Before we—we…" she trailed off. "Anyway, I can't do this with someone who mistrusts me. I just can't. Do you trust me now?"

He cursed himself for being so stupid, for accusing her of contacting his parents. He had hurt her badly. All because whenever he got near his parents, he couldn't think clearly. It had always been that way. For God's sake, he was almost thirty-three. Wasn't it time he let that stuff go? He was close to losing the best thing that had ever happened to him because of his stubbornness.

He stroked the back of her hand. "If I hadn't been so crazy about you, this wouldn't have happened," he said. "I guess you've figured that out. But the world I'd so painstakingly built up got dragged down around my ankles by a lovely woman I was beginning to trust—"

"Beginning to trust," she interrupted. "That says it all. You are so unwilling to trust anyone that when your parents arrived on your doorstep, you decided it was my fault. Just because I own a couple of textbooks they wrote."

"You sang their praises, Ingrid. You adhere to their principles."

"It's true I was trained using their textbooks, but that was the choice of Education NZ, not my choice. It could just as well have been textbooks by Abercrombie or Troughton or…or someone."

"Who?"

"Never mind. What I'm saying is that on very slim evidence you decided that I had—had betrayed you."

He looked at her for a moment, his heart thudding like a jackhammer. Had he made the biggest mistake out of a lifetime of mistakes? "Betrayal is the correct word. I felt betrayed. Only someone who knows me well would understand how I feel about my parents. You're the only person I've spoken to lately about them."

"So it must have been me. How very logical."

"Goddammit, logic was all I had! I daren't let my feelings for you dictate what—"

"What feelings?"

Damn it to the pit. The woman bit like catfish at junk on a streambed. She'd honed in on the very thing he should never have said. Women loved to dissect conversations for every subtle nuance. Hadn't he learned that from his mother and Tania?

He looked down at his size twelves. Shit, he'd forgotten to take off his boots. "I'm sorry about the boots. I forgot—"

"What feelings?"

"Damn it, Ingrid. I can't do this. At this time of my life I have no right to—"

"When *will* be the right time, Breck?"

He bent down and unlaced his boots. Slowly. He straightened up and she was there, in his face, pressed against him, just like she'd been ten minutes ago, the perfume of her skin drawing him in. God, he wanted her. Something of his own. He was weak. Lacing their fingers together he raised her hands and kissed the back of them. He sighed. "Deep down I knew you hadn't contacted my parents. But where they're concerned I'm not quite sane. One day I'll explain. I think I needed an excuse to get good and mad at you. I just couldn't cope with those endless damn daydreams about us…"

"You too?"

He looked down at her. Somehow her head had decided to nestle on his shoulder, with her chin tucked against his clavicle. Her arms wrapped like vines around his waist and he could feel her heart going lub-dup, lub-dup at a brisk canter. Fighting this thing was just too hard. He lowered his head and—

"Daddy, are we going now?"

Breck raised his head. He held on to Ingrid as she tried to squirm away from him.

"You want to go now, do you? That's a pity. Ms. Rowland and I were having an in-depth discussion. We'll finish this another time soon. Very soon." He ignored Kit for a moment, willing Ingrid to meet his eyes. When she shyly peeped up at him he grinned. "Story of our lives." Then he sobered. "Are you sure you want to continue—"

"Yes." Unequivocal. Her hectic flush underlined her affirmation.

He figured he was just as flushed. Not just in the face either. He let go the breath he'd been holding and tipped his forehead to gently touch hers. "Thank you."

"Daddy?"

"Coming, Kit."

"Not quite," Ingrid murmured.

Startled, Breck burst out laughing. He kissed her chastely on the forehead, still grinning, and she leaned into him for a few seconds before pulling away.

"Will I see you tomorrow?" she asked.

Although parts of him were hard, his insides softened like caramel at the anxious question. She was putting it all out there. She had way more courage than he did. Sure, he could take a man down if he threatened someone else, but he was gun shy when it came to laying himself down for a woman to stomp over. "Yes. Tomorrow," he promised.

Chapter Seventeen

Bzzzz. Ingrid opened one eye. Was that her cell phone? What the hell was the time? She snuggled into the bedclothes. It was cold tonight.

But her phone continued to vibrate on the bedside table. She rolled over and snatched it up. "'Lo?"

"Stay out of what doesn't concern you or you'll be sorry." Clunk.

Scrambling in the dark, she located the reading lamp and turned it on. A book thudded to the floor and she jumped, her cell phone bouncing on the bedspread. As her heart pounded painfully in her chest, she scooped up the phone to check the time. 3:30 a.m. Who would contact her at this time of the night to threaten her? Because that had clearly been a threat. Why? What didn't concern her? It had been a man's voice, gravelly and indistinct. He'd been using a landline, judging from the noise when he crashed it back on its cradle. In spite of her confusion, she saved the call carefully. Then she tucked her knees under her chin and pulled the cover up to her ears, her heart still doing push-ups in her chest. The kids told her things all the time, things she didn't want to know. Mostly she just said, "Uh huh," and diverted them on to something else. Which kid had told Ingrid some family secrets that the family wanted hidden? Frantically she cast her mind back over the past couple of weeks, but it was impossible to remember an isolated incident. Heck, she spoke to every child every day. What little kernel of truth had she missed?

She'd "be sorry." Oh, *hell*. This wasn't what she'd envisaged when she began teaching preschool. She'd thought it was going to be fun, that she'd have the pleasure of guiding fresh, open minds and setting them on a course of…yeah, and she'd been naïve.

She really, really wanted to ring Breck but she couldn't telephone someone at this hour of the morning just for comfort. Standing on her own feet was something she'd been good at since she'd escaped Marla and Tom's benevolent dictatorship. "Get it together, Ingrid," she told herself. She would have to tread very warily at preschool over the next few days. As she planned how she'd talk to each child individually to see if anything jogged her memory, her heart settled back into its regular rhythm.

Then she brightened. Breck would be around for the next couple of weeks. He wouldn't let anything happen to her, and he'd be another pair of ears. Not that he didn't have enough troubles of his own, but he was reliable and she trusted him implicitly. Which was more than she could say about a lot of other people she knew.

She clicked off the light and lay back down, and then bounced up again. What if that call had nothing to do with preschool and everything to do with her relationship with Breck? What if the caller meant: stay out of the Kerrs' and Marchants' business? Now *that* was more likely than some disaffected parent phoning her in the early hours of the morning.

Or was it?

She peered at the time on her cell again. 3.45. Wide

awake she glared at the phone, willing the time to be later—much later. She wasn't going to get back to sleep now. Sighing, she clambered out of bed and flicked on the light. Brrr. The winter cold stole her breath. Grabbing her robe off the end of the bed she pottered out to the living room and switched on her laptop. Might as well get some work done.

****

Breck dropped Kit at preschool, and then drove on to headquarters to sort out his application papers. As he turned the corner, he glanced in his rear vision mirror. Ingrid was standing in the preschool driveway, her arm around Kit, watching him drive away. She looked sort of forlorn, as if he'd deserted her. He shrugged. He'd be back in an hour.

But when he returned he found Ingrid seated in her office, gazing into space, still with that lost, puzzled expression.

"What's up, sweet thing?"

She turned and grabbed his hand. "I'm so glad you're here, Breck. I don't know what to do. I didn't like to phone you in the middle of the night."

He sat down beside her. "The middle of the night?"

"Three-thirty this morning, to be exact."

He rubbed his fingers across the back of her hand. "Tell me what's wrong."

She showed him her cellphone with several incoming messages, one timed at 3:30 a.m. precisely. When she explained what the caller had said, he wished he could get his hands on the creep and crush him into little pieces.

"I checked, but the sender's name is blocked."

Of course it was. But Ingrid being Ingrid, had all

her incoming calls on Record. He listened to the message several times, trying to ascertain if anything in particular stood out.

Ingrid looked down at her feet. "At first I thought it must be a parent sounding off about some troubles they had at home that their child had inadvertently spilled to me, then I began to wonder…do you think it has anything to do with—Tania and all that stuff?"

Oh, Jesus. Had he dragged her into trouble? He replayed the message. "I think the voice is slightly disguised," he said after a moment. "It hasn't been changed by a voice changer so much as the speaker is trying to disguise it himself. I mean, he's perhaps talking more deeply than he usually does."

Her lips parted. "How can you tell?"

"I can't, really. It's just that everything would be altered in sync if he used a voice changer, whereas he's just changing some of his words. It's definitely a male."

"I wasn't even sure of that." She touched his arm. "You're going to make a great detective."

He couldn't help laughing. "It takes a bit more than that to pass those damned exams." He stood. "Just in case, I'll forward this to Hull. And if it's the family of one of your kids, then it's just as well I'll be here on and off over the next couple of weeks."

She set him up at her desk so he could fill out the application forms all over again. This time he flew through them. After all, he had a template to copy from, and the brief application designed for long term serving police officers was a breeze. It was a pity Harley Max hadn't given him the correct form in the first place, but Max was well known for scorning paperwork from any department except his own. Breck doubted his boss had deliberately set out to make things difficult.

As he folded the papers and tucked them into an envelope, his cell phone crackled and clicked like dice on the gaming floor of a casino. Incoming text message. He read it and yelled "Yes!" before remembering where he was. He sat down and re-read the message. As usual, Abe and Jace had gone for broke. They were not bringing home a son or a daughter. They were bringing home a son *and* a daughter. Boy, would they have their hands full.

"Good news?" Ingrid asked, hurrying towards him.

"Very good news, Aunty Ingrid." He watched her to see when the penny would drop.

"Abel and Jace?" She bounced a little with excitement and his eyes strayed to the front of her sweater. "Behave yourself," she hissed.

"Yes, ma'am, Ms. Rowland."

"Boy or girl?"

"Both. A boy and a girl."

"Ohhh. Imagine flying for two days from Russia to New Zealand with…how old are they?"

"Ten months and two years. They had a stopover in Singapore. They're almost home."

Ingrid rolled her eyes. "Oooo-ee. Uh…I guess Jace won't get much time to look after Kit now, will she?"

Breck shrugged. Then he grinned. "Hey, I could end up babysitting for them!"

Ingrid laughed. "What a turnaround. So did you get that application done?"

He nodded. "But before taking it into Headquarters, I'll hang around here for a while." He was worried as hell about that phone call and there was no point in pretending he wasn't.

"Now you're babysitting *me*."

"Much more fun." He checked to see if anyone was looking and dropped a quick kiss on her hair. "Okay, water play here I come."

He spent the next half-hour sloshing with a bunch of kids who were comparing the volume of water in the various containers they had. At times, things got a little obstreperous and everyone got soaked. Breck stepped back every now and again to eyeball the perimeter of the preschool grounds. Nothing untoward so far.

Kit wasn't playing at the water bath. He was *four years old*, for heaven's sake, and water play was for little kids. But he kept an eye on his father's antics as he worked his way through his basic math worksheet.

Ingrid and her two assistants flitted from group to group, supervising, advising and consoling. And he'd thought police work was hard! These women must be worn out after a day's work here.

Then he got that prickling sensation on the back of his neck that a good cop never ignores. Dropping all subterfuge, he stared at the grove of trees on the hillside behind the preschool grounds. A male figure was half-hidden behind the lower branches of a pine tree. Who or what was he watching? The second he saw Breck staring at him, he melted away into the trees.

"Gotta go," Breck muttered as he streaked past Ingrid and vaulted over the fence.

"Dad!"

He could hear Kit's piping voice as he slogged uphill and into the trees. He kept running, assuming that the watcher would be running too. With no time for the niceties of careful tracking, he hurtled along, threading between pine tree trunks until he reached the summit.

Then he stopped and examined the terrain. Nothing moved to the south the west or the east. And it was a very good vantage point, so where had the watcher gone? Breck eased back behind the trunk of an extra large tree and hunkered down. He would wait this guy out.

Chapter Eighteen

Forty minutes later he wasn't so confident. There'd been no sound whatsoever apart from the sough of the wind through the branches and the operatic trill of a blackbird bursting to tell the world that it was almost spring. The ground was littered with pine needles, making footprints invisible.

Giving up, he scrambled to his feet and stretched to relieve his cramped muscles. Either the guy was an expert at cat and mouse, or he was long gone. Could he have passed Breck, going back towards the preschool? Breck's pulse cantered. While he was loitering around here, were Kit and Ingrid in danger?

He ran back the way he'd come, pausing half way down the hill to check. All looked serene. Stella Martin was playing ball with a group of kids near the gate, but everyone else had gone inside. He jogged the rest of the way downhill and vaulted over the fence.

Ingrid trotted up to him. She was obviously trying not to look as though she was in a hurry, but one look at her face would give the game away. "Breck, what happened?"

He wondered how much he should reveal. He had to tell her *something* so she was aware she needed to be vigilant, but he didn't want to add to the stress of that middle of the night phone call.

"I thought I saw someone watching the preschool," he explained, choosing his words carefully, "but I think it was just a guy out for a walk. He disappeared before I could catch up with him. A false alarm."

Her hazel eyes examined his face. "You're sugar coating it, aren't you? You raced out of here like a bat out of hell."

"After what's been happening, I had to react quickly."

He prowled out to the front entrance of the preschool but it was the middle of the day and all was quiet. Most people were at work and the only cars in the area looked as though they belonged to local residents. Just the same, he walked slowly past all the parked vehicles along the road, committing one numberplate to memory. In the backseat of the Taurus he could see a picnic rug that had been tossed over some lumpy material. It might be his overactive imagination, but the rug looked as though it had been purposely adjusted to hide whatever was beneath it. He whipped out his cellphone and took a photo, just in case.

But it seemed as though everyone at the preschool had been affected by his actions. As soon as he walked in the door, twenty-five pairs of eyes homed in on his face. Anxiety boiled in the air. He cursed to himself as he saw the worried look on Kit's face, and the wary expression on Ingrid's.

"Oookay now. What's everyone doing?" God, he sounded like his father, full of false joviality. He joined Stella Martin's group to play snakes and ladders and fooled around taking photos of the kids with his camera phone.

As soon as everyone had settled down, he

whispered to Ingrid that he was taking Kit out of preschool early so he could submit his application form. "And how about we repay your hospitality? Come over for dinner." Time to pay his dues. Anyway, he *wanted* Ingrid to see more of their makeshift, hopeful way of existence. And if she couldn't reconcile it with her more orderly life, well then…He drew in his breath as he tucked Kit into his car seat. If that happened, it would not be the end of the world, but it would cut the heart out of him. At least this time he had Kit. Last time he'd been alone.

****

Three hours later he figured things were going along just fine. Ingrid lay on the floor, her head propped on her hands, giving suggestions as Kit tried out a new jigsaw puzzle. And Kit…well, Kit was a happy camper.

Breck enjoyed hearing their laughter as he scrubbed saucepans in the kitchen. Made the place seem whole somehow, as if their four cramped rooms kept the world outside at bay. He whistled under his breath as he tossed out the remaining spinach. He hated spinach and Kit wasn't a fan, either, but he'd figured that from the newsletters Ingrid sent home, healthy food was a priority for her. So he was trying. But he'd bought a packet of parsley sauce to smother as much of the damned vegetable as possible. One thing was for sure. Kit was going to bed *real* early tonight. Breck's stomach tightened in anticipation. He had it all planned out. He'd get Kit off to bed, and then he and Ingrid would stretch out on the sofa and…things would come naturally. He hoped.

But Kit refused to cooperate. There was no way he was going to sleep while Ingrid was around. "Dadd-ee…" he protested.

"It's very late, Kit," Ingrid said. "Remember tomorrow we're going on a trip to the museum." She wiggled her eyebrows at Kit, closing the last of the books she'd been conned into reading.

Kit sighed, outnumbered.

With relief, Breck turned out the light and ushered Ingrid out of the bedroom. "See you tomorrow morning, sport," he called. He stretched. "How about a cup of coffee?"

She was eyeing him but when he caught her looking, she turned away. "I'll make it. You've done all the work tonight."

He stretched out along the sofa, listening to her finding cups and milk. There was something about women and kitchens. He didn't know why he found it comforting to hear a woman chinking cups and humming under her breath. Maybe it was because he associated kitchens with Natasha's warm fuzzies.

"Here you go. Just as you like it. Black, one sugar, right?"

He sat up. Hell, she even remembered how he took his coffee. This woman was a keeper. Why were the two of them playing the wary tango? Well, he knew why *he* was, but why was Ingrid so skittish? He sipped his coffee. Time to stop tangoing and start living. He set down his coffee mug. "So…we've finally got some time to ourselves." Nice one, Marchant. Real intelligent comment.

She smiled and he was a goner. He grabbed her coffee mug, sloshing some of it on the carpet, and dumped it on the side table. Without any finesse he scooted the rest of the way along the sofa, desperate to hold her. "Ingrid," was all he said, but she came into his arms like a homing pigeon. No finesse from her either, thank God. And this time the kiss was even more amazing. The woman *steamed,* for God's sake. He felt the bird bones of her shoulder blades beneath his fingers and shook with the realization that this woman was tiny. Because she tended to come out of her corner fighting, sometimes he missed the fragility, the vulnerability. He softened his clasp and leaned over to turn the table lamp down low. "Are you sure?" He had to ask. Showed his vulnerability too, but a man had to ask. He'd been to too many crime scenes where a man hadn't asked, had taken, and gone too far.

"Been sure for a long time now," she whispered, raising a hand to his face.

She stroked his skin as if she were sampling the texture of something precious. Then, surprising him, she leaned forward and took the initiative. Her soft lips trembled a little, but she didn't pull back. And Breck knew that no matter what happened, he would never forget this night. She was so different from those who'd come before. Gentle. Hesitant. But very determined.

"So sweet," he whispered against her lips and time wound down until it stood still. They explored, they sampled and they laughed a little when they both tried to tug off Ingrid's sweater at the same time and turned themselves into a conjoint octopus. Breck sank into the sensations, relishing them. This was what making love should be. For a second he recollected Tara's ferocious, frenzied lovemaking then dismissed it from his mind. She had no place here.

****

Lord, the man was amazing. She'd never been

made love to with such…well, devotion. He'd found her most sensitive spots and adored them. Breck Marchant was her ideal lover. He was the one she'd daydreamed about, but never expected to meet. Over the past few weeks she'd surmised, but now she *knew*. She'd said it before and she'd say it again. Tania was a double-dyed idiot. "Mmm," she murmured as he worked his way down her body dropping a kiss here, stroking there. She gave herself up to the moment and drifted away on a sea of pleasure.

Coolness on her skin brought her out of her trance to discover she had only her panties and bra on. Her shoes and jeans had disappeared. Her shirt lay tangled on the floor alongside his jeans. Smiling, she spread her hands across his warm chest, savoring the intimacy, then stretched her arms around him, holding all that muscle and skin and *man*. He smelled of soap and warm skin. He smelled of Breck.

"Is everything still okay?" he whispered.

"Oh, *yeah*." Ingrid couldn't help the heartfelt words.

He snorted a half-laugh that changed to a groan as she rubbed her hands up and down his back and clasped that gorgeous butt to tug him against her overheated skin. He exhaled on a long sigh and took her hand to wrap it around himself. She stroked him from root to tip once, twice, and then found herself flat on her back, skin to skin. He tugged off the last of her clothes and she couldn't resist smiling a smug smile. He might be diffident, but he was quick. He ripped open a condom packet with his teeth and Ingrid thanked God that Breck had some sense of responsibility. She seemed to have lost hers the minute he'd laid hands on her.

"Slow. We need to go slower," he muttered.

Damn the man. She was sizzling, but he wanted to do the right thing. The trembling muscles in his arms told her he was forcing himself to slow the pace. She didn't *need* him to slow down. He nuzzled her neck and then, as if time meant nothing, began a slow assault on every nerve point from her face down, down, down…And when he *finally* got to her breast, she was so strung out she shoved herself into his mouth.

"Mmmmf." He rubbed his tongue back and forth across her nipple.

She closed her eyes. Heaven. But she was achy and hot and she wanted him. Sooner. She slithered skin to skin further down the sofa until she reached her goal. And closed her mouth around him.

His whole body jerked. "Ingrid!" It was the plea of a man at the end of his rope. She twitched the condom out of his hand and began to smooth it down over him, but he stayed her hand. "Leave it, honey. Just give me a minute or I won't last." He took a deep breath, then to her shock rolled them off the sofa on to the floor and there she was, on top. She understood that even as he fought for control, he was still trying not to crowd her. His hand slipped between her legs and he slid a finger inside. Delicious pressure, but not enough. "More," she pleaded.

He slid another finger inside her and she simmered. "Breck! You. Inside me. Now."

"God, yes." He tugged her closer and nudged at the gate, then raised her a little, settling her down on top of himself, sliding home as if this was a path they'd taken before. "You set the pace," he muttered between clenched teeth.

Oh, yeah. She pushed up on her elbows, and then plunged. They sighed in unison and Breck whispered, "So, so good. Again..."

But on the next plunge they both unraveled in an uncoordinated upheaval that had them shuddering and gasping. Spread across Breck's body like a blanket, Ingrid listened to their hearts thundering.

Finally Breck sighed. "Ingrid."

She raised her head, heavy as an oversize flower on a stalk and looked into his eyes. "Mmm?"

"Nothing. Just 'Ingrid'."

"Mmm." She nodded in understanding.

"That was..." He trailed off.

"Spectacular? Amazing? Incredible?"

He huffed out a laugh and she bounced on top of him. "All that and more."

Relaxing, they drifted in and out of sleep, draped together. In the kitchen the temperamental freezer ticked and muttered to itself. Footsteps clipped past the door, along the walkway and off into the quiet of the night. Relaxed and sated, Ingrid dreamed and listened to the quiet.

The intrusion of her ringing cell phone was shocking. Her heart jolted as she scrambled off the sofa. After midnight! Nobody *ever* rang her this late. Her mother? Was her mother ill?

"I'll get it for you. Just sit there." Breck was already halfway across the room. He snagged her phone and tossed it to her.

"Ingrid Rowland."

"Trident Security. Ms. Rowland, the alarms at your school have been set off. We're on our way. Do you want to meet us there?"

"Oh those *damned* alarms!" she exclaimed. "Probably another false alert. Thank you. I'll be there in ten minutes."

"Meet who where?" Breck asked.

"Those stupid alarms at the school are sounding again. Someone from Trident Security is on his way."

"I'm coming." He began dragging on his clothes. "Have to bring Kit but he'll sleep through it. He sleeps like a grave digger on double shifts."

They bundled Kit up in his bedclothes and rushed out the door.

Ingrid was really, really pissed off. She had been having the best night of her life with the man she'd wanted for so long, and those dumb, faulty alarms had stuffed everything up. Tomorrow she'd have them pulled out and she'd replace them with another brand. She'd bill her so-called security service provider for the lot. Enough was enough.

As they pulled up in the preschool carpark, the alarms beat a screaming pattern on the cold night air. A car with the logo of Trident Security on it was already parked in front of the main doors. Ingrid jumped out of the SUV cursing under her breath, but when she reached the foyer, all thoughts of firing Trident Security fled.

Shards of glass crunched beneath her feet and there was a great yawning hole in one of the small side windows. The larger one with safety glass was still intact. If whoever it was had managed to squeeze in through the small window then they must be very small. Kids perhaps? For once the damn security alarms were right.

"Kids," the security guard's voice said behind her.

"Looks like." Ingrid unlocked the door and reached inside to turn off the screaming alarm.

"Don't go inside, Ingrid," Breck's voice warned. "There's something wrong. I don't think it's kids."

Ingrid turned towards him and out of the corner of her eye saw a shadow slip past the entrance to the parking lot. "There's somebody out there!" she whispered.

Before she'd finished speaking, Breck was racing across the lot. The security officer brushed past Ingrid and took off after him.

Her heart in her throat, Ingrid walked quickly back to the SUV. The parking lot was lit up like a runway by the security lights, but beyond that was only blackness. Breck and the security officer disappeared into the darkness and she and Kit were alone.

## Chapter Nineteen

Breck's legs pumped frantically as he traversed the same ground he'd run across yesterday. Stumbling over the uneven surface, he fought to keep his footing. Behind him the security officer puffed like a whale, but Breck was grateful for the intermittent beams from the man's flashlight. Ahead of him he could hear thudding footsteps. Then the sound veered off to the right. Back downhill. Was this idiot playing with him?

He ratcheted up his speed, careless of a sprained ankle or worse. This time he'd catch whoever was playing games with them.

Thud. Thud. He was getting closer. His quarry was gasping with labored breaths. And he was no teenage vandal. The footfalls were solid, heavy, those of a full-grown man.

Far off to the right a scream ripped the air. Ingrid.
"Breck!"

Without a qualm he abandoned the chase, leaving it up to the security guard. Switching direction, he pounded back towards the parking lot. He burst out of the darkness into the light and for a second was blinded. Then he heard the sounds of scrabbling feet kicking up pebbles. "Bitch!" someone screamed, and a shadowy figure raced away from his SUV into the darkness beyond.

"Ingrid?" He wrenched open the car door. Nobody inside. Oh, God. "Kit?"

"Daddy?" Kit flung himself at Breck so hard, it felt as if someone had punched Breck in the gut. Grabbing his father's hand, Kit urged him to "Hurry, Daddy. Hurry. Ingrid's hurt. Mommy hit her and hit her and—" He rushed around to the front wheel of the SUV, tugging Breck towards where Ingrid lay huddled on the ground. She looked like a bundle of old clothes someone had tossed away.

"Oh, no." His heart in his throat, Breck knelt beside her, trying to feel for her pulse. The second he touched her she hauled off and tried to slug him. "Ingrid. It's me. Breck. Sssh."

"Mmph." Her hand slid away and her head drooped, but not before he'd seen the massive welt on the side of her face. And the blood on her knuckles.

"Oh, Ingrid." He tried to gather her into his arms but she resisted.

"Hurts," she muttered.

"What the hell happened?"

Kit piped up. "It was Mommy. She came running up and pulled me out of the car. But Ingrid stopped her." He, too, knelt down and laid his chin on the back of Ingrid's neck. "It's all right, Ingrid. Daddy's here now."

"Let me see, Ingrid. I need to know how badly you're hurt."

Reluctantly she unfolded herself and tried to sit up.

Breck sucked in his breath. "Your *mother* did this, Kit? Are you sure?"

Kit nodded.

There was a huge welt across Ingrid's cheek that

would blossom into a bruise by tomorrow. But Breck was more concerned about the mess of matted hair on Ingrid's scalp. It looked as though someone had bashed her with a rock. He swallowed his fear and glanced around, looking for the security officer. Nowhere to be seen. Wrapping his arm around Ingrid, he whispered, "Lean against me, sweetie."

She sighed and relaxed against him, wincing. God, she must have other injuries as well.

"Kit, get my phone."

Kit tugged the cell phone out of Breck's pocket and held it out.

****

Fifteen minutes later, the carpark was swarming with cops. Hull lost no time in fanning out his team around the perimeter. An ambulance sat just outside the circle of crime scene tape waiting to tend to Ingrid. So far she'd refused to be treated until she'd had a look at the damage done to her school. Kit sat, wide-eyed, watching the strobe lights on the police cars and the ambulance.

Ingrid, her hand in Breck's, waited for the go-ahead to return inside the building. Her head alternately pounded and ached, but it was important to see if the school could stay open. If not, she had many phone calls to make in a very short time.

"What time is it?" she mumbled.

Breck moved a little to check his watch. "Nearly 1:30."

"Okay, Ms. Rowland. We've cleared it so you can see where the intruders got in and what they did. But you must stand where I stand. Do you think you're well enough to do that?" Tony Hull was solicitous but firm.

"Lead on, MacDuff," Ingrid said as Breck eased her to her feet.

But when she saw what had happened to her lovely, lovely preschool, fury boiled up inside her. If this was the doing of that maniacal Tania Kerr, she'd hunt that rabid woman down and wring her neck.

The walls of the foyer were sprayed with the message "Warned you, bitch" in several places. In the main room adjoining the foyer someone had attempted to light a fire, but it had burned itself out. Just as well. Jars of paints and colored glues were kept in one corner and although supposedly not flammable, they would have added fuel to the piles of paper and books that had been stacked in the middle of the room.

Ingrid stood in the center of it all like Dido amid the ruins of Athens and turned in a circle. Slowly. Her head pounded and graunched, and her stomach heaved. She didn't know if that was from the bash on the head or the awful thought that she was faced with a phenomenal amount of work to get the school back up and running. What if she couldn't contact all the parents before nine a.m.? How could some of those people make alternate arrangements on such short notice? Sure, the foyer could easily be painted and if she started right now, it might be finished but still sticky at nine a.m. But where was she to buy paint at one o'clock in the morning?

In the center of the floor in the main room a huge hole yawned. No safety inspector would allow children in that room. And they only had another small room that doubled as a computer room. They couldn't all fit in there.

She followed Hull around the edge of the main

room into the storeroom. This was where the paper had come from to start the fire, but the intruders had left most of the room's contents in their neatly stacked piles on the shelves. And when the bathrooms were checked, they looked intact.

"Only bothered with the main rooms," Hull commented. "But the question as far as I'm concerned, Miss Rowland, is what does that writing mean? 'Warned you, bitch'?"

"Detective, I wish I knew. The night before last I got a phone call in the middle of the night—"

"Marchant told me. But you don't know if it's a disgruntled parent or because you're er…associating with him."

"That's right."

Hull stared at her for a moment, reminding her of Breck when he was considering a ticklish problem.

"This whole thing keeps revolving around Tania Kerr. What the hell is she up to?"

"Sir!" A constable crunched over the parking lot and stopped when he reached the crime scene tape. "We've found someone."

Ingrid and Hull stepped outside the main door and Hull held up the tape so Ingrid could squeeze underneath it. As she ducked down, her head pounded and she staggered. She would have fallen if Hull hadn't grasped her arm. "Thank you," she muttered. As she straightened up, Breck strode towards her.

"Sit down, for God's sake, and let the paramedics look at you."

The constable was consulting with Hull in a low voice.

"In a minute, Breck. They've found someone." She

turned to Hull. "Who is it? Is it the person who vandalized the school? Is it Tania?"

Hull looked first at Ingrid, then at Breck. "I'm afraid he's not in a condition to tell us anything. He was hit over the head the same as you were, but he didn't get off so lightly. The paramedics are going to be very busy." With the constable leading the way, Hull strode off towards the bush area where Breck had seen the man the day before.

Breck steered Ingrid towards the ambulance. "I'll find out everything from Tony after you've been seen to."

He hovered between the ambulance and his SUV, trying to keep an eye on Kit and another one on her. Ingrid admitted to herself that it felt good to have someone concerned about her. It had been a long while since someone had worried about her for her own sake. Of course her mother wouldn't like to see her harmed, but she would not be impressed at the undignified picture Ingrid made with blood seeping down over her cheekbone and her sweater torn and muddy. Ingrid was sure that Marla would look neat and tidy on her deathbed. She must be weak or upset or something, because she said as much to Breck.

"Your mother is a neat freak?"

"Well, it's more that she thinks females should always behave in a ladylike manner." She paused and hissed as the paramedic swabbed her head wound.

"Ah, hence the private all-girls school."

"Private all-girls boarding school, actually."

Breck watched the paramedic examine the head wound. "How old were you when they sent you to boarding school?"

"Nine."

"*Nine*? What the hell were they thinking? Were you a handful?"

Ingrid tried to shake her head. "Hold still," the paramedic growled.

"Sorry. No, I think it was because Mother and Tom wanted some time together." Then she subsided. Too much information. Why was she telling the world about her childhood? Breck—maybe. The paramedic—definitely not. She knew why. Her defenses were down, not just down, but down and out. She felt as if someone had found every pulse point in her body and was grinding away at them with sandpaper. She wanted to lie down and sleep but she was too antsy. "I think I'm going to—"

The paramedic held a bag in front of her.

Whoosh!

Great. Now Breck had seen the very worst of her. Perhaps her mother had something after all, about being a lady and maintaining self-control. On the other hand, it was damned hard to maintain self-control when your stomach rebelled. And rebelled. She grabbed the bag again and felt a hand holding her hair back.

"It's okay, Ingrid. I'm here."

Breck. The man was as reliable as sunrise. And he didn't seem the least bit put out. Must be the police training. Perhaps there *was* something to be said for cops after all.

She leaned back against his arm and the paramedic wiped her face with a damp cloth. "Miss—umm, Ingrid, you need to get stitches in this scalp wound. We have to take you to hospital *now*."

Embarrassed, she felt hot tears trickling down her

face. "I don't wanna go to hospital."

"I know," Breck answered her. "But it's for the best. Kit and I will follow the ambulance and wait till you're fixed. And don't worry about tomorrow. Stella Martin and I can handle the museum trip."

"The museum trip! Oh, no! Breck—"

"Ingrid. Shut up and go with the nice man." She shut up and watched as the paramedic winked at Breck.

"I'll get you for that, Breck Marchant," she muttered as she was assisted on to a stretcher.

Chapter Twenty

Breck threw himself down on the sofa beside Kit and yawned. What a hell of a night and day. Ingrid had had to spend the day in hospital since she was mildly concussed. Boy, had she been pissed.

She'd needed to contact her insurers.

She'd wanted to paint the graffiti off the walls of the preschool and get quotes from builders for the reconstruction of the floor.

She'd wanted to supervise the visit to the museum.

She hadn't actually pouted when the nurse pointed out to her that she would not be doing any of those things. She'd just subsided down the bed and looked miserable.

Breck had promised to take up the slack. And he had. Now he could hardly keep his eyes open. How did she do it? He'd contacted Stella Martin at six a.m. and asked her to phone all the parents. They'd hoped that some parents would keep their kids home. But no. Most of the parents were working parents and almost the full quota of kids were at the gate at 8:30, psyched up ready to go to the museum. The bus driver looked terrified at the sight of thirty preschoolers standing in two neat rows waiting to climb on to the bus, so Breck had had to accompany the group, even though the requisite number of assistants were there. He'd hoped to have time to paint a second coat over the graffiti while they were away. He'd been at the doors of the local hardware market when they'd opened at 7:30. At least he'd managed to get one coat of paint finished before the hordes arrived.

At the museum, while the kids stared in awe at the prehistoric section, he'd borrowed Stella's iPhone and spoken to Ingrid's insurance company. Then he'd lined up several builders to quote for repairs. He emphasized the need for urgency, but that backfired on him. The insurance assessor and a couple of builders were prepared to meet him on site that afternoon. So he'd had to abandon Stella and the twitchy bus-driver and dash back to the school. Then he'd reported back to Ingrid. He'd also checked up on the man who'd been hit on the back of the head, but he'd not yet regained consciousness. They were none the wiser who he was or what he had been doing at the preschool in the middle of the night.

After running around like a maniac, he sat down to have a cup of coffee and discovered it was time to collect Kit.

At that stage he decided that a day in the life of a non-working Dad was not for him. He'd rather be setting up a sting to catch a bunch of break-and-enter thieves, or hunker down in wet undergrowth waiting for a hostage situation to simmer down than drive around chasing his tail.

But Ingrid had needed his help. God knows, she'd helped him often enough, but it wasn't a tally thing. He *wanted* to help her.

As soon as Kit was asleep, Breck settled down in front of the computer and sent detailed emails to Raker and Hull about the recent developments. No doubt there was an incident report somewhere in the system about the attacks on Ingrid and the security guard, but neither Raker nor Hull would see them for several hours. He also informed them about the mysterious man in the hospital who carried no ID.

Once he'd done that, he created a document for all the people who might be involved in the puzzle that was Tania Kerr. Angela whoever, Albertine Reynolds and Billy Kerr were the main ones. They might lead him to Tania or they might not. Even if he only managed to make minimal contact with them, they could hold clues to Tania's behavior or whereabouts. He would pass the information along to Hull and Raker. And the next time he saw his ex-wife, he hoped she'd be behind bars. He still swallowed a truckload of saliva every time he thought of Ingrid struggling to protect Kit.

He wondered if Tony Hull had checked out the elderly Ms. Reynolds yet. Glancing at his watch, he saw it was almost ten o'clock. Oh, what the hell. Hull was no timekeeper. He'd still be working.

Hull answered after the first ring. "Yeah? Who's that?"

Breck explained why he was calling but Hull had no fresh news. "Sent some uniforms out. Nobody home."

"When was that?"

"The day after you told us about her. Why are you poking into the old lady's background?"

"Well…since I've been dragged into this drama whether I like it or not, I'd rather be proactive than reactive."

Hull grunted. "Can't argue with that. How much more time do you have on leave?"

"Ten days."

"Go for it then. Keep me up to date. I'll send a couple of uniforms around to Reynolds' place again tomorrow and let you know the outcome. 'Night."

Good. That was Ms. Reynolds covered. Breck would rely on Ingrid to find out what she could about the mysterious Angela. In the meantime he'd delve further into Billy Kerr's background.

****

Ingrid watched the orange glow of sunrise outside the window. She was sharing the hospital room with a garrulous woman who was blessedly still asleep. Ingrid couldn't wait to get back to her own place. Most of all she needed to return to school and see what was happening there. How was Breck coping? Poor little Kit must be beside himself, seeing his mother come at them out of the darkness and try to drag him out of the car.

Ingrid shivered. Tania was more than a loose cannon now. She seemed to have lost touch with reality. Why had she attacked them? Tania had always made sure that she was the sun around whom others revolved, but with her latest escapade she was a wanted criminal. At least before she'd just been missing.

The good thing was that Breck was no longer a suspect in her disappearance. First Tania had contacted his parents; now she had come out of nowhere to attack Ingrid and vandalize the school. Why? Along with all the other parents, Tania had known about the trouble with the school alarm system when it was first installed. It had become a standing joke. Tania had capitalized on that. She didn't miss a trick. Tania was good at capitalizing on anything she could get her hands on. Right down to framing Ingrid for plagiarism at exam time. She'd almost destroyed Ingrid's career before it got off the ground. Tania had been so angry that Ingrid had avoided sharing her assignments with her, that she'd set Ingrid up to take a fall at exam time.

Their final exam consisted of interpretation and attitude rather than cognition, so the students were notified prior to exam time about the type of questions they would encounter. Most students prepared the answers on their laptops. It couldn't have been hard for Tania to access Ingrid's laptop because when she bothered to turn up for lectures, she insisted on sitting next to Ingrid.

Ingrid had found out why Tania had become so chummy when she was hauled into the principal's office and asked to explain how her exam answers were an exact copy of those of 'another student.' It had taken Ingrid several weeks of wrestling with Education New Zealand to clear her name. She'd had to employ an expensive lawyer. Even then they'd delayed their decision so long that the teaching year had already begun by the time they'd exonerated her. Their exoneration had been perfunctory at best, and Ingrid had spent the last few years making sure she didn't put a foot wrong. She had never told her parents, scared of their reaction if they discovered she had become a kindergarten teacher by the skin of her teeth. But perhaps she *should* have mentioned it to Tom Rowland. His team of smooth, vicious lawyers could have eaten Tania alive. Maybe if that had happened, they would not all be faced with Tania's erratic behavior now. Then again, a team of lawyers might not be enough to control Tania. Whereas they would play by the book, Tania had *never* played by the book.

Ingrid wriggled restlessly. God, *everything* hurt. Even so, she would be glad to get out of here. She didn't know anyone who actually liked hospitals, and she was chomping at the bit to get on with her life. There was so much to do. Had the walls at the preschool been painted? What about the repairs to the main room? Had the police caught Tania yet? Her mind ran on a treadmill until a nursing assistant popped in with a cup of tea.

"*Thank* you. I'm sick of doing nothing," she admitted.

The nurse laughed. "That's what most of our patients say. Except, of course, the new mothers with a couple of kids at home already. Anyway, you're going home soon."

And even before breakfast was served, Breck and Kit arrived. They took one step inside the room and Breck held up both hands. "Yes, ma'am. The wall has had two coats of paint. No, the builders haven't yet begun the repairs because the insurance company didn't come till late afternoon. Yes, Kit is fine. Yes, I'm fine. No, they haven't caught Tania yet." He took a breath. "And how are you, Ms. Rowland?"

Kit giggled. He was fine.

"Better now, thanks." She grinned. "You sound like a police report."

He rolled his eyes, then bent over and kissed her. Just a peck, but at the same time he palmed his hand to the back of her neck and rubbed gently.

Ingrid clasped her hand over his for a second and

cast a quick look at Kit. But Kit seemed to take it all in his stride. He hopped up beside her on the bed and announced, "We think Mom's gone nuts."

Ingrid coughed to hide her amusement. "Is that so?"

"Yeah. She must have."

Ingrid understood that was Kit's method of coping with the strange behavior of his mother.

Breck said nothing, just let Kit ramble on. Kit nodded solemnly. "She needs a doctor. But the police can't find her. When are you coming home?"

"As soon as I say she can," a voice said from the doorway. The doctor was doing his rounds early. Perhaps it was part of the new austerity measures. Did he hope to release her before breakfast?

Breck's eyes met hers. He grinned. He was obviously having the same thoughts. "We'll be outside."

"Aw, Dad. I wanted to see what the doctor does when he…" Kit's voice died away as his father hauled him into the corridor.

The doctor's lips twitched. "At that age they're little ghouls. Got one just like that." And he proceeded to give Ingrid a thorough inspection. He wasn't happy with her determination to quit the hospital and go straight to work, but as he said, "I can't stop you. If I try to keep you here, you'll just walk out. I guess stubbornness is your middle name, huh?"

Unwillingly, Ingrid gave a half-laugh. "It's been said many times."

He cautioned her, wrote out a prescription and signed the release form.

"Thank you," she said fervently.

"Breakfast!" The nursing assistant burst into the room with two trays.

Ingrid risked a glance at the congealing oatmeal before saying brightly, "Oh, what a shame! I'm just leaving." She scooted into the shared bathroom as her roomie called out, "So can I have your breakfast?"

"Go ahead." Ingrid knew very well that oatmeal was good for you, but she and oatmeal were on very bad terms.

An hour later she was spitting tacks when Breck dumped her at her apartment with a warning. "No, you will not come to preschool today. Yes, everything is under control. Yes, you will lie on the sofa and take your pain pills and antibiotics. Any questions?"

"Questions? Questions? I'll give you questions!" She struggled to get to her feet but Breck had trussed her up in the blanket from her bed and she found herself rolling forward into his arms instead of poking him in the chest and telling him what he could do with his rules.

"See? Weak as a kitten. You need a few hours rest." Grinning, he kissed her chastely on the forehead and hurried Kit towards the door. "See you later!"

The door banged behind them.

*Grrrrr.* Who the hell did he think he was?

Then she remembered the paint splashes on Breck's wrists and the tired lines around his eyes. While she'd been lying sedated in hospital, he'd been working like a slave on her behalf. Fine, but she wanted to see for herself what condition the preschool was in and see how Stella was managing with the small space available until the builder had completed the repairs. Perhaps she could phone the builder and hurry him along.

Then she realized she had no idea who Breck had contracted to get the job done. Damn it all, he'd taken over so completely, he'd squeezed her out. For some stupid reason she felt like crying. "Remnants of concussion," she told herself. "Stop feeling sorry for yourself."

Well, she'd promised Breck to find out about Angela, Tania's friend or cousin or whatever she'd been. That was something useful she could do. She struggled to her feet and went to find her laptop.

Chapter Twenty-One

Breck's cellphone warbled and vibrated. He scooped it up with one clean hand while the other kept wielding a paintbrush. "Marchant. Oh, hello Raker. Oh, no. Poor woman." He rested the brush on the lid of the paint can.

Raker's men had been unable to contact the elderly Miss Reynolds and had begun to question her neighbors. What they'd learned had given them cause to force an entry to the woman's home where they'd found her body. She'd been dead for at least a week.

"What did the neighbors say, exactly?"

"That on the 6th she had a couple of visitors. The only person who ever came to see her was her grand-niece, but this time the niece brought someone with her. It sounded to the next door neighbors as if Albertine Reynolds objected to the newcomer because there were raised voices, then the visitors left abruptly."

Albertine Reynolds had been bludgeoned to death. And she'd lain in her own congealed blood for a week. She would have been there longer if it weren't for Breck's identification of her numberplate on the getaway car outside the Kerr home.

"Was there a car in her garage?" he asked.

"Yeah. An old unregistered mini with no numberplates. Listen, Marchant, you do good work.

Tony Hull contacted me. He told me you're applying for the detective division. Hope you've got your application under way."

Breck felt a glow in the pit of his stomach. Maybe he *would* make a halfway decent detective. Then a thought struck him. "Before you go, Raker, did you get a clear description of the grand-niece?"

"Yeah, and that's one of the reasons I'm calling you. This grand-niece sounds awfully like your missing ex. Could there be a connection?"

Breck drew in a breath. "I was going to contact you about that. Look, I haven't a clue what is going on with Tania, but she's popping up everywhere. Did you read the memo I sent you?"

There was a rustle and a thump. "Got it. Hang on a minute." After a short silence Raker muttered, "Shit! What's with the woman? Just as well you ditched her way back."

"Yeah," Breck answered laconically. He'd have to come clean with Raker and Hull and give them a few more details about Tania. He took a deep breath. "Look, I need to tell you a few things about Tania. Should have told you before but…I could never prove anything. And in trying to protect our son, I made a huge mistake."

"Huh? Look, I'll see what Hull is doing and if it's possible, we'll all meet first thing in the morning. I'll be in touch."

Raker had sounded intrigued, and no wonder. As a cop, Breck should have known better than to hide anything from investigating officers. Talk about treading a thin line. But Tania had been his wife for more than three years and while they'd been together, although she'd given him hell, she'd been a good mother to Kit. He'd let her walk all over him for the first couple of years because he was unsure about the unwritten rules of marriage. With his background he'd had no yardstick to measure their marriage by. He wasn't weak, he told himself, just ignorant.

It wasn't until he saw how Abel and Jace interacted that he'd begun to have doubts about his own relationship.

Worst of all, he hadn't known about the way she and Marty had treated Kit once she'd moved in with Marty. But he laid that squarely at his own door, not Tania's. If he'd been more assertive and less unwilling to rock the boat, he doubted that Tania would have neglected Kit to such an extent. He'd made it easy for her.

That day when he'd discovered those papers in the laundry cupboard, he'd not known whether to believe her glib explanation or not. After all, who keeps documents belonging to someone else? By that stage of their marriage, he was unwilling to take anything she said at face value. She'd snatched them and said "Oh, for heaven's sake, Breck. Pull yourself together. What do you *think* I'm doing with this stuff? When I bought the business, these were sent to me with all the other stuff." She had purchased a small distribution business and the garage was permanently full of boxes of leaflets. Breck had had no way of disproving her words, but when she'd gone out "to meet some friends for a drink—nobody you know" he'd gone back to check on those papers.

They'd been moved, which he'd expected, but he hadn't expected to find them by chance when he was putting his work clothes away. To his shock, he'd found them jammed at the back of his chest of drawers. Wondering why one drawer didn't close properly, he pulled it out to investigate.

Then all sort of scenarios had zipped through his mind. Insurance? Was she setting him up to take a fall for something he didn't yet know about? If so, the documents must be incriminating.

Once he'd read them carefully he'd boiled with fury. They were incriminating all right. The documents contained information that Tania had no right to—nor any other person who was not the original owner. They were a mix of unpaid bills, some amounting to hundreds of thousands of dollars, and letters from well-known public figures containing startling disclosures. Breck had been rattled to see a note from Auckland's Deputy Police Commissioner written on plain paper to a woman, obviously not his wife. The letter revealed emotions that Breck was sure the DPC would rather not have disclosed.

The only possible explanation was that his wife was a blackmailer.

But he had not been able to prove it. When she'd returned home he'd held out the papers and demanded an explanation. What he got was a wife who screamed vitriol, so he'd taken a deep breath and did what he should have done long ago. "Get out," he'd said.

And she had, with alacrity, but she'd taken Kit with her. "I wouldn't leave a cat with you," she'd snarled. "You know damn well you don't have a clue about bringing up kids. He's way better off with me."

And he'd been certain she was right so he'd kissed Kit goodbye and watched them leave.

It had been four months till she'd let him see Kit

again.

****

Next morning Hull and Raker listened to Breck's story but as Hull said, "It doesn't alter anything apart from the fact that we want to get our hands on Tania Kerr even more than we did before. We'll worry about the blackmail stuff when we find her."

Raker asked, "How's your boy holding up? He must be a bit shaken after his mother tried to drag him out of your vehicle like that."

"Surprisingly well," Breck answered. "He seems to have washed his hands of her since she attacked his favorite preschool teacher."

"*Your* favorite preschool teacher too, I hear." Hull wiggled his eyebrows and Breck grinned.

"Uh, huh." There were no secrets among cops. They were the biggest gossips on the planet.

Fortunately Hull's cell phone rang before he could delve any deeper into Breck's life. Beck felt awkward discussing his relationship with Ingrid. It was so new and shiny and filled with hope that he almost didn't dare go there.

"Great. Thanks for that. We'll be there in a half-hour." Hull flipped his phone closed. "The hospital has finally brought that bashed guy out of his induced coma. They said we can question him now, but they gave the usual provisos. Not too long. Don't stress the patient, blah blah."

Breck grinned. Hull was not full of the milk of human kindness when he was seeking information.

"You coming?" he asked Breck.

"Me? Uh…sure."

And when they walked into the hospital room,

several of Breck's questions were answered. The guy in the hospital bed was almost bald and his thick neck and huge hands hinted at his chunkiness.

"Name?" Hull barked.

"Billy Kerr." His hands twitched and he took a good hard grip on the bed sheet.

Breck pushed forward. "*You're* Billy? I've been searching for you."

"No kidding."

Breck turned to Raker. "This is the guy who was at the Kerrs' place last week. And I'm sure he was the guy who clobbered me in our underground carpark a while back."

"Prove it."

Breck smiled. "Got your coat all neatly tucked up in an evidence bag, buddy. And although I don't like using my son, Kit got a better look at you than I did when you ambushed us." He shrugged. "Seems to me, you've got no cause to be cocky."

Billy Kerr sat back, the smug look wiped from his face. He looked from Raker to Hull and then back to Breck.

"Where's Tania?" Raker asked.

"Bitch." Billy's chin tucked into his chest. His shoulders rose and fell as he inhaled shakily.

"Took you for a ride too, did she?" Breck said.

"You'd think after all I've done for her..." Billy trailed off then burst out, "The bitch bashed me on the head and left me to die."

"*She* was the one who cold-cocked you?" Breck had long suspected Billy was Tania's accomplice, but why had she tried to get rid of him? Billy was right. He could have died, left alone in the cold with a severe head wound. But since he hadn't died, she'd left him swinging in the wind, because at the moment Billy was the main suspect for the school vandalism. Tania must have wanted to make sure she was well rid of him. Just another of her dupes.

But why had Tania tried to grab Kit? He opened his mouth to ask Billy, and then shut it again. He was here under sufferance. Hull and Raker were riding this pony.

Raker nudged him. "Go on. Spit it out."

"Uh…Billy, what does Tania want with my son? She tried to snatch him tonight."

Billy shrugged. "Must be running out of money."

"Oh." How stupid of him not to realize that Tania still regarded him as a cash cow. Even though she couldn't 'kidnap' her own son since she still officially had custody, it wouldn't stop her from holding Kit's freedom over Breck.

Hull and Raker settled down to interrogate Billy and Breck stepped away from the bedside. He peered out of the grimy hospital window, listening as Raker tapped away on his iPad and Hull held out a recorder in front of Billy, garnering everything they could about the puzzle that was Tania Kerr. It seemed as though the bang on his head had released Billy from his thrall of loyalty to Tania.

"Where do you think she'll be now?" Raker asked him.

Billy frowned. "Doubt she'll be at my place, so I don't have a clue."

"And your address is?"

Billy told them. As Breck had surmised, it was close by Billy's martial arts studio.

Hull nodded to Raker and left the room, flipping open his cell phone as he went. The hospital room fell silent, Hull's murmur cut off by the door.

Billy looked from Raker's face to Breck's. "What happens to me now?"

Breck shrugged. He didn't give a damn. "Not my problem." He could still feel Kit's trembling as they huddled together in the dark of the parking garage, tensing for the next blow. Billy Kerr could go to hell.

"Why did Tania contact my parents?" he asked, before he could stuff the words back into his mouth.

"Your *parents*?" Billy's incredulous tone said it all. Another one of Tania's little schemes that her cohort had no idea about.

"I'm more interested in why you went to the preschool center last night." Hull had come back into the room.

Billy opened his mouth, and then shut it again.

Hull raised a supercilious eyebrow. "Suddenly you've gone silent. Why?"

"She hated that preschool teacher," Billy burst out as if the words had been yanked out of him. "Really hated her. Don't know why. And then she learned that Marchant and the woman were seeing each other."

Breck gritted his teeth. "The woman is called Ingrid. And how could Tania have known? We didn't exactly advertize it."

Billy shrugged again. "She's been watching you for ages. Knows all about you."

"But why?"

"You dumped her. Said she'd get her own back one day."

Breck thought for a moment while Hull and Raker

said nothing, just waited.

"So this thing at the preschool was killing two birds with one stone."

"I'm more concerned with what she'll do next." Hull glared at Billy. "I bet you know."

Billy attempted an insouciant shrug, but his injuries turned it into a shrinking twitch. "All I know is that she's leaving, and before she does, she wants to get her own back on everyone who's ever crossed her."

"Christ. The way she sees things through a glass darkly, that could be a list as long as your arm." Raker sounded as if he had had quite enough of Tania. "She's way out of control and we have to find her. God knows who her next victim will be."

"You said she was leaving. Do you mean leaving Auckland or leaving New Zealand?"

Billy stared at them. "How should I know?"

"You were going with her, weren't you?" Hull asked.

Billy colored. "Yeah. Well, I thought so."

"Got a passport?"

"Doesn't everyone?"

Breck was startled when Hull grabbed Billy by the front of his hospital gown and growled, "Don't frig around with me, you little toad. *Were you going overseas*?"

"J-Just to Australia."

"How did she plan on squeezing more money out of me from Australia?" Breck asked.

"She…she was gonna—"

At the expression on Billy's face, the three men stilled.

"She was gonna what? What, Billy?" Breck stalked

over to the bed and loomed over the hapless Billy. "What was she gonna do after that? She wasn't going to give Kit back to me, ever, was she?" He had to stop right there because he was choking up with anger.

Billy cleared his throat nervously. "She had some scheme going. She knows someone who wants a kid."

Breck opened his mouth and shut it again. He was conscious of a great weight pressing down on his head that made it hard to think, impossible to articulate. He tried again. This time his voice came out as a croak. "She was—she was going to *sell* Kit? But she's his mother!"

Billy nodded. "Yup. That gave her the right to do as she liked with the kid."

"What about your kid? I bet you're Bobby's father. Was she going to give *him* away too?"

Billy blanched. "Of course not."

"But you can't be certain, can you, Billy?"

"Where are the children?" Raker demanded. "Where are Pixie and Bobby?"

"At my house, of course."

"So you have a baby-sitter."

Billy shook his head. "Pixie keeps Bobby in line. They don't need no baby-sitter."

Breck thought of all the years he had said that Tania was good with kids. And he thought of how he'd had to impose on Jace and Abe's goodwill so that Kit could be cared for while he rushed around trying to solve the Tania puzzle.

"It's an offence to leave children under the age of fourteen on their own," Raker commented. "But I guess Tania knows that."

"Is it?" Billy looked genuinely shaken.

Breck reflected that he'd always thought Marty was a dimwit, but hell, Billy was worse. Why had Tania thrown in her lot with the Kerr men? Control, he supposed. They had been easy to control.

And he hadn't been, so she wanted revenge because he'd edged her out of his life. But she'd still managed to control him from afar. She'd used Kit.

"What happened when you went to see Mrs. Reynolds?" Hull asked.

Billy huddled inside his hospital gown. "Who?"

"Tania's great-aunt."

"Oh. Her. Old bitch wouldn't let me in. So we left."

"Why wouldn't she let you in?"

"Said I looked like a crim. Me!"

Breck shifted from one foot to the other. Billy's indignation would have been funny if Ingrid and Kit were not at the mercy of Tania. This wasn't getting them any closer to finding Tania and Breck just wanted the questioning to be over. It wasn't providing any useful information.

"So you went back and bashed her head in just to get even. When did you do that?"

"Fuck! I never! What are you talking about? She—" Billy's whining ground to a halt as he realized the implications of Hull's comment. If it was possible, Billy turned ever whiter. "Tania? She-she did that?"

"Okay, Billy. We're going to your place now to see if Tania has turned up. Got a key, or do we just kick the door down?" Raker's face was expressionless.

Billy almost leapt out of bed. "No! Don't do that! I'll give you the garage door remote." He fished it out of the tray where his personal possessions had been tossed and they left him huddling under the bedclothes, looking miserable.

## Chapter Twenty-Two

Ingrid trawled through the registered preschool teachers' website looking for the Angela she'd known at university. She couldn't bring the woman's surname to mind, but she would know it as soon as she saw it. She leaned back in her chair. Lord, her back ached. And her head ached. Even her teeth ached. Bloody Tania. Perhaps she should wait till tomorrow to do this.

Pushing herself to her feet she made her way back to the sofa. Her cell rang, startling her.

"Stella! How are things? How are you coping with—?"

Stella warbled on cheerfully.

"You are? Doing just fine without me? Perhaps I should take a couple of weeks off…" She snorted with laughter as Stella growled, "You dare."

"I'm looking for a teacher named Angela something or other who trained with me. Can't remember her other name but—she *what*?"

"Don't you recall?" Stella chirped. "Angela Briscoe. She applied for a job here several months ago, but we're fully staffed and couldn't take her on. I remember her because she said she had trained with you."

Ingrid snapped her fingers. "Briscoe, that's it. Please tell me we kept her résumé."

"Yup." There was a rustling sound as Stella leafed through a bunch of papers. "Here she is."

Ingrid tapped Angela's details into her iPhone. "Thanks Stella. I should be back at work tomorrow, and if not tomorrow, then the next day."

"Make sure you're well, first. Oh, by the way, you had a couple of visitors today," Stella said. "Your stepfather and some other guy."

Ingrid felt herself growing tense. "Oh, my God. Did my stepfather see all the damage?"

"Relax girl. I guided him away from the main room and he said he was glad we were doing some redecorating. He didn't see the real damage."

"Thanks Stell. I'm in no shape to go a round with my parents at the moment. This other guy, did he leave a name?"

"No. Just shook his head and smiled when I offered to pass on a message."

Now what? Ingrid wasn't sure she needed any more surprises right now. "How old was he?"

"Umm…in his early fifties, I'd say."

"Oh! He wasn't an inspector, was he?"

"No. He would have presented his credentials."

Ingrid thought of a couple of arrogant inspectors who rode roughshod over the regulations. "Not necessarily."

"Well, he wasn't one I've met before. But he knew the rules about strangers in preschools. He didn't engage with any of the kids, didn't linger at all. He said we have a very nice preschool and that he'd be in touch with you."

In spite of Stella's assurances, Ingrid chewed her lip worriedly. Pedophiles were a preschool teacher's greatest nightmare. "Could you file a report about it, Stell?"

"Already have. Must say he didn't seem…never mind."

"I know. But thanks for everything, Stell. See you soon."

Stella was a godsend. She knew the rules but wasn't fazed by them. Sometimes she wasn't a very shrewd judge of character, but she made up for that by her can-do attitude. Ingrid reflected that if her circumstances were different, if for example she was more solvent, she'd like to appoint Stella as her manager so that would leave her free to do other things.

*Like what,* a little voice asked. Yeah, well, she'd lived and breathed Rowland Private Preschool for so long that she'd subjugated all those long ago desires and interests and now she could hardly remember them.

Let's see. She could join a club and play tennis. Uh, huh. Always wanted to do that. Running around after a bunch of kids kept her fit, but she wanted *pleasure* with her fitness. Of course, there was one pleasure that would keep her fit. Breck could help her out there. She grinned to herself. Speaking of desires…

She really, really wanted to know what he thought about her. He was one of the most tight-mouthed people she'd ever come across. The joke was that most people considered her to be quiet and secretive. Most people hadn't met Breck Marchant. She so hoped he'd pass that entrance exam with flying colors.

Boy, how she'd changed. Once she would never have considered going out with a cop. Now it was all she thought about.

Then she remembered something else she wanted

to do as soon as she could. She wanted to trace her father. Now that she'd met Breck and knew a little about Abe, she thought maybe her ideas about cops had been skewed by her mother's outlook. There was no doubt that Marla Rowland tended to see the world from a less-than-impartial point of view. She often failed to understand what others were feeling to the point where she lost friends through her inability to empathize. When Tom had discovered that his goddess had feet of clay, he'd simply worked around the difficulties and pretended they did not exist. But Ingrid had known her mother a lot longer than Tom had, and she could not be so forgiving. Losing her best friend at age eight due to her mother's snobbishness "not quite our sort of people, darling" and her first boyfriend at age fourteen "nowhere near good enough for you, darling", Ingrid had begun to question, albeit silently, some of her mother's opinions. And lately she'd come to wonder more and more about her absent father, the cop.

Why had he never attempted to get in touch with her? Had he jettisoned her into the too-hard basket along with her mother, or had Marla prevented him from seeing his daughter? After seeing the situation between Tania and Breck, she no longer assumed that her father had washed his hands of her.

Pulling her laptop closer, she went looking for a man she hadn't seen in twenty-two years.

Chapter Twenty-Three

Breck clicked off his cell phone and chucked it on to the bed. "Yes!" he yelled, punching the air.

"Daddy?" Kit pounded into the bedroom.

"Everything's fine, Kit. Just fine. I passed the exam. I'm gonna be a detective!"

"Cool!"

"Yeah, cool." He'd phone Ingrid. Then he'd phone Jace and Abe. He dialed Ingrid's number and she picked up immediately.

"You got it, didn't you?"

He grinned, marveling at how she knew what he was calling her about. "How did you know?"

"Your number came up in more ways than one."

He snorted with laughter. "In the words of my son, you are so cool."

"Yeah, I'm so cool I didn't realize that the woman we've been looking for has been right under my nose all the time."

"What woman? You don't mean Tania?"

"No. Not bloody Tania." Her petulant tone said it all. "Angela—Angela Briscoe."

"How do you mean—under your nose?"

"She applied for a job at the preschool recently but because we had no vacancies, we didn't pursue the matter. Fuck it."

He heard a thump on the other end of the phone as if Ingrid had slammed a book down. She rarely swore, so he knew how angry she was with herself.

"Hey, Miss Rowland. Forget about trying to be perfect."

"I *have* to be, don't you see? They're still watching me."

"Who? What?"

"Never mind. I didn't mean…"

"Ingrid, who's watching you?"

"Oh, shit."

Lord, the little fairy princess had really let loose. "Look, Kit and I are coming over now."

He clicked off the phone and bundled Kit into the SUV. "I think Ingrid needs us," he explained.

"Is Mum there?" Kit looked worried.

"No, no. I think Ingrid is still sick. We'll look after her."

And when they arrived, he was glad he hadn't wasted a moment. She'd left the door unlocked *again* so they barreled in to where she sat at her desk, her head on her arms and her face as pale as milk.

He was curious about her comment that someone was watching her, but she looked so ill he couldn't possibly mention it right now.

"Come on, sweet thing. Bedtime." He pulled the chair back and plucked her out of it. She sagged against his chest and sighed as Kit struggled to tug down the bedding. Breck braced one knee on the side of the bed and gently eased her down. There was no fight left in her. He'd seen the many moods of Ingrid but he'd never seen her quite like this. She shouldn't have left hospital so soon, but he understood her anxiety to quit the place.

"Just go to sleep and you'll feel better when you wake up."

"Will you be here when I wake up?"

He had to bend down to hear her words because she was mumbling and shivering. "Of course. Are you cold?"

"C-cold, cold."

"Okay." He tucked up all the blankets around her and turned on the electric blanket.

And in a heartbeat, she was asleep. He hovered, wondering if he should set his watch to wake her in an hour, in case this was residual concussion. His instinct was to let her sleep, but if he was wrong…

He flipped open his phone and called Jace and Abe and explained his predicament. "They wouldn't have let her leave hospital if she still had a concussion," Jace said. "But if she got battered by bloody Tania, she's probably still feeling sore. Might be emotionally drained too."

"Yeah. She's had a helluva week." Breck was going to explain further, but he heard a baby's murmur in the background. It was the sort of cry that said, "Hey! I'm waking up. Where are you?" So he just said, "I'll call you later." He would stay here beside Ingrid to make sure she was okay. Kit had discovered Ingrid's stash of resource books and was happily fingering through them, exclaiming now and again when he recognized a word.

An hour later Ingrid was still asleep and Breck was resigned to staying for the night. He prowled around her kitchen, trying to find something suitable to eat. But Ingrid seemed to subsist on pasta and apples and neither appealed to him. "Kit, would you be all right if I went out to buy some dinner? If you don't like being alone, you could climb up on the bed beside Ingrid. Is that okay?" He was always careful to give Kit options, because when Kit had lived with the Kerrs, he hadn't had any options.

"S'okay." Kit was absorbed in a puzzle book and didn't even glance up as Breck left.

He found a 7-Eleven and stocked up quickly, not giving much thought to his purchases. Time was of the essence, because leaving an invalid and a child on their own was not a great idea. As he braked to a stop in the parking area outside Ingrid's apartment, he saw that the outside light still shone down on the welcome mat. Everything looked secure. Breathing a sigh of relief, he collected the groceries and juggled them while he fit the key into the shiny new lock.

Inside, the lights were all off. Kit must have crawled into bed with Ingrid. He grinned wryly. So much for buying the makings for dinner. He would be the only one eating.

Flipping on the kitchen light he dumped the paper sacks on the counter and tiptoed into Ingrid's bedroom so as not to wake the two of them.

But when he went to pull up the covers over the two bumps in the bed, he stopped short, his heart in his mouth. Pillows had been mounded in the bed to look like sleeping figures.

Kit and Ingrid were gone.

****

"Shit!" He grabbed his cellphone and called Raker. "Raker, I'm desperate."

"What? What's happened?"

Breck gabbled an explanation. At the same time he

feverishly searched the apartment for clues. The quilt on top of the bed had been wrenched off and lay on the floor near the doorway. He picked up the puzzle book that Kit had been working on and it came apart. It had been ripped in two. Worst of all, where Ingrid's head had lain on the pillow was a large red stain. Either her head wound was bleeding again or… *Please God…please don't let my maniac ex-wife hurt her. I'll do anything you want, God; just keep Ingrid safe.*

"But how did anyone get in if the door was locked?" Raker asked.

"Good question." Breck prowled through the apartment and found the answer. The bathroom window was shattered.

But that led to another question. How could Tania overpower two people and hustle them away in the short time available? Sure, Ingrid was sick, and it was possible Kit might have obeyed his mother's orders, but it was still a stretch for one person. "Raker, she had help."

"Just thinking that. Be right over."

Breck rushed out to the parking lot and checked for marks on the fine stone chipwork. Directly behind Ingrid's Fiesta there was a large pool of oil. *If* it belonged to whoever had taken Ingrid and Kit, then the car was sick. But it might just as well belong to one of the other resident's cars. Something to check out later.

He went back to the bathroom and pored doggedly over every possible clue. He examined every scratch and nick on the surfaces near to the window and every splinter of glass. He measured where the broken glass had landed and came to the conclusion that because the damage was not extreme, that whatever implement had been used must have been muffled with a blanket or something similar. And because he was so meticulous, his ferocious attention to detail driven by a dread that pressed down on his stomach, he found the blood spot. A mere smidgeon, but definitely a blood spot.

Raker rushed in and they got down to business.

"The only good thing about all this, is that we've got the cell phone number she contacted your parents with," Raker commented as he watched the SOCOs at work. The scene of crime officers didn't find anything that Breck hadn't, but one of them painstakingly scraped the blood spot into an evidence bag and hurried off to compare it with the blood types on the preschool records that Ingrid kept on her laptop.

If it wasn't Ingrid's or Kit's blood, then it belonged to one of her captors. Breck hoped like hell that the kidnapper had hurt themselves badly, but the drop of blood was so miniscule there wasn't much chance of that.

"Looks as though they've nicked themselves hopping in through the window," the second SOCO commented. "They must be mighty small to squeeze in through that little space."

Breck thought of the school break-in. And he thought of Tania. Perhaps, but it would be a tight squeeze.

Raker interrupted Breck's frantic thoughts. "Not much more I can do here. I'll go back to Central and check the coordinates of that phone call your ex made to your parents in case she's returned to the same place. Another thing I thought of…how about we get Hull to revisit the old lady's house? Tania might have returned there."

"Possibly. Must be running out of hidey-holes by now. Are you sure Miss Reynolds really was Tania's great-aunt?"

"Ninety-nine percent. How about you go along with Hull and see if you can find anything in the house that relates to Tania?"

Raker was giving him a task to prevent him from going off half-cock. Okay. He was wound up so tight his teeth were aching from being clenched. The whole damn fiasco was his fault. He should never have left Kit and Ingrid alone. And after lecturing Billy about the very same thing, too. The only solace he had was that it was unlikely Tania would harm Kit. She wanted to use him as a bargaining tool and anyway, Tania wouldn't harm a child. Would she? Breck swallowed hard. Once upon a time he could never have envisaged her harming *anyone*, but now…

Ingrid, however, was in deep trouble. Not only was there a history between them, she'd also frustrated Tania's attempts to grab Kit. Tania would be out for blood, and from the mess on Ingrid's pillow, she'd already drawn some. Sweet Ingrid who didn't live life on Tania's level would be no match for his vicious ex-wife. If only he could work out what had set Tania off on her murderous rampage, they might be able to *do* something. Shit, there was nothing on earth so bloody frustrating than not knowing where to turn. All the time the clock was ticking. Apparently Tania had killed before, so what was stopping her from doing it again?

He sat in Hull's unmarked Toyota Camry clicking his fingers till Hull murmured, "You gotta learn a few relaxation techniques, Marchant. You're driving me crazy."

"Sorry." His gut churned and burned and he had to do *something*. He resorted to tapping his foot until Hull said with exasperation, "Look mate. You and are I going to have a falling-out if you don't stop all this twitching. I can't begin to understand what you're going through, but you need to chill out."

"Chill out? That crazy bitch has my son and my—friend!"

"Well, you were married to that crazy bitch for a few years. Do us a favor and think about where she might be. Think of the places she went while you were married."

Hull was right. Constructive thinking was more use than sitting around tense and fretting. Tony Hull wasn't unsympathetic. He just told it like it was. The best thing he could do right now for Ingrid and Kit was to explore every possible avenue.

"Well, if we strike out at Billy's and at the great-aunt's, then we should take a look at Ingrid's laptop. She was searching for someone named Angela, a friend of Tania's. That's another lead."

"See. There you go. I understand about Ingrid and young Kit, but once you cut it down to lines to tug on, then you're helping them constructively. Here we are." Hull drove into Ms. Reynolds' driveway and parked the car in front of the garage. The house was old, about sixty years or so, and was constructed entirely of timber. Some of the timber had rotted around the eaves and the garage door did not quite shut. It looked as though sixty summers of sun had warped the timber, and sixty winters of rain had swollen it.

When it became apparent from the rubbish accumulated in every room that a thorough search could take days, Hull called for more manpower. They didn't have days to spare.

Two hours into the search, Breck discovered the first clue. In a desk stuffed full of legal papers and memorabilia, he spied the corners of some photos sticking out. He tugged at them and they came loose and fluttered to the floor. As he bent down to pick them up, he felt a tingle down his spine. The top photo was of two young women—two Tanias. The photo looked to have been taken about ten years ago. The women were not quite identical, but to a casual observer, they looked alike. Attached to the photos were a couple of pieces of paper.

"Fraternal twins," Breck muttered to himself. Hull!" he yelled.

Hull charged down the stairs, looking like an eager bloodhound. "What? What? Hope you've got something. There's nothing upstairs."

Breck held out the photo then shuffled through the papers that were attached to it. Birth certificates for Tania and Angela Bedloe. Bedloe? He thought he'd married a woman named Tania Davidson, a woman whose parents and sister had been killed in a car crash when she was a baby. Perhaps she'd been married before she met him and just hadn't wanted to mention it. He leaned against the desk. This was Alice in Wonderland territory. Natasha had read that book to him and he'd often wondered how Alice coped with life after Wonderland. Did she come out the other side okay, or did she live the rest of her life questioning reality?

Hull grabbed the pile of photos and the birth certificates from him. "Holy shit! Guess the old lady was her great-aunt after all."

"This explains why I found no birth certificates at the Kerr's house."

"Uh, huh. But like you, I can't understand what all this is about. Why does a perfectly sane woman suddenly go off her tree and start murdering her relatives, set up others to take a fall, and end up kidnapping people? It's bizarre."

"I'm wondering a hell of a lot more than that. I'm wondering who I married. Tania or Angela?"

Hull leaned against the desk beside Breck. "Uh, Marchant, all I can say is…holy shit! What a hell of a conundrum."

He was about to say more when his cell phone warbled like a thrush's early evensong.

"Yeah? Cool. Send two of 'em here to the old lady's place and we'll meet the others…where?" He turned to Breck. "Been given another four staff. So now we've got a real task force. Where d'you think we should go next? I'm thinking we should—"

Breck interrupted. "I'll return to Ingrid's place. Did anyone check her laptop yet?"

Chapter Twenty-Four

His instincts had been right. When he booted up the laptop, he saw that the last file she'd been working on was named 'Angela Briscoe.'

"There," he said softly, pointing to the attached résumé. "An Angela Briscoe approached Ingrid's assistant about a job at Rowlands four months back. Looks as though Ingrid has dug further. I've got Stella's private number because we had to liaise over the vandalism repairs. I'll give her a call."

Stella was kicking up her heels at a noisy pub and he had to shout to get her attention. The background noise receded as she searched for a quiet corner. She freaked out when she heard that Ingrid and Kit were missing but proved to be an excellent witness. She remembered clearly what Angela looked like, how she spoke, what she said and even what she'd been wearing.

"How come you remember all this?" Breck asked. "Not that we're not grateful, but few people remember details like this."

"Because she said she'd trained with Ingrid and was a friend of hers, so I was extra careful. But there were no teaching positions available so I filed it and just mentioned it in passing to Ingrid. Hey, I tell you who she looked like. Like that Tania bitch who's causing all the trouble. Looked a little like her, but she was much nicer."

"Nicer?"

"Yeah. Polite. Not aggro like Tania. And she was shorter than Tania."

It was interesting that there was no photo with the résumé. Many people forwarded a photo of themselves when applying for a job, but Angela had not. But why had Angela approached Rowlands? Why would she want to teach at a preschool where her likeness to Tania would at once be noticed? It was as if one twin was pulling one way; and the other twin was pulling in the opposite direction. One wanted to be noticed; the other needed to stay hidden.

"Thanks Stella. I'll be in touch." Then Breck turned to Hull. "This address that Angela gave. Let's go there."

****

As they drew up outside Angela's house, Breck noticed a silver Taurus in the driveway. It was the one that had been parked along the road from the preschool on the day he'd seen someone watching the school. He peered inside. The checkered rug was still on the back seat but this time it was folded. There didn't appear to be anything beneath it. He said as much to Hull who was intrigued with Breck's sleuthing. "Don't know why you didn't join the detective division before. You've got the right mindset."

"Obsessive attention to useless details, you mean?"

Hull grinned. "Something like that."

"Don't know if I'd be quite so obsessed if it didn't involve Kit and Ingrid."

As they approached the front door, they separated.

Hull went around the back while Breck waited for the other two team members to arrive. The house was in darkness. Street lights reflected on the windows and Breck could see that none of the blinds or curtains were drawn. He began to doubt there was anyone inside. God, he so wanted this over. He wanted to hold Kit and Ingrid in his arms again, keeping them safe. He sure as hell hadn't kept them safe so far. Were they inside this house?

Two figures loomed out of the darkness. The other team members had arrived at last. One was carrying something that looked like a tomahawk.

"Hull is around the back," Breck whispered.

For an answer, one of the men held up his cell phone and pointed to it. They were already up with the play.

The cop with the phone marched past Breck and banged on the door. "Police! Open up."

Nothing. Not a whisper.

He banged harder.

Still nothing.

Breck's stomach dropped away. Not with disappointment. With fear. If they didn't catch up with Tania and Kit and Ingrid soon, God knew what would happen to Ingrid. Then his thoughts scurried to a standstill. What if it wasn't Tania who'd taken them away? What if it was Angela? Bad twin or good twin? Which was which?

A splintering sound cracked the suburban quiet as Hull and the police constable hacked their way through the back door.

"They've been here," Hull said as he opened the front door. "But it's not a crime scene. All of you look around. Find out where they've gone."

Breck took the staircase in big strides. There were two bedrooms and a bath upstairs. In the small bedroom he found a stuffed toy that didn't belong to Kit and a pile of bandages. A wet towel speckled with blood lay in the sink. Had someone dressed Ingrid's wound?

He reported to Hull who was poking around in the kitchen. Hull nodded. "They can't be more than fifteen minutes ahead of us. The coffee in these cups is still lukewarm. Two cups." He turned on the two cops. "*Find* something, anything. Hurry!"

"At least at this stage Ingrid and Kit are still alive," Breck muttered.

Hull said nothing.

Breck opened his mouth, and then shut it again. Oh, Christ. Hull thought that they might have been alive fifteen minutes ago, but he obviously didn't hold out much hope about how long they'd stay alive.

"I can't give you false hope, Breck," he said gruffly. "We don't have any idea of the sort of people we're dealing with here. The whole scenario is warped—a sort of good versus evil. Sure, it looks as if one sister is holding the other back, but for how long?"

"Sir?" One of the constables held out a small piece of paper. "I found this on the bottom stair, and there's another piece just inside the back door."

So much for being the great detective. In his anxiety he'd run right over it, Breck thought to himself.

But it was he who found the next piece of paper, at the end of the paved garden path leading to a small gate tucked away in an unkempt hedge. On the other side of the gate was a narrow lane, not wide enough for a vehicle. Hull stopped them from going any further by yelling "Halt!" like a drill sergeant. "From herein we use SOCOs. Someone's leaving us breadcrumbs."

From Alice and Wonderland to Hansel and Gretel. But this was no fairy tale. "We're wasting time," Breck said through gritted teeth. Well, he wouldn't interfere with their scene, and there were other ways around this.

He peeled off from the group and jogged around to the front of the house. Running along the sidewalk, he kept parallel to the lane as much as possible. When he came to the intersection where the lane met the sidewalk he paused. Now what? The streetlights lit up the walkway clearly and he could see right to the open gate at the end of Angela's garden. Tall shadows stretched through the gateway on to the lane where the team waited for the SOCOs to arrive.

Too much waiting. Always waiting. Ingrid? Kit? His heart thumped and strained and it had nothing to do with his short sprint down the sidewalk. He hunkered down, forcing himself to slow his breathing.

And there it was, right at his feet. Another breadcrumb. They had come out of the laneway and crossed the street. He stood. He should call this in. He should. If he stuffed this up, he'd lose everything.

The clock in his brain ticked on inexorably.

Was Tania watching him even now? One sister could take Ingrid and Kit while the other kept a lookout. Except that wouldn't fly. Ingrid and Kit together would be too much for one person. Ingrid might be sweet-natured, but she was a fighter. She'd already proved that she would fight not just for herself, but also for Kit.

But Kit…what would Kit do? Would he automatically obey his mother, or would he try to protect Ingrid? He thought his mother was sick, not evil, so he might do as he was told. Except…how was he reacting to two Tanias? Would he know which was which? Breck wasn't sure he'd know one from the other himself unless he faced both of them side by side. How could he expect Kit to work it out?

Hands on his hips, Breck turned in a circle. After they'd crossed the road, where had they gone? The obvious answer was that they'd had another vehicle stashed away.

Aside from vengeance, what did Tania hope to gain from kidnapping both Ingrid and Kit? For hours now he'd tried to fathom that out. As for killing her great-aunt, it was obvious the woman had kept records about her two great-nieces, but so what? All families did. Why should that have been a bone of contention unless…unless they'd been kept as a form of blackmail or control. Even then, that was mighty thin reasoning. No. The great-aunt must have been killed for another reason. Or, more chilling, for no reason at all.

He tried to think back to when he and Tania had been married. Naturally they'd had to produce birth certificates prior to their marriage. He must have seen Tania's birth certificate but he could remember nothing about it, except that her surname was Davidson, not Bedloe. Heavens, how many times had Tania been married? Or was it a case of how many birth certificates did she have?

Okay, he understood that she saw Kit as a way of screwing money out of him along with the double-edged sword of vengeance. But she wouldn't hurt Kit, would she? She'd been neglectful in the past, but that was a long way from harming him. Besides, he was her son, and although it appeared she was not the conscientious mother he'd always assumed her to be, she wasn't all bad.

But—Angela? She was an unknown quantity.

He rubbed his forehead. What a can of worms.

Poor Ingrid. He'd give a lot to know about the issues between her and Tania. Was there a way to find out? And would it help him to find them?

He paced across the road, head down, looking for more scraps of paper. Was it Ingrid or Kit who had left a paper trail, or could it possibly be the good twin?

Further down the road a dog handler's van drew up to the curb, followed by the SOCO's SUV. Okay, he couldn't delay any longer. He phoned Hull. "Get them to come down the road further. There's another scrap of paper down here." He clicked off before Hull could tear strips off him for going off on his own.

Then he saw it. A heap of dark clothing had been pushed under a roadside hedge further along where the street abutted the main road. He'd take a look first before calling the team in case it had nothing to do with their investigation.

He glanced around. Groups of sparrows and blackbirds settled down to roost in a stand of trees at the far end of the street. Their twittering mutters sounded almost cozy on the still night air. At this hour most people were eating dinner or lounging in front of TVs and computers. It was too chilly to be outdoors.

Breck stopped and took another look around. Nothing.

He didn't approach the bundle of clothing directly by walking down the sidewalk. Instead, he walked down the center of the street so as not to disturb possible evidence. He'd come close to destroying a valuable clue already so he'd better get this right. Hull was giving him yards and yards of slack because of the circumstances, but if Breck stuffed up anything else, he'd be sent home with a flea in his ear.

As he came parallel with the clothing, he could have sworn he saw it move. Bullshit. He was so stressed out about Kit and Ingrid that he wasn't thinking straight. Needed to do some of Natasha's deep breathing exercises.

He took a step back and—a woman's hand stretched out from beneath the clothing, fingernails clutching at the damp earth. A muffled moan startled him into action. "Ingrid?"

As he rushed towards her, footsteps thudded down the road. The troops had arrived.

Chapter Twenty-Five

"We've got the last bit of paper. What's up down here? Christ, Breck, you're—shit!" Hull stopped dead when he saw the twitching fingers stretching out from beneath the pile of clothing. "Ingrid Rowland?"

The hand stopped moving.

Hull raised his eyebrows at Breck, stepped forward and hunkered down. "Ingrid? It's Hull and Marchant. You're safe now." He gently tugged on the bundle of clothing. "Marchant, get a flashlight. Can't see a damn thing."

Breck tugged his tiny penlight out of the inner pocket where he kept it. "Here. Try this. I'll call for something bigger."

There was a strange gargling sound from Tony Hull. "Paramedics. Quickly!"

Breck juggled his cell phone in one hand and the flashlight in the other. The beam fell on a bloodied mess then bounced away when the 111 call went through. Breck jabbered out directions then redirected the flashlight beam back on to the huddled heap in front of them.

"She's bad, Breck. Very bad. See for yourself." Hull stood aside.

Breck crouched down. "Ingrid? I'm here. We're getting help." Then he reared back as the bloodied head rose and glared at him out of its remaining eye.

"Nnnn-nn," it said.

Breck tried to reconcile the pulpy red mass in front of him with Ingrid's face. "Oh, shit, shit, shit." He leaned forward again. "We'll get them, Sweetie. Help is on its way. Ingrid—where's Kit?" He reached out to touch her but his hand hung in the air when she tried to raise herself again and whispered, "Nnnn-nn…" Her voice died away as her body sank down and went slack. She was unconscious.

She was also naked, the paramedics discovered, when they eased her on to a gurney.

"I have to go with her," Breck said to Hull.

"Of course. We'll keep searching for your son. We've got the e-experts at Central going through records now and we'll keep following the paper trail. On top of that—" The ambulance doors slammed in his face and the siren wound up to a screech.

Breck sat on an upturned bucket that seemed to serve as a seat while a paramedic struggled to stabilize the patient. As he cleaned Ingrid's eyes and nose and the features finally became clear, Breck stiffened in shock. "That's not Ingrid! It's Tania!" Or was it Tania? Could it be Angela?

The paramedic looked at him. "Don't give a damn who she is, buddy. She's in bad shape."

Breck pulled out his phone and tried to get hold of Hull. "Turn that bloody thing off!" the paramedic yelled. At the same time he kept up a running commentary for the driver who was reporting Tania/Angela's symptoms to the hospital.

"No! Another woman's life is at stake and so is my son's." As soon as Breck gave voice to his fears, he realized just how precarious those lives were. If a woman did this to her sister, what would she do to others who got in her way?

Breck gave his back to the paramedic and the woman on the gurney and texted Hull while the paramedic's attention was diverted. He hoped Hull could understand his cryptic message: 'This one not Ingrid…Tania!' That was the best he could do at the moment, but as soon as Tania/Angela was stabilized, he intended to screw whatever info out of her he could.

To make sure he had access to her, he signed her in as his wife. With all the blood and bruises, he couldn't tell who she was. But she wasn't Ingrid, and for that he was thankful.

He waited outside A&E, fretting, fretting, as the emergency team worked on her. What was happening to Ingrid and Kit? Several times medical staff approached him for information about 'Tania's' background. He told them all he knew, which wasn't much. Tania's secretiveness was her downfall. And if this wasn't Tania, then her twin must have the same background.

An hour later a woman doctor approached him. "Mr.…Marchant, is it?" He nodded.

She glanced at the police insignia on his sweater. "Your wife has some traumatic injuries. She's been severely beaten. We are stabilizing her before we remove her spleen. I suspect one of her kidneys will need to be removed also. Someone has whaled on her with a cricket bat or something similar. Her left wrist and cheekbone are broken, as if that side was exposed to her attacker. Do you know what happened to her?"

Breck shook his head. "We've been looking for her

but never expected to find her in this state. It's possible her sister did this to her."

The woman looked shaken. "Her *sister*? Hell. Well, I'm not sure how physically strong she is, but her recovery will be very slow." She glanced at her watch, her shrewd grey eyes flicking to his face and away again. "There's no point in waiting around here. If you leave a contact cell phone number, that would be best. It will be hours till we know the results of the exploratory operation."

"Oh." There went his chances of finding out where Kit and Ingrid had been taken.

"Thank you, doctor." He shook her hand. Her face looked pale and tired, as if she spent too much time indoors. Her weary expression hinted that she'd seen almost everything that human beings could do to themselves and others.

As he left the hospital to search for a cab, his phone rang. "Any news?"

"You're not gonna believe this, but whoever is dropping breadcrumbs, and it must be Ingrid or Kit since the twin you're with has been bashed up by the bad twin, then they've done an excellent job. Breck, wherever they went, they went on foot!"

"What?" Breck thought quickly. "That's to our advantage. Dogs?"

"Soon. Doing fine with the paper trail so far. Got the dogs on standby. Marchant, one of them is dragging their feet. Can't tell who it is, but it looks as if it might be Ingrid. Prints are too big for young Kit. Presume she's trying to slow them down. Or she's injured."

"Doesn't make any sense though for them to go on foot. Although…" He remembered the getaway car on the night he'd searched the Kerr house. "Angela's a lousy driver. Can't be Tania because she's a good driver. Well, whoever I was married to was a good driver," he added. Who the hell *had* he been married to? Tania or Angela? And if he thought *he* was puzzled, what about poor Ingrid and Kit? Especially Kit.

"It's to our advantage, so don't knock it," Hull said. "Wonder where they're headed? So far we've reached Alberton Road. Does Tania have any contacts in the Mt. Albert area?"

"Hell, I don't know. Let me think. Umm…hold on. My parents live in Mt. Albert. Could she be heading there to ask for help?"

"Surely not. Why would she do that?" Hull sighed. "Weirder and weirder. Okay. Give me your parents' address and phone number."

Breck knew both, but he rarely had cause to contact his parents, unless you counted a five second phone call at Christmas time. Naturally they never phoned him. "Shouldn't Raker be brought up to speed?" he suggested. "He might have something we don't."

"Already done. He was driving out of town for the weekend when I told him that Ingrid Rowland and your son had been kidnapped, presumably by Tania. Judging by the screech of tires, I guess he's on his way back here."

They had barely arrived at his parents' house when Raker drove up, accompanied by a constable. "Helluva twist," he said to Breck by way of a greeting. "Guess you didn't know your wife had a sister?"

"Tania told me she died in a car crash along with her parents."

"We checked. The parents are dead, certainly, but no mention was made of anyone else in the car."

"Just another lie."

"Yep."

"Marchant, stay here. Raker, with me." Hull was all business suddenly. Breck was startled to see Hull check his Glock and slide it into a shoulder holster. What the hell was he expecting?

Breck slid down low in the back seat of the Camry so he could angle his head to get a good view of the front door area of the house. Behind the Toyota, Raker had parked his vehicle leaving enough space for a speedy getaway. And behind that was a patrol car, all its lights turned off.

He closed his eyes. *Please* let Ingrid and Kit be all right. That mad bitch who'd attacked her own sister might well be hurting them, hurting them badly. He envisaged the pulverized face of the sister he'd found and shuddered.

And what of his parents? Where did they fit into all this? Had Tania run to them for help? Did they know that Tania had a twin sister?

It was a long shot anyway, wondering if Tania had come here. She'd used them as a mouthpiece before, but that might be the extent of her relationship with them. Worst of all, if Ingrid and Kit weren't here, *where the hell were they?*

He heard the front door open. Easing quietly up in the seat, he peered out the side rear window. A pool of light showed Hull and a constable standing on his parents' doorstep, but he couldn't see if they were talking to anyone. Raker and the other two constables must have gone around the back of the house. He hoped

Hull realized that the grounds were extensive. The house was set on an acre, and if Tania/Angela was hiding out with her captives in the grove of trees at the rear of the property, they'd be hard to find. It would make for an easy getaway through a neighbor's property, provided her captives were mobile. God knows what state they were in. And God knows what mental state their captor was in.

The front door clicked shut. Breck stuck his head up again but Hull was nowhere to be seen. He and the constable must have been admitted to the house.

Breck stayed where he was. That was all he had to do. *Not* help. Harder, far harder than anything he'd ever done. He rubbed a hand over his face, listening to the whiskers scratching. Inside the car it sounded loud.

Suddenly the car door exploded open. A bloody hand reached out for him but he was already on the move. Scrambling backwards, he burst out of the other door and ran like hell.

****

His lungs heaving as if he'd run a marathon, he hurtled towards the rear of the property where Raker was. He couldn't see a damn thing. It was full dark now and there was heavy cloud obscuring the moon. Whoever had tried to get into the car was no longer chasing him.

Unable to find Raker, Breck doubled back and crouched down behind the garden shed. He could hear nothing, which was odd. Where the hell was Raker?

A slight breeze kicked up and stirred the leaves on the trees, and from a long way away Breck heard a sobbing cry. "Please!"

He half rose to his feet then sat back again. Where

had the cry come from? Who was it? It was a woman's voice but it hadn't sounded like Ingrid. However if she was badly injured…

His mind raced around in circles. Was it a trap?

Easing past the shed, he rushed towards a clump of bushes and hunkered down again.

Nothing.

What had happened to Raker and the two constables with him? It wasn't as if they were facing a gunman. If Tania/Angela was here, she could hardly take on Hull, Raker, three constables and Breck. So why weren't Hull and Raker doing something?

Were his parents home? He looked up towards their bedroom window at the top of the house. There were no lights on. There seemed to be a dim light downstairs in the dining-room, but it wasn't an ordinary light. More like a flashlight. There was definitely someone in the room, because every now and again, an elongated shadow passed in front of the light.

He eased closer, knowing he could tuck in next to the passion fruit vine climbing over the loggia to hide.

Now, just one last sprint—

"Marchant. Stop."

Breck rocked back on his heels. "What?" he hissed. "Where the hell are you?"

Out of the darkness, Hull and a constable appeared at his elbow. "Right here. We went in the front because the door was slightly ajar. Just got in and heard a disturbance upstairs so we raced up there only to hear someone lock the door behind us. Thought Chambers was going to have a heart attack."

The constable, Chambers, smiled wanly.

Breck tried to grin but he was just too damned

tense and anxious.

"Any hiding places in your parents' house, Marchant? Because I tell you; we looked up and downstairs and even outside, and there's nobody to be seen. Yet someone tried to lock us in. And rather than escape out the back door, they went to ground. Raker was keeping watch at the rear of the property and they didn't go out that way. There are too many of them to have slipped past us."

"Uh, let me think. Where's Raker now?"

"Just sent him to stake out the front, since we've got the back covered."

Thank God. Breck had wondered if Raker was another casualty of the Tania/Angela team.

Then he stomped down on the dark fear that only reared up when he was confined in small, dark places. "Hull, there is a place where someone can hide, but it's too small for four adults and a kid."

"Maybe it's no longer four adults and a kid."

Breck's heart lurched at Hull's words. "Let's work on the assumption that it's four adults and a child, shall we? My child and girlfriend are in there somewhere."

"Sorry. And your parents."

"Yes, and my parents." But they weren't Breck's priority.

"So where's this hidey-hole?"

"Under the stairs there's a cupboard. But at the back of that cupboard there's a crawl space. I guess maybe two adults could fit in there."

"Great place for kids to play," Hull commented absentmindedly.

*Yeah, fantastic place. He'd been sent there often until his parents realized that shutting him in the dark alone still didn't improve either his learning skills or his 'truculent manner.'*

"Okay, let's just you and me get in there, being as quiet as we can, and we'll take a look under the stairs." Hull made it sound like a Boys Own Annual adventure.

"I wonder what Angela is armed with," Breck murmured.

"You reckon it's Angela?"

"Yeah. Just remembering some things. Trying to put them together. Tell you later."

"I see. Don't suppose your parents own a gun of any sort?"

Breck snorted. "Hardly. My father always planned on talking criminals to death."

"Oh. One of those. My uncle's like that. So who do they call when they're in trouble? Cops. Anyway, at least that takes the heat off. If Angela or whoever got her hands on a firearm, we'd have a massacre on our hands. Wish I knew what made her tick."

"You and me both."

Both men fell silent for a moment, and then Hull said, "Okay. Let's go. Here, take this. Just in case."

"This" was Hull's back-up weapon, a little snub-nosed .38 special.

Breck blinked. "Oh, okay."

Hull turned and set out towards the back door of the house, Breck following closely behind.

A rustle from the undergrowth had them both freezing. "Help. Please help."

Hull grabbed Breck's arm. "*Don't.*"

Christ, didn't Hull have any faith in him? This was probably a trap.

"Come out where we can see you." Hull called out.

"Sssh-hh. C-can't move."

"That's Ingrid," Breck hissed at Hull.

"You'd better be right, boyo." Hull led the way with his Glock and flashlight.

Big lavender bushes grew beside the path and it was here they found her. "Oh, God." Breck crouched down and peered at the mess of blood and skin that was Ingrid. His stomach heaved.

"Bw…" Her voice faded away.

"Beaten the same way as the other one," Hull opined. He doused the flashlight.

Breck was too busy dialing 111 to answer.

Hull crushed his hand over Breck's stumbling fingers. "We still have people to save, Breck. We have to flush out Angela. If the ambulance comes roaring in here, that could spell the end for young Kit and your parents."

"But Ingrid—" Breck bit off the rest of his words. How could he choose between Kit and Ingrid? Fuck his parents and Angela. But Kit? He slid the cell phone back into his pocket and knelt down beside Ingrid again. Oh, God. Flicking on his penlight he tried to assess her injuries, but all he could see in the narrow beam was a blood-spattered arm, crooked protectively over her head. "Give me the fucking flashlight." He snatched it from Hull and then wished he hadn't. When he saw the full extent of Ingrid's injuries his heart wept. "I'm here, sweetheart. We'll get help for you." He turned the beam off.

The arm over her head trembled but he didn't dare touch her. How badly was she hurt? Then he remembered that blood-covered arm reaching into the car only a half-hour ago and groaned.

"What?" Hull whispered.

"She's been wandering around injured for a while. She tried to get into the car and I thought it was Angela. I bolted. She wanted my help and I failed her. Now I *still* can't get help for her because of the others. Shit, shit, shit." He punched the air uselessly.

"K-k…"

"Kit? Where's Kit, Ingrid?"

She moved a little and he took the risk of clasping her fingers.

"Come *on*, Marchant. We need to go *now*. We can't afford to delay any further. Leave her. She'll be safe here."

"Fuck you. Call one of the others to look after her. I'm not moving till you do."

Hull sighed and murmured into his cell phone.

A minute later Chambers moved quietly into place beside Ingrid. "Ms. Rowland, I'm Constable Chambers and I'm going to take care of you till Mr. Marchant gets back."

Breck nodded to him and followed Hull towards his parents' house.

## Chapter Twenty-Six

The Pirates of Penzance had nothing on Hull. He definitely moved with cat-like tread. Breck followed him, wondering how the man moved so stealthily. Some members of the AOS could take lessons from him. Breck concentrated on keeping his breaths shallow and making sure that as they neared the back door, he didn't stand on anything that would make anyone aware of their presence. If Angela had been on the lookout, she might have seen the flashlight beam when they discovered Ingrid, but hopefully she'd think they were waiting for reinforcements to regroup.

Or she might not be here at all. She could be long gone. Pray God she hadn't taken Kit with her when she fled.

As they stepped into the kitchen, the capricious spring weather covered their approach. The wind was rising, soughing through the big trees on the perimeter of the property.

Hull turned and gestured to Breck to lead the way. This was a route Breck remembered very well. From the punishment under the stairs, to the warmth and relief of Natasha's kitchen where she'd left their dinner simmering in the oven.

Every step towards the cupboard dragged at his feet, told him not to go there. He swallowed and reached for the intricate door fastening. Hull nudged him and indicated his penlight but Breck didn't need light for this lock. It was a double cupboard and after he turned the key, he set to work untwisting the length of wire holding the two small doorknobs together. There was no sound from inside.

Breck's heart was almost suffocating him. Between the dread of what he might find inside and the fear of having to return to that lonely, black space, he could scarcely breathe. God knows, he'd had to crawl into many small places since he'd joined the cops. But this one was different. This one was the sum of all his childhood fears.

"Have you got it open?" Hull breathed in his ear.

Breck nodded and yanked the door open with more force than necessary. He cannoned backwards into Hull. And something catapulted out and whacked him in the stomach. He and Hull went down in a tangle of arms and legs. "Christ," Hull muttered as he leapt to his feet. But Breck was already grasping his aggressor. "Kit!"

"Daddy?"

"Oh, God. Kit." Breck wrapped his arms around Kit and refused to let him go. "Are you all right?"

"Daddy." Kit collapsed against his father, sobbing quietly. "She put us in the dark. She smacked Ingrid and smacked her."

Time was of the essence, but Breck shut out everything except his shivering son. "I'm here now, son. And Detective Hull is here. We'll sort things out. There are police outside too. Did she hurt you?"

"J-just once. Ingrid screamed at her. So did the other lady."

"Marchant, ask him—"

"Don't hurt him, you bitch!"

Someone else was in the cupboard. The words were aggressive, but the voice was quavery. Sounded like his mother.

"It's okay, Mother. I'm here now. Where's Angela?"

"Gone. Sh-she locked us in here—"

"Hull. Quick! Make sure she's nowhere near Ingrid."

But Hull was already rounding up the troops and calling an ambulance.

"You can come out now," Breck told his parents.

No reply.

Kit whispered, "I think she's frightened of the dark. She keeps shivering."

"What about…Grandpa? Is he afraid of the dark too?"

Kit shook his head. "He went with Angela. Are Ingrid and Mommy okay?"

"Not sure, son. Tell you what, you hold the door open and I'll climb inside. I'll use my penlight." He wriggled into the cupboard and pushed his way on his hands and knees into the storage area at the back of the cupboard. "Come on, Mother. Take my hand."

"Breck, I'm so, so sorry. All those years ago when we…however did you breathe? I can't *breathe*."

Her voice was rising again and Breck knew that if he were to drag her out now, she'd resist him. He bore down on his fears and wriggled into a position beside her. "No need to worry. Together we can do it." His years in the AOS had taught him to identify with the victim. And his mother was a victim. No doubt about it.

She hadn't cooperated with Tania or Angela. Why hadn't he ever picked up on the strange vibes between his father and his mother? Because he hadn't wanted to see his mother in a favorable light, that's why.

He placed his penlight on the floor so that they had a little light, and he could feel his mother's breathing gradually slow down. "Keep holding that door open, Kit."

The dusky grey light at the doorway beckoned.

For the first time in his life he took his mother's hand. "Hold on to me. When you feel better, we'll crawl out of here."

"Daddy?"

"It's okay, Kit. Grandma and I are getting ready to come out now."

"Just crawl, Grandma," Kit advised. "Crawl towards the opening."

"Good advice. Come on, Mother." But as Breck tugged on her hand, his mother suddenly collapsed against him. Hell. It would be better anyway if she were unconscious, he told himself. But it was going to be difficult to drag her out and time was wasting. What was happening outside? More importantly, was Ingrid going to be okay? He snatched up the little flashlight and shone it on his mother's face. She was sheet white. Well, he didn't feel so chipper himself. He hated this place and the sooner he got them out, the better. As he placed the penlight at a strategic angle, his heart jumped.

A stain of red was spreading over the front of his mother's shirt. Oh, God. "Mother!" He'd never called her Mom and even now, he found it hard to call her anything warmer. "*Please*. Come on. We have to get out of here." He braced his feet on the end wall and pulled. She was a dead weight, and he paused, sweating and gasping, then tried again. Clenching the penlight between his teeth, he gradually eased her closer to the doorway.

Suddenly the room and environs lit up, brightness bouncing off the walls.

"Sir?"

"Chambers?"

"Yessir. Ms. Rowland's on her way to hospital. Thought you'd like to know. She's bad, but they got her stabilized."

Breck tugged again and gasped, "My boy?"

"He's right here, sir. No problems."

The cupboard was stifling. Sweat ran down his face in rivulets and stung his eyes. One more pull should do it.

"Here. You hop out. We'll do that."

Raker and Chambers tried to edge Breck aside but he clung fast to his mother's shoulders. "No. She's mine. Nearly there." He needed to do this. Had she been injured, trying to protect Kit?

Gasping, he floundered on the tiled floor, his mother half across him. Eager hands checked her out and Raker rang the paramedics.

"Kit?"

Kit collapsed against Breck, his arms winding around Breck's neck.

"Easy, son. Can't breathe."

His chest heaved with the effort of dragging in great lungfuls of air. "D-did Grandma get hurt protecting you?"

"That woman, *not* Mummy, hit me and Grandma

shoved her. She punched something into Grandma's chest and Grandma coughed."

Breck examined his son's face. He thanked their lucky stars that Angela had only slapped Kit. A blue bruise and a red patch on his cheekbone were the only marks on him. Of course there was no telling what Angela had had in store for Kit, but all that mattered was that she hadn't been able to carry out her plan.

As the paramedics tended his mother, her eyelids fluttered.

"Punctured lung," one paramedic muttered, listening to her attempts to breathe. They propped her up and loaded her on to a gurney.

"Which hospital?" Breck asked them. "We're just leaving to see someone else who—"

Raker grabbed his arm. "We've arranged for both Ingrid and your mother to go to Carlton General. I'll take you and the boy now. Leave Angela to Hull and his men."

"There's another problem. Where the hell is my father?"

"Does young Kit know?"

Breck hoisted Kit up on to his shoulders where he clung like a monkey. "Kit, did you hear what Sergeant Raker just said? You told me that Grandpop went with Angela. Where did they go?"

"He lives here."

"Yeah." Breck waited.

"He kept talking vand she said, 'shut up, you old fool.'"

In spite of the circumstances, Breck couldn't help grinning. "Sounds like Grandpop."

"He likes Mommy. He doesn't like the other one."

"Uh, huh." Breck was starting to wonder just how much his old man liked Tania. They'd always got on well, but… "So then what happened?"

"That woman hit Ingrid and punched her. Grandpop made her stop." Kit swallowed tears, and Breck put up his hand and held tight to Kit's. "Then they just left her there on the f-floor. They went outside and Ingrid moved." His eyes big and round, Kit reiterated it. "She moved!"

He'd obviously thought Ingrid was dead.

"She whispered to Grandma and me that she was going to get help. She got away, Daddy!"

"Then what happened?"

"They came back and got very angry. They shut Grandma and me in that dark room."

"Sounds as though Angela kept Kit and your mother for insurance while she made her getaway. She must have thought Ms. Rowland had got clear away," Raker suggested. "Still doesn't tell us where your father is though."

Breck didn't much care. It was past time he went to check on Ingrid and his mother.

Chapter Twenty-Seven

Kit stretched out across Breck's knees while Breck held fast to Ingrid's hand. His body was cramped like a corkscrew but he wouldn't let go of either of them. They needed him as much as he needed them.

The boy wuffled gently in his sleep. Breck envied him. He was way too anxious about Ingrid and his mother to fall asleep. It had been a twenty-two hour day so far and would be another few hours yet before Ingrid and his mother were out of the woods.

"How is she?" Raker put his head around the door.

"The old head wound reopened and caused most of the blood. Lost a tooth. Broke a finger. Could be worse. Brain damage is a concern though, so soon after concussion," Breck whispered.

Raker winced.

"Got a BOLO out for Angela?"

"Yeah, but we remembered you said she was a terrible driver. We figure she'll ditch the car and stick with public transport or just go on foot. Seems to be what she's comfortable with. We woke Billy up and had a chat. Angela was their driver that night you went to the Kerrs' house. He'd only just learned that Tania had a sister and next minute he found himself in a car with her going to toss over his brother's house. I think her driving terrified him more than her attitude."

Breck snorted in amusement. "Did you tell Billy that Tania is so severely injured she's not expected to live?"

Raker shook his head. "He didn't want to know anything about either of them. He's got the two kids and he has his hands full."

Oh, hell. He hadn't given a thought to Pixie and Bob for days. That was something else that would have to be faced. Bob might be all right with his father, but Pixie had nobody.

"I'll see how—"

"*How dare you!* That's my daughter in there and I have every right to see her!" An irate but carefully modulated voice spoke in the corridor outside.

Out of the corner of his eye, Breck saw Ingrid flinch. "Raker, she's coming round. Get someone."

"Gladly. That's her mother out there."

Shit. He was too damned tired to deal with Mrs. Rowland. He'd left a message on their answerphone. Reluctantly. Last time Ingrid had been adamant that she didn't want her parents notified that she was in hospital. This time he'd felt obligated to let them know. The specialist had mentioned possible brain damage. Anyway, her mother was cited as next of kin on her medical insurance.

"Oh, shit," Ingrid murmured. "Is that my mother?" Her hand twitched in Breck's clasp.

Breck snorted with both relief and amusement. "Darling Ingrid. We're here. Kit and I are here."

"Who called her?"

"I did. Your condition is serious, sweetheart. Just lie still."

In a flurry of white coats the ward doctor and head

nurse rushed into the room followed by a woman Breck presumed was Ingrid's mother. He wondered where the stepfather was. Mrs. Rowland was immaculately dressed and made up even though it was getting on for four a.m.

"I demand to know what has happened to my daughter."

"Please be quiet, madam. I'm trying to listen to your daughter's heartbeat. Ah…" The doctor sounded satisfied. "Good. Ms. Rowland, do you know where you are?"

"Bloody hospital again?"

"Ingrid!"

Breck and the doctor grinned while the nurse giggled and pretended to fiddle with the IV tube. Breck moved aside to let the doctor check her over, but as he let go her hand, Ingrid panicked and tried to grab his fingers.

"Breck! Don't go. Please."

"I'm not going anywhere." He lurched to his feet, pins and needles attacking his shins and calves after sitting still for so long. Kit murmured and tried to make himself more comfortable by wrapping himself around his father's neck. Half strangled, Breck staggered over to a corner of the room and plopped down on the visitors' chair.

"Can you remember what you were doing when you got hurt?" the doctor asked.

It seemed that Ingrid's memory was perfectly clear. "Uh, huh. I was trying to punch someone but she hit me first. She had one of those"—Ingrid's voice trailed off as she searched for a word—"those knuckle dusters."

The doctor grunted while Mrs. Rowland stared

with horror at her daughter, her attractive face looking distraught.

"How many fingers am I holding up?"

"Fifty-two. Doctor, I'm fine. My head hurts, my face hurts and my leg hurts. But I can see okay and I can hear okay. I can even think okay. When can I go home?"

Breck got up and walked over to the bed. "This time, my girl, you are not going home until the doctor gives the all-clear without having his arm twisted. Right?" He turned to the doctor.

"*This* time?" Mrs. Rowland said at the same time as Ingrid muttered, "shit." She seemed to have woken up belligerent. Breck didn't mind at all. It was good to know she was her usual fighting self with a bit more edge. She might need that edge if she was to cope with the pain that was to follow as she recovered. And, of course, her mother. He almost wished he hadn't contacted the Rowlands, but he knew he'd done the right thing.

Just then Mrs. Rowland's gimlet stare alighted on him. "Are you the person who telephoned us?"

"Yes, Mrs. Rowland."

"Thank you for letting us know." She didn't state the obvious: that Ingrid certainly wouldn't have told them about being injured.

"Is that your son?"

"Yes." Kit was in danger of sliding off his shoulder and Breck hitched him up.

To his surprise, Mrs. Rowland walked over and brushed the hair off Kit's face. "A good-looking boy," she whispered.

Breck knew she was dying to ask what his

relationship with Ingrid was, but good breeding was holding her back.

"He goes to Ingrid's preschool," he explained. "Ingrid and I are friends." And that was as far as he was going to go. He leaned down and whispered, "Ingrid, I need see my mother. We'll be back soon. You're safe now."

"Oh! W-What happened to her?"

"Angela happened to her."

"Oh, no! Is she here in this hospital?"

The doctor finished making notes on Ingrid's chart while the nurse tucked in the edges of Ingrid's blankets. "Sleep," the doctor said firmly. He indicated the drip. "Otherwise…"

Ingrid got the message. She whispered, "Bye," to Breck and obediently closed her eyes.

Must be very ill. Last time in hospital she'd been far from obedient.

As Breck turned to leave, Mrs. Rowland said, "I'll hold your son while you visit your mother."

Breck eyed her. She might be Ingrid's mother, but he didn't know her. More to the point, neither did Kit. After the night he'd had, if he woke up being held by a stranger, he might panic.

"Thank you for the offer, but if he wakes up—"

Mrs. Rowland nodded, her lips firm, but Breck was unsure whether or not he had offended her. As he strode past her, juggling Kit into a more comfortable position, he stole a look at her. Her fingers plucked at her Oroton handbag and she glanced around as if wondering what she should do. Breck felt a little sorry for her.

At the nurses' station he was making inquiries about his mother when his cell phone rang. "Marchant."

"Raker. Got some bad news."

His chest tightened. His mother or his father?

"Tania didn't make it, Breck."

"Oh." He didn't know how he felt. The woman who had led him a dance for years and who had done her best to wound Ingrid was dead. At least…he hesitated as he walked in the direction of his mother's room. Had it been Tania who'd attacked Ingrid at the school? Kit had said that 'Mommy' attacked Ingrid, but what if he was wrong? What if it had been Angela? The end result was the same. Ingrid had been badly battered.

But…would they ever know the truth? Because when Angela was caught and brought to account, as soon as she learned her twin sister was dead, she'd blame everything on Tania. He held no brief for his ex-wife. How could he give a damn? But he hated injustice, and he'd have to work hard to see that Angela paid for what she'd done.

Then he shoved thoughts of the sisters aside as he came to his mother's room. Drawing in his breath, he tiptoed towards her bed. Even from several paces away her injuries shattered him. A student nurse sat sentinel at her bedside. There was a tube leading to a suction device that sucked the air out of her lung, or so he presumed. It made a horrendous slurping noise as if it was sucking out her blood. She was unconscious, white as parchment and seemed to have shriveled up so that she looked more like a child than a woman.

"You're her son?" the nurse inquired.

She spoke in a normal tone as if her patient could hear her. So he didn't lower his voice. "Yes. Can we just sit here for a while?"

"Sure. I'm supposed to let the doctor know when

someone arrives to see her, so I'll just do that now. Won't be long." She rustled out of the room leaving him with a sleeping son and an unconscious mother.

The suction machine continued its obscene slurping and Kit mumbled and muttered in his sleep. Breck's arms were beginning to ache and cramp in spasms so he eased Kit on to the chair and covered him with a spare blanket from the end of the bed. He stretched his arms out for a few minutes then wandered over to the window but all he could see were the lights in the room reflected back and his own grim, exhausted face. In a cupboard he found a pillow that he propped up against the side of the bed. Sitting on the floor and resting his head on the pillow, he found he could just reach his mother's hand. He would go back to Ingrid's room soon, but first he had to find out what the doctor thought about his mother's condition.

He must have dozed off because the next thing he heard was a sharp, loud voice demanding, "Come on, man. Wake up."

His reflexes had taken such a beating over the past twenty-four hours that it took him a few seconds to react. He scrambled shakily to his feet and shook his head. "Sorry." Walking over to the wash-basin unit in the corner he splashed cold water over his face. "I'm Mrs. Marchant's son."

The doctor held out his hand. "Alan Edwards. I see you're a cop. Bet you've done as many hours as I have, huh?"

Breck wished Dr. Edwards would lower his voice. Kit was wriggling restlessly. He tried to respond to the doctor's comment but he was just too tired and anxious. "How is she?"

The doctor walked around to the other side of the bed and adjusted the suction machine. Then he checked the drip and stood for a moment looking down at Breck's mother. "Something or someone slammed into her so hard they cracked her sternum and collapsed one of her lungs. These sorts of injuries usually occur during road accidents."

Breck shook his head. "No accident. Believe it or not, it was another woman with a powerful punch and a knuckle duster."

"Christ." Edwards shook his head in disgust, his untrimmed wavy hair bouncing about. "She'll be on the suction for about another three or four hours, and we'll keep the drip going for a couple of hours after that. From then on she'll be on some strong painkillers. Can't let her go home for a couple of days 'till her breathing's stabilized. Do you know if she's allergic to anything?"

Breck shook his head, feeling lower than a snake's belly. Shouldn't he know stuff like this about his parents? "I think she's okay with most things. I'm not really sure, because we've been estranged for years." There, he'd said it. He'd admitted that their relationship was non-existent.

The doctor flicked a look at him and shrugged. "You're here now. That says enough. How long can you stay?"

"I have to get back to see my-my partner." He didn't know how to describe his relationship with Ingrid. What did you call a woman who put herself in harm's way to protect himself and his child? She was more than a friend.

The doctor frowned.

"She's in 245," Breck explained.

"Oh! I thought you meant you had to get home. Hell's delight! You've had a great time tonight, haven't you?" He ran his eye down the chart in his hand. "Is that Ms. Rowland?"

Breck nodded.

"I'm on her team, but her main doctor is Dr. Tole."

"We've met. Dr. Tole is having a hard time keeping Ingrid in her bed. She's not fond of hospitals. This is her second trip in a week. And she must have cited her mother as a referee because Mrs. Rowland arrived and umm…"

Dr. Edwards grinned. "Sometimes the people we use as referees are about the last people we want to see. Have you got anyone to look after the boy?" He nodded towards where Kit snorted in his sleep.

Breck shook his head. "I guess the two of us will be bouncing back and forth between Ingrid and Mother like yo-yos."

"Got a suggestion. When you've appeased Ms. Rowland, go home and get some sleep. Don't come back till you've had a shower and a meal. Your mother won't be ready to talk to anyone till the afternoon."

Breck glanced towards the window. The afternoon? He glanced at his watch. God, it was morning already. Five a.m.

"I'll instruct the staff to mention that you've been waiting by her bedside and that you'll return later."

"*Thank* you." Breck's comment was heartfelt. He was torn in so many different ways it was hard to know what his priorities were. Angela had to be caught. His mother and Ingrid had to be comforted. Kit had to be looked after.

## Chapter Twenty-Eight

But when he returned to Ingrid, he knew that this was where his priority lay. Ingrid was his future. His hospital-phobic lady had her eyes closed, but her bruised face was turned towards the door, as if she had been waiting for him. There was nobody else in the room so he lay Kit in the visitor's chair and sat down on the end of the bed. Without opening her eyes, Ingrid stretched out her arm, wincing, and he clasped her hand in his. "Oh, Ingrid darling. I promise you'll never have to go through anything like this ever again."

One side of her mouth rose. "With your job, who knows? Got something to tell you."

He leaned forward. "About?"

"Mother called my father. Said that if I was getting involved with police issues, he'd better handle it."

Breck blinked. "Your real father?"

"I guess you'd call him that. The correct term is 'natural' father."

"Very PC. What will Tom Rowland say?"

"Now *there's* my real father, to all intents and purposes. Sort of. He finds me hard to understand. But I think Marla has a lot to do with that. There's quite a wall between Tom and myself. He tries to scale it with dollars."

"When did you last talk to your father?"

"About…I was five. Just learned to use a phone. I answered it one evening when Marla was in one of her depressive moods and wouldn't come out of her room. He seemed…nice. Asked about my day, stuff like that. He didn't ask about Marla which was good. If I'd told him that she hadn't come out of her room for two days he'd have been over like a shot, and then Marla would have *really* gone off her trolley."

"She seems very calm now. No anxiety."

"Yes, Tom has been good for her. Not sure if he's been quite as good for me, but I'm not the one who matters."

"You matter to *me*, Ingrid. Because of me you've had a terrible time and I feel so damned guilty—"

"Sssh." Her grip on his hand tightened. "It's not just because of you. Tania and I crossed swords a few years back. She almost torpedoed my career, but I managed to scramble back on board. Because she didn't quite stymie my work, I guess she's been lying in wait to finish off the deal. I knew when she enrolled her kids at Rowlands she had a plan."

"But whoever would have thought she'd conceal Angela's existence so well?"

"I've been wondering where Angela has been for the past few years. Perhaps she lived with the great-aunt."

"Or a mental health facility."

"Oh! I hadn't thought of that."

"Excuse me. Uh…Marchant?" Harley Max stood in the doorway.

"Sir." Breck let go Ingrid's hand and stood. "Did Raker call you…?" His voice got tangled up in his throat. Surely Max wasn't *Ingrid's father*?

At the same time, Ingrid asked, "Dad?"

This changed everything. Harley Max? Of all people. Max was one of the most difficult characters he'd ever had to deal with.

"This is awkward," Harley Max commented. "I gather you two know each other?"

Ingrid and Breck nodded. Warily Breck edged towards Kit, ready to pick him up and beat a hasty retreat. "I'll leave you two to get er…acquainted."

But Ingrid piped up. "No. I want you to stay, Breck. Please."

Harley Max looked as though he'd like to sit down. Breck gestured to the place where he'd been sitting and Max collapsed on to it. "Ingrid. I'd resigned myself to never seeing you again," Max began.

Ingrid interrupted. "Before you go any further, I know that Marla and you made a bargain that you'd stay away. But I'm not four years old anymore. For the past month I've been poking around trying to find out where you were. You're not in the phonebook. You're not on Facebook. I was going to try to coerce Breck to find out which branch of the police you worked in. But I see you know each other."

Breck felt his face heat up. "Hell, he's my boss, Ingrid."

Ingrid's expressive eyes lit with unholy glee. "Oooh, that's awkward."

"Used to be his boss, Ingrid. He's in the detective division now."

"I know. I guess you're the person who gave him the wrong application form."

"What?"

"Never mind," Breck and Ingrid said in unison.

Max smoothed his receding hairline. "How are you really, kiddo? This is the second time you've been in hospital in the past week. What's going on?"

"Have you been keeping tabs on me?" Ingrid stared at her father with her head on one side.

"Of course I have. What do you think I did? Walk away?" Max's voice rose in indignation.

"I've never been sure."

"What did she tell you?"

"That cops make terrible fathers. That you were never home."

"Sounds familiar," Breck commented, even though he was not part of the conversation.

Harley Max looked up from where he was drawing patterns on the bedspread. "You and that Tania woman? Did she say the same thing?"

"Yeah. And more."

"That terrible father thing is a load of bullshit," Ingrid intervened. "Kit has never been so happy than since he's been with you. Bet he couldn't sleep like the dead if he'd still been with Tania. Probably have to keep one eye open to see what was going to happen next."

Max got up and walked over to Kit. "So this is the young guy some of the drama has been about? Looks peaceful."

Breck knew Max was trying to divert attention away from the awkwardness of meeting his daughter. He could understand that. Must be damned difficult. It was damned difficult for him, too. Now he didn't know where he stood. Would Max try to intervene in the burgeoning relationship between Ingrid and Breck? After all, Max knew some of Breck's secrets and insecurities. Probably already decided that his daughter needed someone better.

Breck tried to rub the headache away from between his eyebrows.

Ingrid, being Ingrid, refused to be diverted. "Where do we go from here, Dad?"

"Uh…wherever you want to."

"That's a cop-out and you know it." She grinned at her father.

*She's gonna wrap him right around her little finger.*

Breck watched Max regroup. "Yeah. I guess it is. Can I say you get your directness from your old man? Definitely not your mother."

Ingrid snorted in amusement. "Oh, I agree. The other night I was bleeding all over the place and feeling sick as a pig and Breck got to watch me hurl. I figure any man who can hang around during that is a keeper. So I told him about Marla's insistence on behaving like a lady even when feeling ill."

Max whitened beneath his tan. "I didn't hear about that. What happened? Are you telling me you've been attacked *twice* by that nutty woman?"

"Relax, Dad. It's all over now. At least it will be when they catch her." Ingrid absentmindedly patted her father's hand.

He held on to her fingers. "You'd better tell me what this is all about. I can't make head nor tail of it."

"Okay. Breck, could you tell him? I'm a bit woozy. Don't forget to tell him there are two of them." Ingrid settled back against her pillows, the bruises standing out purple on her waxy skin.

"For heaven's sake, Ingrid! Will you lie down and

rest!" Breck rushed forward and eased a pillow out from behind her. "There. Sleep."

Her face was becoming more and more distorted as the swelling over her cheekbone intensified around the bruising. He turned down the bedside lamp and Harley Max clicked off the main switch by the door, just as the nurse bustled into the room.

"Two men to look after you," she said brightly.

"Mmm," Ingrid mumbled.

"Just a little pinprick…and there!" The nurse sounded triumphant.

Breck wondered if she'd expected Ingrid to leap out of bed and say, "No, no, I don't want pain relief!" He rolled his eyes at Harley Max who grinned back.

"Would one of you hold this, please?" The nurse held out an ice pack.

Harley Max looked at Breck.

Breck tried a tired grin. "You do it, Dad."

Max knelt down by the bed and tenderly pressed the pack to Ingrid's swollen cheekbone.

As the nurse bustled around the room flicking infinitesimal flecks of dust off the bedspread and cabinet, Breck picked up Kit and settled himself in the chair. With the lights lowered, the room took on a more peaceful air, less like a hospital room and more like someone's bedroom. The door shut behind the nurse and Breck allowed himself to relax. Harley Max could take up the vigil now.

****

He woke with a jolt an hour later.

"Daddy! Bathroom."

"Uh? Oh…okay."

He staggered to his feet still clutching Kit, but Kit

was happy to scramble down and potter off to the bathroom by himself. Breck stretched and glanced across at the bed. Ingrid's eyes were open and she was watching him, smiling a little. Her father was stretched out on the floor, fast asleep, using one of her pillows as a headrest jammed up against the wall.

"Good morning," Breck whispered. "How do you feel now?"

"That injection sure worked. I can't see straight, but I don't feel any pain."

The rattle of crockery outside the door had Max scrambling to his feet just as Kit came out of the bathroom. A nursing assistant shoved open the door and edged her way in with a cup and saucer. Kit screamed and threw himself at Breck. "It's her!"

The 'nurse' flung the cup away and launched herself on to the bed. But Harley Max beat her to it. By the time Breck had managed to grab the flailing arm holding a knife, Max had covered her like a sticky blanket. He pinned her other arm and both of her legs beneath him and hung on like a limpet. Breck pressed the red alarm button, and juggled with his phone to redial Raker. Shaking, Ingrid pulled herself up as far as she could in the bed, perching on top of her pillows.

Angela's strength was amazing. She heaved like a wrestler trying to dislodge Max. Without a qualm Max angled back and kicked her in the back of her knee. Her feral snarl alerted Breck just in time as she snapped her head around to bite his hand. He punched her. No Marquess of Queensberry rules for this bitch. Even so, it took the combined efforts of Harley Max, Breck and Raker to subdue her. Raker was the only one who had handcuffs and they were grateful when hospital security and a constable rushed in three minutes later.

Breck left them to it and raced to his mother's room. But all was serene. His mother was still unconscious, the suction machine muttering to itself as it kept her lung clear. Angela must have made Ingrid her first port of call. For some reason, Tania and Angela thought of Ingrid as their Nemesis. He glanced out the window down into the courtyard where Raker and a couple of constables were struggling to stuff Angela into a police van. From four stories up he could see her lips moving as she screamed invectives.

Thank God for that. He scorned the elevator and hurtled back upstairs to Ingrid's room. Poor Kit and Ingrid had had a fear-filled three days and he could only hope that Harley Max had toned down his abrasive style enough to soothe them.

He needn't have worried. As he walked along the corridor he could hear a buzz of excited conversation. Ingrid's room was so full of nursing staff agog to hear her story, that there was scarcely room for Breck to fit in a corner. Kit was enthusiastically munching fingers of toast while Ingrid, holding fast to her father's hand, was giving a blow-by-blow account of how her father and her 'fiancé' had saved her. She had the grace to look embarrassed when she caught sight of him lounging in one corner, grinning at her antics. Over the past few weeks, in spite of everything that had happened, her self-confidence had taken a huge leap upwards. Not surprising when you considered what she had been through and survived. Disagreements with her parents and the challenge of running a preschool took second prize to fighting off a couple of murderers. He watched her as she persuaded Kit to sit on the bed beside her. Kit, too, had grown in confidence over the past few weeks.

Then he caught a scowl from Harley Max and decided to make himself scarce. He wished Ingrid hadn't jumped the gun and mentioned her 'fiancé.' He and she had a lot of problems to sort out before their relationship went anywhere permanent. And judging from the look on Max's face, he intended to keep them well apart. Okay, couldn't blame the man. He'd only just met his daughter after a space of twenty-four years. He wanted to spend time with her. And he wanted her to have the best future possible which might not translate to being Brechon Marchant's 'fiancé.'

Breck pushed himself away from the wall and scooped up Kit. "Let's go visit Grandma, then we'll go home and have a sleep and a shower."

Kit pouted at having to miss some of the excitement but he went willingly enough. Like Breck, he had had enough of being confined in a hospital room.

Breck blew Ingrid a kiss and turned to leave.

"Just a minute, Marchant."

Uh, oh. Looked as though Harley Max was about to play the heavy father.

"What's this thing between you and my daughter?" Max demanded as soon as they were out in the corridor.

Breck grabbed a fistful of confidence and held on fast. "Still feeling our way, sir. Been too busy fending off weird people to discuss a future together, but that's what I want. Even if you or her mother objects." Breck looked his ex-boss in the eye. Hell, this was the first time he'd felt glad he'd resigned from the AOS. Max wouldn't be able to rip chunks off him every time he got into one of his moods. And after Ingrid's little mention of her 'fiancé,' Breck figured he was in with a chance. It amused him to see Harley Max assume the role of father as if he'd always been in Ingrid's life, but it was good, too. The interesting thing was that Tom Rowland hadn't come to visit her. Perhaps when Marla had contacted Harley, he'd felt de trop.

As he and Kit climbed into the SUV, Breck thumbed his cell phone. "Hull, it's Marchant here. Heard anything from my father yet?"

"Nothing at all. We've got a cordon around the house because we're still sifting through the evidence, and he hasn't come home. He works from home, doesn't he?"

"He used to. I don't really know. I can't ask Mother because she's in an induced coma. Might be able to ask her tomorrow."

"Today or tomorrow?"

Breck looked at the volume of traffic on the road and the streaks of sunrise in the sky. "Yeah. Today." He yawned. "I'll let you know if I hear from my father, but I doubt he'll come anywhere near me. Seems to me he and Tania might have—oh, I don't know. Just my suspicious mind."

"Crossed my mind, too. He won't have heard yet that Tania's died and that her sister's been arrested."

"Tony, I don't really give a shit."

"I understand. Get some sleep. If I see your father, I'll give him your love."

"A roundhouse followed by an uppercut was more what I was thinking."

Hull chortled and clicked off.

## Chapter Twenty-Nine

Five hours later Breck was dragged out of sleep by the ringing of the phone. "Got him," Hull said.

Breck heaved a sigh and blinked. "Who? What?"

"Your father. Trying to skip the country."

Breck sat up in bed, dislodging Kit who was stretched across his legs. "Whaaa-at? Nah. He hasn't got the guts. Why?" He had so many questions he couldn't get them all out.

"Apparently he and Tania were headed for Australia."

"Oh, of course. Poor old Billy. He did the dirty work, and then Tania and my father were going to disappear. Still don't understand where Angela fits in." Nor could he get his head around the idea of his father deserting his mother for Tania.

"We're slowly getting to the bottom of it. Let you know more as it happens. How's your mother?"

"Should be off the suction machine by now. I'll phone and find out. She'll be in a lot of pain for the next couple of weeks."

"He never even asked about her."

"No. He wouldn't."

"My father would go nuts if anything happened to my mother," Hull said.

"He's never been what you'd call an attentive

husband or father. I thought most fathers were like that till I went to school." Breck hadn't meant to spill his guts but for some reason he found himself trying to explain his dysfunctional family to Tony Hull.

"He's shattered about Tania's death though. Just looked at me when I told him. Said I was lying because that's what cops did."

Breck sighed. "Well, looking for remorse from him is not going to work. Frankly, I don't give a shit. I've got Ingrid and Kit and my mother to look out for."

Hull laughed. "And from what I hear, you've got Harley Max on your tail, too."

Breck sniggered. "Could have knocked me down with a feather when I found out *he* was her natural father. Terrifying. But he and Ingrid seem to be jelling together just fine. Only trouble is, with Max's big mouth, the whole cop shop will know every detail of my life from now on."

"Have a talk to him, Breck. I would. You're a private person and he's a gregarious one. So he has to be taught where to draw the line."

"Oh, I will. Got an idea Ingrid will back me up."

Hull gave a huff of laughter. "I'll back you up. Remember you'll most likely be in my team as from next month. I've asked for you, and they usually give us the staff we want."

"Thanks. I'd better buy some clothes that don't make me look like a cop."

"Won't make any difference to the seasoned crims. They can spot us a mile off even if we're in pjs."

Breck had a mental image of a bunch of cops in striped pajamas pinning down a dealer in an alley behind a bar. "Thanks for your call, Tony. I'd better get the day started before the sun goes down."

But by the time he'd roused Kit, put on a much-needed load of laundry and got them some breakfast, the sun was already well down on the horizon.

"We're vampires, Dad," Kit observed.

"Yeah. Living by night at the moment. Be glad when all this is over. Who do you want to visit first—Grandma or Ingrid?"

"Ingrid."

That was to be expected. He didn't really know his grandmother. *And whose fault is that?* No. He'd done the right thing in keeping Kit away from his parents. He was feeling guilty at the moment because his mother was injured. He'd have to make sure that her future was secure. He hoped to God she didn't decide to do something stupid like forgive his father and spend the rest of her life waiting for him to get out of prison. The charges against Jeremy Marchant hadn't yet been tabulated, but Breck knew they'd involve blackmail and intention to defraud at the very least, possibly even assault, although he couldn't see his father throwing a punch. But who knew? The man had always been an enigma. But he certainly wouldn't be cavorting around the lecture circuit for a good five years at any rate. After that it was doubtful if any of the educational authorities he'd contracted to would want to see him again.

He thought even less of Jeremy Marchant when he saw the strain on his mother's face as she struggled to raise herself on her pillows. He'd like to knock the living daylights out of his father, and he wished he could punch Angela the way the vicious bitch had punched his mother. Angela must work out like a demon at the gym to pack a massive wallop like that. He wondered if Hull had found Angela's specialized knuckle-duster yet. It had probably been purchased from Billy Kerr.

"Is Kit all right?" his mother whispered. The nurse had explained to him that talking would be difficult for a few days.

"Hush, Mother. Don't tire yourself. Kit is just fine, thanks to you and Ingrid. He's sitting on Ingrid's bed at the moment, eating her chocolates. She's on the level above this one."

There was a short silence, and then she said fretfully, "I wish you'd call me Mom."

He looked at her for a moment. "I guess that will take a while." He needed to meet her halfway, but he was tempted to say her request sounded more like a complaint.

"*He* didn't like that sort of thing. Too colloquial." The venom in her voice surprised him, and he wondered how many years she'd kept her resentment bottled up. He'd decided years ago that she thought the sun rose and set on his father. Perhaps he had it wrong. But surely she'd had a choice?

"Okay, Mum." He took her hand. "I want you to get a good night's sleep and I'll see you in the morning. Then we can make some plans."

"Plans?" she whispered.

"Yes. He'll be going to prison, so things will change."

He was startled to see an upturn in the corners of her lips. "Prison." She savored the word. "All right, son. Bring Kit to see me tomorrow." She released Breck's hand and lay back on the pillows stacked behind her.

As he left, a nurse brushed past him, a tray of instruments in her hands. "Just giving her something to help her sleep. Your visit seems to have done her good. She's smiling."

Breck looked back. His mother *was* smiling. Give it time and things would sort themselves out.

****

"So when are you going to make an honest man of me?" he asked, half an hour later. Ingrid was contemplating her array of floral tributes and grapes. Kit appeared to have eaten all the chocolates.

"Uh…" She stammered, reddening. "Look, I didn't mean to box you in or anything. When I said that my father and my fiancé had rescued me from the ghastly Angela, I didn't mean—well, I didn't expect you to…" She trailed off.

Harley Max had apparently gone to work and Kit was at the end of the hospital corridor admiring the self-serve confectionery cabinet.

Now was his chance. But Lord, he was jittery. His stomach jumped and quivered and the hand he held out to her shook like a leaf in a gale. "Ingrid, I'm terrified. I've never proposed before. With Tania things just sort of happened. And I haven't got you a ring yet. And—"

She leaned forward awkwardly and planted a wet kiss on him. "Shut up, Marchant. Do you love me?"

"You know I do."

"No. I don't *know*, but I'd hoped. There's nothing else to worry about then, is there?"

"Oh, yes there is. I haven't heard the magic words from you yet, and then there's your father." He shuddered. "The father-in-law from hell."

Ingrid burst out laughing. "If you could see your face! You know I love you, you double-dyed nitwit. Do you think I'd have put myself through the last eight weeks if I didn't? I could have walked away."

"Has it only been eight weeks? Hell, that'll be something else your father will have against me." He groaned.

She laughed. "He doesn't have anything against you. Says you're one of the best operatives he's ever had. But he'll never tell you that face-to-face. Actually, I'm quite glad I've only just got to know him. If he'd been around while I was in my teens, I'd probably have pulled my hair out trying to live up to his standards as well as Tom's expectations. And then there's Mum…" She rolled her eyes.

Breck rubbed his forehead. A few weeks ago there'd been just Kit and Breck. Now there was Kit and Breck and Ingrid and Mom and Harley Max and the rest. He hoped to God he could cope with them all without stuffing up too often. No doubt he'd manage. After the past few weeks he could probably handle anything.

Ingrid took his hand. "You'll cope," she said, reading his mind. "You'll do just fine. And I still haven't had the bended knee thing. How come you didn't propose to Tania?" She was referring to his comment about never having proposed before.

He shook his head. "She sort of proposed to me. Still don't know why. Backup in case her schemes went wrong, I guess."

"No. She saw a man of value and she wanted him."

Breck could feel himself reddening. "Uh—"

"So come on. Propose before Kit gets back."

"Yes ma'am." Feeling like seven kinds of idiot, he got down on one knee beside the bed. "Dear Ingrid, will you do me the honor—"

"Look girls! A proposal!" A bevy of nurses clustered around the doorway, exclaiming and laughing. The lone male nurse amongst them cast Breck a sympathetic look.

Red-faced, Breck clambered to his feet. "Ingrid, can we do this later?"

Eyes brimming with laughter, she peered at him from behind the bed sheet. "Poor Breck. Never mind. I consider myself proposed to. The answer's yes."

"I should bloody well hope so," Breck muttered, sotto voce.

The nurses moved on and Kit took their place. "What's happening, Daddy?"

"Ah, hell."

"Daddy! You swore!"

"Mmm. Hi, Kit. How about we go get you a salad to counteract all those chocolates?"

"Okay."

The great thing about Kit was that he was fond of food; it didn't really matter what the food was, he ate it. Breck surmised that the boy had gone without quite often when he'd lived with the Kerrs.

"Hey guys," Ingrid whispered. "Could you bring me a salad? I'm real sick of sloppy baby food."

Breck looked at the side of her face where Angela had thwapped her. It was the opposite side to where Tania had bashed her several days ago which was fortunate, but it meant that now her entire face was a huge swelling bruise. He could understand why the hospital was feeding her soft foods. Probably thought she had a couple of loose teeth underneath all that purple. "You think that's a good idea?"

She did her eye-rolling thing and Kit smirked.

"Please. I'm desperate."

Common sense told him it was wiser to wait a couple of days before she had solid food, but the pleading hazel eyes won out over common sense. Something told him she was always going to have this effect on him. He sighed, and then grinned. Actually it was a damn good feeling knowing she was going to be around, working her wiles, for the years to come. He kissed her goodbye and went out to find a Salad King.

Chapter Thirty

Three days later, Breck, Ingrid, Harley Max, Tony Hull and Raker all squeezed into Max's office. Ingrid still didn't feel up to par, but when she'd stared into the mirror this morning the bruises had looked as though they were beginning to fade. Her swollen face had already gone back to normal. The suspected broken cheekbone hadn't eventuated, for which she was thankful. It had been difficult peering over the swelling beneath her eye socket.

The men looked a lot better too. Amazing what a couple of nights' sleep could do. Breck looked relaxed, his feet hooked around the rungs of a stool that her father kept in the corner. It still seemed odd thinking of Harley Max as her father. The only regret she had was that Tom Rowland was no longer interested in her. He had dropped her like a hot coal once Marla had contacted Harley. For twenty-one years he had been the only father she had known. Sure, he was demanding. He wanted results for his investment. That was the way he saw relationships. But he was well meaning in a grim sort of way, and Ingrid hoped that with time, Tom would be able to adjust to the changed circumstances.

"It's bloody frustrating," Detective Sergeant Hull said, yanking on his tie. "Whatever we come up with, Angela Briscoe swears that everything was Tania's idea. It was Tania who worked on Breck so that he'd marry her because she needed a cast-iron respectable background. She probably thought that having a cop for a husband would come in handy. It was Tania who set up Billy Kerr to do their dirty work, and it was Tania who arranged to have Marty Kerr removed. Of course it was Tania's idea to set fire to the preschool and to attack Ms. Rowland. Naturally it was also Tania who decided to kidnap her own son so she'd have a measure of control over Breck if any of her schemes went awry. And of course it was Tania who had a long-term affair with Jeremy Marchant."

"Busy woman," Ingrid commented.

"Yes, and that brings us to you, Ms. Rowland. Both attacks on you have been exceptionally violent. Why?" Hull's sharp grey eyes bored into her. "What do Tania and Angela have against you?"

"Not Angela. It's what Tania has…had against me. The trouble is, when I thought I was talking to Tania, it might well have been Angela. Tania was often in peculiar moods during our preschool training. Strangely enough, she was good with kids. But she rubbed a couple of our lecturers up the wrong way, didn't attend more than half of the lectures, and kept trying to copy my assignments. When I tried to avoid her, she took pleasure in seeking me out. I could see by her smug expression that she enjoyed riling me. She knew she made me uncomfortable and that I didn't have the guts to call her on it."

"And? There must be more to it than that."

"She downloaded my final exam answers from my laptop and passed it off as her own work. So much so that I was called on to explain how my answers and 'another student's' were identical, word for word. It pissed me off that they approached me first before they questioned Tania. They threatened to fail me. Three years' work for nothing. All because of Tania Bedloe. I didn't take it lying down. I told them how Tania only befriended me when an assignment was due. I also told them that I thought she had some sort of mental health issue." She turned to Breck as if he'd objected. "I was fighting for my future, and I pulled out every stop."

He nodded.

"When you mentioned mental health issues, what did they say?" Hull inquired.

"Nothing. She was a chameleon. It was her word against mine, and she was more plausible. She'd had plenty of practice. I was the one the Board labelled with mental health issues." She shivered and wrapped her coat around herself. "Fortunately a couple of my lecturers stood up for me. It became a 'he said,' 'she said' standoff and in the end they grudgingly gave me a pass. But not the grade A I had earned. I was given a grade C aegrotat pass. I've been fighting ever since to keep my school up to the highest possible standard. Rowlands is subject to snap inspections as well as the usual one each semester."

"Sounds to me as if *you* should have a grudge against Tania, not the other way around," Hull commented.

"You'd think so. But that's not the way Tania saw it. She gave them a spiel about her childhood and apparently they sent her to a private clinic for a couple of months to recover." Ingrid curled her lip. "She had them wrapped right around her little finger."

"So several years later when I enrolled Kit at your

preschool, I played right into her hands," Breck said, groaning. "I'm so sorry, Ingrid. If only I'd known…"

She patted his hand. "You weren't to know. For years I've hidden the fact that the registration of the preschool hangs in the balance and that I'm at the mercy of a bunch of inspectors." She grimaced. "My mother and stepfather would have a fit if they knew that their investment was shaky."

Harley Max shifted in his seat. "Leave it to me. I'll sort things out with the Education Board. Once they hear about the real Tania, I guarantee there'll be no more snap inspections."

Ingrid smiled at him gratefully. He might have been late to the party, but he was coming through when she needed him most.

Breck asked what everyone was wondering. "So where do we go from here?"

"Tony and I will carry on questioning Angela," Raker said. "She's lawyered up, so it won't be easy to sift through the facts. The sisters created such good smokescreens that we've got great gaps in our knowledge. Apparently they lived with the great-aunt until Tania went to university and Angela then became a full-time caregiver for the aunt. It seems the aunt was mainly confined to a wheelchair. Reading between the lines, I'd say that Angela was unemployable. Can't see any employer lasting for more than five seconds through one of Angela's rampages. She hasn't mentioned a career or any job applications. Just said she went straight from school to looking after the aunt."

Ingrid frowned. "That doesn't seem right. She's twenty-six by my reckoning. Looking back, I think she took Tania's place often during our preschool training.

There were days when Tania suddenly became irritable and resentful. Her personality didn't change so much as become more of the same. Yet both Angela and Tania managed to cope on a day-to-day level with the work, so you can't say that Angela is totally unskilled."

"It might pay to see if Angela has spent some time in long term mental therapy," Breck suggested. "That would explain the missing years and months."

Hull nodded. "One thing we've learned is that the twins were orphaned at a very early age. After the parent's car crash, the great-aunt applied for custody of them. They were only two. Lord, that poor woman must have had her hands full."

"And got murdered for her pains," Ingrid murmured.

Breck, who was sitting beside her, stretched out his hand and took hers. She saw her father glance at them and look swiftly away. She grinned to herself. Breck was becoming more relaxed around Harley Max, which was a good thing. She did not want any awkwardness between them in the years to come.

"It looks as though Tania was the brains of their little schemes and Angela supplied the brawn if it became necessary. Unfortunately Tania couldn't control Angela towards the end," Raker said. "She literally bludgeoned Tania to death, and would have done the same to you, Ingrid, if she'd found you. Just as well you crawled into the bushes."

Ingrid shuddered. "I managed to escape from the house while she was chasing Tania, but then I didn't know what to do. Kit and Mrs. Marchant were still inside, and I wanted to try to get them out. But I had no idea where Angela was."

"She was outside casting around looking for you. Fortunately we found you first."

"Thank Constable Chambers for me, would you, Detective Raker? He was wonderful. He knew just what to say and do."

"I'll tell him. He's a promising individual."

"Is that Andrew Chambers?" her father inquired.

"Yes. And you can keep your hands off him," Raker retorted. "No need to encourage him to join one of the AOS squads. We need him where he is. Anyway, he's never expressed an interest in joining your mob."

Harley Max examined his fingernails as if nothing could be further from his mind.

"Your father poaches all the good ones," Senior Sergeant Raker explained to Ingrid.

She grinned. If the team was at the stage of bickering and cracking jokes, then everyone was recovering. She knew they'd pussyfooted around some of the facts so as not to upset her, but ultimately everything would have to come out in the open so they could tidy up any collateral damage caused by the twin sisters.

"How is Billy Kerr?" Breck asked.

"Shattered."

"Yeah. I guess that pretty much sums it up," Breck agreed. "I feel sorry for him, even though he probably had a hand in the death of his brother. But he's not the brightest bulb in the pack and he's been coerced by those sisters into doing things he'd never have imagined all on his own."

"That's why they never tried the old switcheroo when Tania and you were married," Hull commented. "You'd have picked up on it, but Billy and Marty were none the wiser. Angela only got in on the act once Tania married Marty Kerr."

****

Two hours later Breck and Ingrid arrived back at his apartment, wrung out from sifting through the complicated mess that had been Tania and Angela Briscoe's lives. Ingrid flung herself down on the sofa, heedless of bruises. "Thank goodness that's over. When will you collect Kit from Jace's place?"

"Soon. Abel started his new job today, and poor old Jace is juggling a baby, a two-year old, and Kit. Before I do that, you and I are due a little talk. No. A *big* talk." He sat down and tucked his arm around her. "Miss Rowland—or should that be Miss Max?"

"You know that old saying? I don't care what you call me, just call me."

He grinned and rubbed his thumb in circles over the top of her hand. The tingles started up, same as ever. Probably on Level Four by now. God, she had it bad.

"Well now, Miss Rowland, I seem to remember you accepting my hand in marriage."

"Yes, I remember something like that. Of course I was on medication at the time."

"Hah! You don't get out of it that easily."

Laughing, she threaded her arms around his neck. "Got no desire to get out of it."

His hands smoothed up and down her back as he moved in for one of those deep kisses that turned her brain to molasses and lit fires where no man had ever been able to light them before.

He sighed and held her tighter. "Ingrid, you are the best thing that ever happened to me, and I'll always want you in my life. But—"

"But?" She kept her head down.

"I have a bunch of responsibilities that could make things difficult for us. There's Kit, my mother, a new job…"

She put her hand across his mouth. "So what? Everyone has hurdles they have to get over. We'll just have one or two more than most. We both have good jobs. Best of all, Kit is a fantastic kid. My dad is on our side too. When your mother recovers we can find something for her to do so she's not totally reliant on us now that your father is, uh, not around."

Breck snorted in amusement. "That's a nice way of saying I have a jailbird for a father." He shook his head. "Who would have thought it? Whoever could have anticipated that the great know-it-all, Jeremy Marchant, would get sucked into Tania Kerr's schemes? What was he thinking? Hell, what was Tania thinking? I can't see how my father would have been of much use to her."

Ingrid shrugged. "She might have wanted to use him as another way to keep a hold over you."

"Then she didn't do her homework. My father and I rarely encounter each other. How could he possibly have any influence over me? We exist on different planets. I can see why she wanted to use Kit to screw money out of me, but that's where it stopped. When we were married, okay, I lent her a cloak of respectability I guess. But after our divorce, what use was I to her?"

Ingrid looked down at her feet. "You're a cop. And cops can be turned. You could have been very useful in some of her schemes."

"Hah! If she'd tried to milk me for information, I'd have told her to piss off."

"I know that, and you know that, but Tania didn't think like we do. I bet she was sure she could inveigle you into supplying information."

Breck's forehead creased. "But what schemes did the sisters have afoot that needed information from the cops? They were small time blackmailers, not drug dealers or human traffickers."

"Perhaps they planned on er…growing their business," Ingrid suggested.

Breck grinned. "You sound like a member of the Chamber of Commerce. Anyway, to hell with them. Y'know, I lay in bed last night wondering how to juggle everything in my life without short-changing us. You and I deserve some time together."

"We do. Any suggestions?"

"First things first." He eased her to one side and poked his fingers into his shirt pocket.

"A ring!" she exclaimed with delight. "You have a ring for me, haven't you?"

"So much for surprises." He opened the little silver box. "If it's not right, we'll change it straight away. Be honest. Say what you think."

Before looking at it, she ran a hand down the side of his face. "If you chose it, it will be just right."

It was.

"Oh!" A simple baguette cut emerald. No diamonds. No muss. No fuss. "Breck, you are so damned *clever*."

"Sometimes."

"Always. You understand people. You get them, their motivations and stuff like that. You're gonna make a hugely successful detective." Clutching the ring-box in one hand, she wreathed her arms around his neck, tugging his face down. "And best of all, you get me." She planted a lush kiss on his lips, and then as he started to respond, drew back with a giggle. "You should have seen the expression on your face when I used that magic word 'clever.' Nothing wrong with being clever, you know."

He rubbed one hand over his thigh. "Uh, Ingrid. I spent a lot of years being told I was dim-witted, so it's taking me a while to adjust."

"Yup. And it's time you got over it. Now how about sliding this gorgeous ring onto my finger?"

He looked at her for a minute, and then gave one of his slow, bone-melting grins. As he slid the lovely ring on to her finger, he murmured, "One day I will be as good for you as you are for me. I'm working on it."

"Silly man." She nestled her hand into his, and the emerald glowed and smiled between their twined fingers. "I wouldn't be here now if you weren't the best thing that's happened to me."

****

Breck thought back to the day several months ago when he'd responded to the AOS call-out only to discover that his own son was the subject of the emergency.

He stroked Ingrid's hand and wondered how he'd managed to luck out. He'd found himself a fantastic woman, his son was on a level road to a secure childhood, and he'd engineered a reconciliation with the mother who'd been a stranger to him for more than a decade.

The icing on the cake was a career that held a promise of success and enjoyment.

Life didn't get much better than this.

"What are you thinking about?" Ingrid was watching his face.

"Us."

She snuggled closer. "Right answer."

## A word about the author…

Our family was all born in New Zealand and now live in Queensland, the sunshine state of Australia. Nobody else in my family writes, but in the latter part of the nineteenth century, my antecedents published newspapers and were authors. Blood will out, as they say.

I've always written—poetry and short stories as a child; then later on in life as our kids grew older I began writing novels, probably to counteract the stultifying boredom of being a legal executive. Later still, when I discovered I loved recruitment, my twelve-hour working days were made even longer by a sudden drive to write and write and write, usually between 8 p.m. and midnight. I was doing two things I really loved, and the hours involved became irrelevant.

I'm glad TWRP has offered to publish *Innocent Hostage* because I think readers will enjoy reading a suspense novel set in New Zealand, a place of fragile beauty and hard-working people.

Find me at: www.vonniehughes.com

~*~

**Other Vonnie Hughes titles
available from The Wild Rose Press, Inc.:**
*LETHAL REFUGE*

* 9 7 8 1 6 2 8 3 0 6 2 9 3 *